THE ATLANTIS CODES

BOOK 1 OF THE ATLANTIS LEGACY SERIES

LARRY HAMILTON

The Atlantis Codes
Copyright © 2020 by Larry Hamilton. All rights reserved.

Published by Hamilton House Books
www.HamiltonHouseBooks.com

Printed in the United States of America
ISBN: 979-8-9861176-0-2

"Atlantis"

The continent of Atlantis was an island
Which lay before the great flood
In the area we now call the Atlantic Ocean.
So great an area of land,
That far from her western shores
Those beautiful sailors journeyed
To the South and the North Americas with ease,
In their ships with painted sails.
To the East, Africa was a neighbor
Across a short strait of sea miles.
The great Egyptian Age is
But a remnant of the Atlantian culture.
The antediluvian kings colonized the world.
All the gods who play in the mythological dramas
In all legends from all lands,
Were from far Atlantis.
Knowing her fate,
Atlantis sent out ships to all corners of the earth.
On board were The Twelve:
The poet, the physician, the farmer, the scientist,
The magician, and the other so-called Gods of our legends…
Though Gods they were.
And as the elders of our time choose to remain blind…
Let us rejoice
And let us sing
And dance and ring in the new
Hail Atlantis!

CHAPTER 1

Anna Maria Island, Florida
Present Day

Trouble is coming. Coming by land…coming by sea. Coming for you… coming for me.

Matthew Flannery leaned over the kitchen sink, resting both palms on the faded-yellow, gold-flecked, Formica countertop which housed two well-worn stainless-steel basins. He chewed the inside of his lower left lip, a lifelong habit, and peered out the small two-pane window above the kitchen counter. He never tired of gazing at the postcard scenery that beckoned just outside his small but comfortable bungalow located on a white sand beach on the Gulf of Mexico. The story-and-a-half dwelling wore a coat of sun-faded yellow paint with white trim. A modest widow's walk circled the center of the roofline with just enough decking to accommodate a couple of lounge chairs and a small table. A brick paver lanai lay out back facing the water, always partially obscured by blowing sand from the beach.

It occurred to Matt that he had not cleaned the kitchen window in a while. The milky haze that builds up on windows facing the ocean was starting to cloud his view. He made a mental note to take care of this problem, perhaps as early as tomorrow. If not tomorrow, soon. Matt lived on island time.

The first time his father brought the family to Anna Maria Island, Matt was eight years old. He knew even then he would return to live on the island someday.

And so he did. It was for him…simply paradise.

Matthew was summoned back from his island daydream by the grinding of the blender, winding up like it was about to take flight.

Matt was preparing a Saturday afternoon margarita with great care. He did not like his margaritas too limey or too strong. No puckering. He preferred a balance of tangy and sweet, topped off with just a dash of orange juice to round off the bite. And, of course, he only used premium gold tequila.

He removed the container from the base of the blender, pried off the lid, and tipped the container forward, dribbling a little on the tip of his tongue to be sure it met his exacting standards.

Ah, yes! His taste buds approved.

He reached into the overhead cabinet and pulled out his favorite margarita glass, a treasured souvenir he had purchased at a Jimmy Buffett concert. It was a tall, thick glass tumbler and the heaviness of it felt good in Matt's hand. It featured Jimmy Buffett's smiling face wearing his trademark sunglasses with the word "Margaritaville" colorfully printed below his image. Matt anxiously stuck his glass into the ice dispenser in the refrigerator door and filled the glass three quarters of the way to the top with cubed ice. Never crushed. He then moved the glass to the kitchen island and slowly, with an air of ceremony, poured his masterpiece over the frosty cubes.

Grabbing the full glass of perfect margarita, Matt swished it around and over the ice to chill it, swung around the corner of the kitchen island and headed toward the living room sofa. He had been looking forward all week to watching the traditional end of season football game between his beloved University of Florida Gators (his alma mater) and their rivals, the Florida State Seminoles. The annual grudge game was about to begin and he did not want to miss the kick-off.

Matt was gliding across the threshold that separated the kitchen from the living area when he abruptly froze in his tracks…

CHAPTER 2

Matt's Bungalow
Anna Maria Island

MATT HAD NOT HEARD a sound or noticed the slightest movement, yet there in front of him, at the end of the hallway that led from the front door to his kitchen, stood a man the size of two. The stranger was not smiling and did not appear likely to be a representative from the local Welcome Wagon.

With the margarita precariously balanced in his left hand and body suspended in mid-stride between the kitchen and sofa, Matt stared at the intruder. He quickly sized up this ominous stranger who had appeared out of nowhere.

The intruder was dressed entirely in black. His head was big, bald, and shiny. Pale white skin covered it and ruddy red splotches were scattered here and there like continents on a world map. A small gold earring hung from his left ear. No facial hair at all. Looked like Mr. Clean gone to the dark side.

Matt guessed the man to be at least six and a half feet tall. Matt stood six feet even and had to look up to see the stranger's eyes. The man's neck and torso were so thick and muscular that his tee shirt was stretching valiantly to keep from ripping out at the seams. The hulking man's arms bulged as large as a normal man's thighs, resembling bionic arms transplanted into his shoulder sockets. His legs could pass for small tree trunks. His chest resembled two concrete blocks pressed side by side, complemented by rows of bricks directly beneath. He wore a skin-tight tee shirt made of the stretchy compression fit material that athletes wear, loose fitting dress slacks, and heavy, thick-soled shoes polished to a high gloss. The massive fellow could have been a character straight out of a James Bond movie. But, this was not a movie. The situation was all too real. Matt did not know what to make of the man's cliché appearance or his sudden interruption of the afternoon's scheduled festivities.

The unexpected visitor was straight-faced, stoic, and stood menacingly at the end of Matt's hallway.

The uninvited guest's dark, unrevealing eyes stared without blinking into Matt's wide-open, enquiring, and blinking steel grey eyes. A hint of a menacing smile, or maybe a snarl, started to form on the stranger's large and bulbous face as he flexed his oversized biceps for effect. A small trickle of perspiration rolled down the side of the big man's forehead. He seemed to revel in the tension he was creating in the room, allowing it to build and expand before he spoke.

I need to act as if I'm in control of this situation whether I am or not, Matt reasoned with himself.

Using the calmest, deepest voice he could muster under the circumstances, Matt broke the silence.

"Who the hell are you and what are you doing in my house?"

The man-mountain narrowed his eyes a bit, then responded in a deep voice that sounded faintly Russian or East European.

"Do not play dumb with me, foolish man. You know why I am here and you know what I came for."

Matt searched his mind at warp speed for an answer that might make some sort of sense. While continuing to balance the margarita in his left hand, Matt pulled himself up to his full height and shot back a reply in the hope that he sounded braver than he felt.

"Look asshole, I have no idea who you are or why you're here, but I recommend you move on down the road because you obviously have me confused with someone else! My name is Matt Flannery and ..."

Big Baldy interrupted.

"I know who you are, and be assured, this is *not* a case of mistaken identity. I have waited a long time to possess what you are hiding. Now, give me the code keys without delay and I might let you live…or at least I will kill you quickly, so you don't suffer."

A sickening smile spread over the stranger's face as he seemed proud of his little speech.

Matt's mind spun furiously, referencing anything in his brain that might explain what codes this stranger might be referring to.

Surely, he doesn't mean the codes to my home security system? Hell, I don't even have one. Anyway, this guy could just rip the damn door off the hinges and come in any time he wanted! My home safe? Nothing in there but my passport, house and boat documents, and some old relics Grandpa left me.

Nothing made any sense. Matt concluded that this fellow had come to get something that Matt could not produce, and man-mountain was not going to be happy about that.

It seemed obvious this visitor would stop at nothing, including tearing him and the entire house apart, in an attempt to find these "codes" or "keys" or whatever it was that he came for. It was not going to end well for Matt as things currently stood.

*I have to level the playing field somehow…*He pushed down the cold, growing fear welling up in his stomach that threatened to paralyze his arms and legs. He took a deep breath and decided he had to neutralize the invader somehow and let the police sort out this mystery later. Otherwise, the odds did not seem favorable that there would be a "later".

Matt countered again in an effort to buy time.

"Look Mister, I'm telling you, you're in the wrong house and talking to the wrong person. I don't have any codes or keys, don't know anything about these codes or keys, and don't want to know. I have a ballgame to watch so get your ass out of here before I call the cops!"

Even as the echo of his words died out, Matt realized how weak and impotent the ultimatum was. He felt the icy fingers of fear threatening to paralyze him again.

CHAPTER 3

Matt's Bungalow
Anna Maria Island

BIG BOY GLOWERED DARKLY at Matt as a tide of red began to spread upward from his thick neck, working its way to the top of his large head. The man's spreading crimson flush reminded Matt of a thunderstorm slowly approaching from far out at sea.

The scowling man growled through gritted teeth and began to speak.

"All right tough guy, have it your way. You're not as smart as I thought and you are a disappointing adversary, unworthy of my talents. They should have sent a little girl to take care of you. I generously offered to do this the easy way, but you seem to prefer a more painful ending to your pitiful existence. You will beg me to accept the code keys after you become intimately acquainted with the Pearl Persuader."

As he finished his sentence, Big Boy reached into his left front pants pocket and produced a switchblade knife with pearl handles. He flicked it open with the touch of a button, extending the knife to its full murderous length. The blade flashed in the sun's rays streaming through the kitchen window. The killer menacingly waved the knife in small circles, making sure Matt got a good look at it. He then took a measured step towards an astonished and bewildered Matt…

CHAPTER 4

Capital City of Aquatica
Ancient Continent of Atlantis

The members of the National Assembly were all present for this historic occasion. The Assembly had convened to debate the future course of the Nation of Atlantis. It was a watershed moment in the glorious history of Atlantis and it's people.

The soaring, ornate Chamber of the Assembly echoed with numerous animated conversations taking place among the one-hundred Assembly Members who represented the four prime states of Atlantis. Some were attempting to change the opinion of Members who did not share their viewpoint on the upcoming debate. Others were enthusiastically affirming to those they agreed with, that of course, they were choosing the wiser path for Atlantis.

The Assembly was composed of elected representatives from each of the four prime states, twenty-five Members per state. All Members belonged to one of two political parties that had evolved over the years.

In years past, there had been multiple political parties sending representatives to the Assembly. Over time, consolidation had occurred and now only two factions remained and they shared control of the nation's government.

The two parties were known as the Visionaries Assembly and the Guardians Assembly.

The parties had historically worked out policy and legislative differences in a peaceful manner. Until now.

King Lemurius and Queen Alshura were present for this momentous occasion. As symbolic figureheads of the nation, they possessed no power to legislate and could cast no votes in Assembly decisions. Nevertheless, they were an impressive sight and remained a source of great pride and inspiration to the people of Atlantis.

The King was a regal figure clothed in flowing robes of purple trimmed in gold and multi-colored jewels. Atop his head sat a golden crown adorned with four great gemstones of different colors, denoting the four sovereign states of Atlantis. His long reddish-brown hair flamed before the Assembly, his dark beard short and perfectly trimmed.

Queen Alshura was stunning as usual. Her Majesty was dressed in a magnificent flowing dress shimmering with shades of turquoise, aqua, and deep blue to reflect the watery heritage of her people and their kingdom. Atlantis was completely surrounded by water and the oceans had always played a significant role in its history and culture.

To complete the Queen's ensemble, a stunning platinum tiara had been carefully woven into the curls of her long, thick, black hair. The tiara showcased four sparkling blue gemstones that matched the colors woven into her gown while also paying tribute to the four states of Atlantis.

The King and Queen were said to be descended in part from the Ancient Ones who had created the civilization of Atlantis including the technology that enabled the citizens to live in comfort and elegance. The Ancients had intermarried with only a select few native women and men at first, producing hybrid offspring which became the genesis of the Royal lineage. Intermarrying then became more commonplace and the bloodlines of the two peoples eventually blended and after many years, produced the current citizens of Atlantis in all their great diversity.

The Ancient Ones had intended Atlantis to be a shining city on a hill, spreading light to the whole world—when the world was ready and able to embrace that light.

Depending on the outcome of this evening's debate and subsequent vote, many feared the intentions of the Ancients was about to be pushed aside in the name of progress and vanity.

CHAPTER 5

Matt's Bungalow
Anna Maria Island

MATT WAS NOT ONE to shrink from a fight. He had spent ten years in the U.S. Navy and had more than held his own in the mix-it-ups and bar-brawls that seem to be an inevitable part of a seaman's life. Yet, nothing he had encountered during those scuffles had prepared him for this.

The devil had appeared without reason or warning.

Matt was a resourceful man. He understood that he had to gain a strategic advantage over this menacing monster advancing toward him before it was too late.

As he quickly took inventory, he realized the only weapon he possessed was the tasty margarita he had so carefully prepared and the Buffett glass that held it.

This could end up being a waste of a perfectly good margarita.

As he tightened his grip on the margarita in his hand, he glimpsed his old Louisville Slugger baseball bat leaning in the corner a couple of feet to his right. A plan began to form in his mind.

Matt was a standout baseball player in high school, excelling as a power hitting center fielder. He was blessed with a combination of speed and power rarely seen outside of professional baseball. Matt was a strong defender, fast on the bases, and turned a lot of fastballs around for extra bases and home runs. His power was generated from strong wrists and bat speed. Matt had continued to play in the Navy leagues as well as local amateur leagues to keep his skills sharp. He possessed a keen batting eye, quick reflexes, and the strong wrists that enabled him to generate a fast and powerful swing. In the next few moments, Matt was going to need those skills more than ever. His life depended on them.

Big Boy took another menacing step toward Matt while flashing an evil smile, showing his unnatural mouthful of shining white teeth. He taunted Matt with a surreal East European version of Bob Seger's "Come to Papa". It was like something out of a bad "B" movie. All this as he tossed his knife back and forth from one hand to the other; the long, thin blade catching the window light in glints and flashes. He was taking his time and enjoying himself while looking forward to finishing what he came to do. Perhaps a little overconfident this one. That could work to Matt's advantage.

Matt tried to ignore the distracting flitters of light reflecting off the moving blade, so he could focus on his opponent. There were several trails of sweat running down the predator's face now. He was gearing up for the torture and kill. Matt fought down his fear once again, remembering that he had an important game to watch and he did not have time for this bullshit!

He took a deep breath, tensed his body, and launched…

CHAPTER 6

Aquatica
Continent of Atlantis

MINISTER LETURIS ROSE FROM his ceremonial seat positioned to the front of the Assembly, high enough for all to see. He was dressed in the ceremonial robes of the Assembly Leader, rich burgundy with gold braided trim down the front and around the collar and cuff areas. Leturis was a tall, stately man with a magnetic presence and intelligent green eyes. He was Director of the Visionaries Assembly, the majority party. Therefore, it was his duty to preside over the Assembly proceedings.

A hush fell over the room as the Minister straightened himself to his full stature and cleared his throat to speak.

He looked around the room at members of both parties. He studied their faces. Colleagues and friends he had known for years and he loved them all for who they were and what they represented. The decisions that were demanding to be made were momentous, setting the course for Atlantis and the wider world for centuries to come. The nervous anticipation permeating the room was evidence this was understood by all who were in attendance. He felt the weight of the future pushing down on his shoulders but shook it off and forged on. He had to be resolute.

In a soaring voice, Minister Leturis proclaimed the proceedings to be open and that the debate would now commence. After a nod of respect and recognition to the King and Queen, he set forth the parameters of the discussion.

"My honorable brothers and sisters of the Ancient and Great Nation of Atlantis. Today, we gather to discuss the future course of our beloved country and to choose how we will interact with the world around us for the next millennium."

"Over the last few years, there has been a growing debate over the future course of Atlantis, who we see ourselves to be as a people, and what our place in the world should be. The rising tenor of this debate can no longer be ignored, nor can action be delayed. We must determine a clear course at this moment in our history. One direction and one destiny. Then we must all set forth together, a united Atlantis, on that chosen journey. We must do this now before rancor divides us any further."

"Today, we will present both views of the issue at hand and decide whether to call for a Citizen's Referendum. As you know, the Referendum allows all Citizens of Atlantis to vote on this matter and the will of the people would prevail."

"This Assembly Meeting is being telescreened nationally and a holiday has been declared for all Citizens, so they may watch our deliberations and hear both sides of the issue. Thus, we honor the magnitude of the issue before us."

"As the appointed Director of the Visionaries, I will now present our vision for the future of Atlantis. I will then allow Minister Tiborus, the honorable Director of the Guardians Assembly, to offer their vision for our great nation. Let us begin…"

CHAPTER 7

It is now a proven fact that margaritas can be an effective weapon when properly employed.

With a quick thrust of his wrist, Matt fired the citric acid and alcohol mixture straight into Big Boy's surprised eyes and it stopped the man dead in his tracks. The intruder let loose a string of expletives and threats as he struggled to clear the liquid from his stinging eyes. Tears were flooding down his face, leaving him blinded for the moment.

Matt took full advantage of the man's inability to see and lunged forward, slamming the thick bottom of the glass tumbler into the man's nose as hard as he could without breaking his own wrist.

Matt noticed Jimmy Buffett grinning at him from the side of the glass as if to show his approval for a job well done. Matt felt like a pirate for a fleeting moment.

The thick glass bottom drove hard into Big Boy's nose and Matt heard the sickening crunch of shattering cartilage. Blood exploded out both nostrils of the man's crooked and newly deformed nose. Howling screams of rage were emanating from the bleeding and bellowing trespasser. He was swearing and making horrific promises to Matt, going into great detail about what he was going to do to him even as a crimson stream of blood poured freely from his disfigured nose.

But Matt did not have the time or inclination to listen to sweet talk from his new acquaintance. There was work to do.

CHAPTER 8

Aquatica
Chamber of the Assembly

MINISTER LETURIS' VOICE RANG out again in the Chamber, authoritative and mesmerizing.

"The Visionaries Assembly is just that—we are true visionaries! We hold forth a grand and glorious revelation of what Atlantis is destined to be. A destiny that is our moral obligation to fulfill. It is apparent that we hold the high ground in this world in every respect. Technologically, culturally, governmentally, militarily, and philosophically. Are we not bound by virtue to share our wealth and wisdom with all the peoples of Earth?"

"Some of you argue that every culture and nation should chart their own course and not be unduly influenced by us or our way of life. You say we should adhere to a policy of non-interference. I ask you today, what has this hands-off policy done for our fellow men and women around the world? They suffer disease, poverty, tyrannical rule, a base existence devoid of higher pursuits. Are we to stand by and do nothing to elevate their way of life? We can show them a better way and I say we must!"

A murmur of enthusiasm rippled through the Chamber.

"Of course, this would have to be done systematically or our technology would create chaos in their unlearned hands. Therefore, we have formed a plan to disseminate our knowledge and culture in an orderly and uniform fashion, kept carefully under our control. There will be resistance from many countries in the beginning because they have no concept of the value in what we are bringing to them. But in the due course of history, they will see that we have given them a gift of transformation that will change their lives for the better…forever!"

More excited rumblings from the Chamber.

"I declare to you, my fellow citizens, this is our divine right and manifest destiny. Moreover, I believe it is our *obligation* to better mankind. They will thank us some day for what we will do for them. We must bring a new era of hope and prosperity to the entire world! We are the only nation who fully understands what is best and what is possible for the people of this planet and we are the only ones who possess the means to perpetuate it."

"This great adventure will not only transform the neighboring world but will also galvanize our beloved Atlantis. It will bring us closer as a people by giving us a common cause to work toward, together. A cause worthy of our people. We will be energized as never before! We will do things we have never done and create things we have only dreamed of."

"I implore you now, Citizens and Leaders of Atlantis, join me in this great cause. Let us change the world for the better and let that change begin now!"

Intermittent shouts of enthusiasm and agreement floated up from the Assembly Members.

"Minister Tiborus, I yield the floor to you."

CHAPTER 9

Matt's Bungalow
Anna Maria Island

WHILE THE FURIOUS ASSASSIN struggled to clear his vision, Matt slid nimbly to his right and grabbed the familiar handle of his lucky bat. He squeezed it hard with his strong hands. Matt felt a new sense of empowerment surging through him, daring to believe the battle might be tilting in his favor. This old scarred and blemished Louisville Slugger was a weapon he knew how to use well.

Big Boy was attempting to gather himself and regain his momentum. As he began stumbling forward, hampered by his blurred vision and throbbing nose, he parried the Pearl Persuader with wild swings in an attempt to wound his target with a lucky sweep.

Matt felt the familiar warmth and shape of the bat in his grip, aligning the trademark straight up as he had always been coached to do. He calmed his mind and body as he had so many times in the past when he had stepped into the batter's box against a tough pitcher with the game on the line.

This game was definitely on the line. Game tied, bottom of the ninth, two outs, runner on third. Clutch time. Matt stared at the reeling giant who was moving forward again, stabbing at the air with his blade, still determined to turn Matt into shark bait.

It was time to hit a walk off home run at Big Boy's expense.

Matt balanced his feet into a textbook batting stance, cocked the bat back and behind his head to the optimum hitting position, and took aim at Big Boy's head as if it were a giant softball. Matt's left leg stepped toward the target, his hips rotated to generate power and speed, held his swing until the last possible moment, and in a blur, he unleashed his wrists and bat in an upward arc. The bat made solid contact with the left side of his adversary's head.

Matt heard two distinct sounds at the same moment the bat struck its target. The first was like that of a heavy hammer smacking into a watermelon. The second was the sharp crack of the wooden bat snapping off at the handle.

The assassin's eyes rolled up and back as the force of the blow staggered him into the wall where the hallway opened into the kitchen. His knees buckled and he was heading down. In an effort to stay on his feet and stabilize himself, he grabbed for whatever he could get hold of, dropping his knife in the process. He stumbled backwards into a floor lamp which immediately buckled and broke. His back side landed squarely on top of a low, thin wall table with a glass top. The metal frame of the table surrendered under his bulk and the glass top shattered, scattering shards of glass around the floor and putting the killer on his back. He tried to get to his feet but tripped over the broken table, pitching into the wall so hard that a framed print of one of Matt's favorite Navy ships, the old battle wagon USS Iowa, bounced off it's wall mounting and joined the wreckage on the floor. Sharp pieces of glass from the tabletop were now imbedding into the faltering man's palms as he put his hands on the floor to steady himself in a vain attempt to stay on his feet. He was painting bloody smears on everything he touched.

The stunned intruder vaguely mouthed the words, *"What the hell?"* as he struggled to make sense of what was transpiring.

It was not supposed to happen like this.

This world class hit man had never in his wildest dreams expected to find himself facing defeat at the hands of this amateur. He was being bested by a target he was expected to easily chew up and spit out after getting what he came for.

The only thing he was spitting out at the moment was his own blood.

CHAPTER 10

Aquatica
Chamber of the Assembly

Minister Tiborus walked to the podium with eyes focused down on his notes, looking like a man who was carrying the weight of the world on his shoulders. He believed he was. In fact, he was certain of it. He looked rather lost in his roomy ceremonial robes. He had become increasingly thinner and slighter of build as the years passed. His robe was also deep burgundy but with silver trim work, designating him as the Leader/Director of the Guardians, the minority party.

Tiborus was an elder statesman who had carried the trust and soul of the people of Atlantis in his heart for many years. It had been a life-long love affair. They loved him and he loved them back. He had always endeavored to be their conscience and implored them to be the best version of themselves they could be, both individually and as a nation. It had been his life's work and personal mission. For the first time in his role as a servant of his cherished people, he feared he could no longer call forth their better angels.

Trying to blunt the momentum the Visionaries had created with their shiny new world vision, had been like attempting to hold back a rushing river with one's bare hands. Tiborus knew the Visionaries meant well, but this was a dangerous, slippery slope they were moving toward, and this was his last chance to stop the growing madness taking hold of his countrymen.

"Minister Leturis, my fellow Assembly Members, King Lemurius and Queen Alshura, and all the great Citizens of Atlantis, I greet you on this historic and momentous occasion."

"I ask that you not underestimate the importance of the subject we are addressing today. This is not one of our sporting contests we are speaking of, but rather the future of our people as well as those of the entire world. The excitement that has been generated for this misguided initiative is contagious and intoxicating. I understand that. I feel your desire for greatness and common purpose. But in our enthusiasm, we must not lose sight of who we really are and what is morally right."

"We are the beneficiaries of a wealth and quality of life that we did not create on our own. It came to us from our Founders; the Ancient Ones who stayed with us for a season, living among us, and becoming one of us. They mixed their own blood and essence with ours through marriage and childbirth, creating a permanent bond with us. They imparted many gifts to us from their advanced civilization and entrusted it to us as a legacy to enjoy and protect."

"The Ancients viewed us at first as their children, then as their brethren. We were not forced to accept or use the gifts they offered. We certainly were not commissioned to force others around the world to do so. We worked and grew alongside the Ancients but were always permitted to exercise our own free will…without coercion. And, we have continued to accept their ways as our ways even until today."

"The Ancients always offered us a choice. Nowhere in the wise instructions from the Founders are we asked to evangelize the world to our ways or force our culture and technology upon others."

"Now, we are considering a path that would not only have us impart our technology and culture to other nations, but do so with or without their consent, in whatever way that we decide is best. Is playing God to be our new national identity?"

"Who are we to judge what is acceptable or desirable in the lives of other peoples? Are they less happy than us because they don't have telescreens or more outwardly comfortable environments? Given a choice, I assure you that many of them would not trade their simpler lives for the more complex ones that we embrace."

"This is not to say that over time we cannot share our inheritance with other cultures, but "share" is the key word. We should not force our ways on people, calling it our God-given duty and moral obligation as a justification to decide the course of others. They too are our brothers and sisters and deserve the right to exercise free will, just as we have."

"We have existed peacefully as a nation for thousands of years without major conflict or rancor with our neighbors. This was the truest and highest legacy of the Ancient Ones. Will we now recklessly abandon all the values that define who we are as Atlanteans? I declare to you that all nations and all people have a right to self-determination."

"If we embark on this new path, we will never be the same as a nation, or as a people. Once we start down that road, we can never go back. We will have lost our way and sacrificed our innocence on the altar of self-righteousness."

"Other nations will not view us as the saviors that you imagine us to be. They will see us as an occupying force and reject us out of hand. We will never be able to gain that moral high ground again and we will never be viewed in the light that we are now. We will be remembered as just another power-hungry nation imposing its will on those who are deemed inferior and weaker. Is this the oppressive burden we want to leave for our descendants? That they be global caretakers? Nation builders? Always suppressing bitter conflicts with our conquered neighbors?"

"I implore you to search your own heart and listen to your conscience, each and every one of you, and let the wisdom you find there act as your moral compass as we determine what is the right and just path for our wonderful Atlantis to follow in the future. May Spirit bless all of you and protect us from ourselves."

The Assembly Hall had grown hauntingly silent as those who had gathered there considered Minister Tiborus' words. You could sense the weighty silence hanging over the entire nation as those at home felt the ominous heaviness of his prophetic warnings.

After pausing to look deeply into the eyes of his peers and countrymen a last time, he quietly shook his head, gathered his notes from the podium and shuffled back to his seat, stumbling once causing a gasp to escape from the onlookers. His shoulders were slumped and there was a palpable sadness about him—as if he sensed the inevitable.

Minister Leturis returned to the podium, then called for a vote to decide if a Citizen's Referendum would be held.

The Chamber was now shrouded in a more subdued mood. The air heavy with the weight of decision.

Nevertheless, the motion carried.

The Citizens of Atlantis would decide their own future… their own fate.

The Referendum would be held in two weeks.

CHAPTER 11

Matt's Bungalow
Anna Maria Island

MATT GLANCED DOWN AT the broken bat handle he was still squeezing and noticed his hands were shaking from the large dose of adrenalin that had been released into his system. He glanced over at his unknown nemesis, feeling certain the intruder would be unconscious after being on the receiving end of such a powerful blow to the head. Matt was shocked to see instead, that Big Boy was just shaking his head as if recovering from a bad hangover.

Matt watched incredulously as the dazed and bleeding giant fumbled around the floor, and in a stroke of luck, recovered the knife that had bounced away when he crashed into the wall.

Matt could not believe this guy was not only conscious, but still determined to kill him.

Sonofabitch! This Neanderthal is indestructible. He's hell-bent on gutting me and ransacking my house even if it kills him, or me, or both of us!

Matt now knew, without a doubt, that only one of them would walk out of there alive on this day.

Matt surveyed the broken, jagged bat handle that he still gripped in his hands. It had sheared off at an angle leaving a sharp, protruding wedge of wood on the end. Matt glared at the recovering menace rising up from the floor and knew what he had to do and he had to do it now, before his enemy could recover.

It was judgment day for one of them…

CHAPTER 12

Atlantis

THE NATIONAL REFERENDUM WAS not even close. A landslide victory for the Visionaries Party. Despite the heartfelt pleading of Minister Tiborus, the populace could not resist the hard pull of destiny and national purpose that had been laid out by the Visionaries.

In recent years, life had waxed routine for the Atlanteans. They had overcome most of the environmental and cultural challenges that had kept them engaged and united in years past. The timing was perfect to capture the people's imagination and recruit them to a new and exciting national and personal mission. And so, it began—a feverish crusade to create a new Heaven on Earth.

It was not the first time, and would not be the last time, that Hell would ascend to Earth disguised as Heaven.

CHAPTER 13

Matt's Bungalow
Anna Maria Island

MATT FLIPPED THE BROKEN bat handle upside down, grasping it with both hands, the jagged end pointed towards the floor. He let out a primal scream of anger and disgust at what he was being forced to do.

He charged his adversary with all the swiftness and aggression he could muster. He tried not to think about the act he was going to commit. Matt had contributed to the taking of lives from a distance in his time with Naval Intelligence but had never taken a human life this way, up close and personal.

No time to think about that now. Have to keep moving forward. Him or me.

Big Boy heard the yell and sensed the rush of movement in front of him and looked up with bloodshot, unfocused eyes. Shock and disbelief registered on his pale face, sharply contrasting with the deep red blood splattered all over it. The mysterious visitor tried to focus on what Matt had in his hands and could see enough to know something bad was coming and he needed to stop it.

He swung his blade wildly from side to side in a desperate attempt to keep Matt at bay. The blow to the head had caused his vision to blur but he still hoped to get lucky and slice into an artery or organ somewhere in Matt's body. That would even the odds again and perhaps he could complete his mission. The

Leader of the Brotherhood would be pleased and he would return a hero after all.

But this death match was not to be decided by luck.

Matt turned sideways, presenting a smaller target, keeping away from the moving and slashing Pearl Persuader. He stepped to the left and moved behind where the man was half-sitting and half-standing.

It was time to finish this thing.

As Big Boy cursed and flailed at him in a panic, Matt drove the jagged tip of his trusty bat handle deep into the right side of the struggling man's neck. The makeshift spear severed the jugular vein, causing a spray of blood to cover everything close by, including Matt. With a final ripping, digging motion, the wooden tip tore through the man's windpipe, deciding the contest once and for all.

The assassin tried to scream but was quickly stifled by blood gurgling into his throat and filling his lungs.

Ivan writhed in agony and rage, choking on his own blood, his red eyes wide open and wild. He dropped his knife and had both hands around his throat, trying to stem the flow of blood squirting out of the open gashes as his heart continued to pump furiously, but to no avail. He could not accept that he had been outmaneuvered by this nobody and did not want to believe what he already knew to be true. He had failed The Brotherhood and himself. He would die alone and in shame.

CHAPTER 14

Atlantis

ATLANTIS WAS ELECTRIC WITH renewed purpose and unbridled enthusiasm. Many of those who originally voted against the Visionaries' plan, now found themselves caught up in the new national fervor. The dissenting voices had been drowned out, resigning themselves to watching the frightful drama continue to unfold.

The mighty wheels of Atlantis were now turning at a fever pitch. A continental machine without limitations. Without restraint.

The Assembly had authorized the formation of a research and development group comprised of the top scientific minds from all of Atlantis. Dr. Sarontin, the National Minister of Science, was chosen to oversee this elite scientific body. It would be known as the Supreme Council of Science.

The purpose of the Council was to find ways to better harness the tremendous power source the Ancient Ones had built for Atlantis.

Until now, the power source had only been used for peaceful purposes and had sustained an abundant lifestyle for Atlanteans, requiring little effort on their part. The central energy plant was appropriately named, the Life Source. The Ancients had constructed transmission conduits and control nodes throughout the entire continent. The power distribution system had required little maintenance or expansion by the citizens over the many years since the Ancients departed. It was designed to be self-generating and self-maintaining.

Because the scientists of Atlantis had not been required to learn more about how the Life Source operated in order to benefit from it, much was unknown about its inner workings.

This would have to change quickly if the new world order were to become reality.

And change it did.

CHAPTER 15

Matt's Bungalow
Anna Maria Island

THE BLOOD SPURTING FROM the dead man's neck covered much of Matt's faded Gators tee shirt and khaki shorts. Scattered, random patterns of red on nearby walls resembled a form of horrific modern art. Matt's feet and sandals had become small islands surrounded by dark pools of blood fed by the silent stream still bubbling from the intruder's severed jugular. The would-be assassin had at last fallen silent, his body limp, eyes fixed and lifeless.

It was finished.

As Matt squinted at the neck wound, as if someone else had inflicted it, he noticed the assassin had three small triangular or pyramid-shaped tattoos on his neck near the neckline of his tee shirt. Curious.

Where had he seen those before?

CHAPTER 16

Atlantis

THE BIGGEST CHALLENGE FACING Atlantis in implementing their global plan, was how to project political power worldwide in a way that would make resistance futile and minimize the pushback from all countries.

The intention was to make this a peaceful transition. The only way the Atlanteans knew to keep it non-violent was to build a massive military machine that could be deployed simultaneously around the globe in a show of power that would force worldwide acquiescence.

Of course, this military presence would be gradually withdrawn once the other nations accepted their place in the Atlantean New Age.

Since most of the knowledge and experience that had been gained by Atlantis' technicians and scientists had been used for peaceful applications, there was limited military tech available. A few battlefield weapons had been developed just to make sure neighboring countries did not consider a hostile move against Atlantis, but nothing on the scale required for this initiative.

Therefore, the new research facility reflected the mission before them. It was named the Special Weapons Research Center (SWRC) and would be located on the outskirts of Aquatica. Here, the researchers would focus on reverse engineering the Life Source and creating weapons and delivery systems that would inspire shock and awe worldwide.

This would guarantee a peaceful transition to the New Age of Atlantis!

CHAPTER 17

Matt's Bungalow
Anna Maria Island

MATT NOW TOOK A moment to consider the surreal drama that had just taken place in his home. The full impact of the deadly invasion was beginning to sink in.

Matt knew he should not be alive right now.

As the adrenalin rush began to subside, he felt the frigid fingers of shock and disbelief creeping into his extremities and dulling his mind.

Who was this crazy man who had just tried to filet me? And what the hell was this code or key he was willing to kill me for?

Matt could only conclude the assassin had made a mistake and assaulted the wrong man. Nothing else made sense. Matt knew he should feel good about his own quick thinking that had staved off sure death, but as he looked down at the bloody hulk on the floor, he only felt sick to his stomach.

CHAPTER 18

Hawthorne, Florida
25 years earlier.

MATT'S GRANDPA FLANNERY WAS a robust man who always seemed larger than life when viewed through Matt's youthful eyes. Even now in his early sixties, Grandpa Flannery exuded a confidence and sense of humor that could only come from a man who had lived well and done so for a long time. Someone comfortable in his own skin. At ease with his place in the world he inhabited.

On this hazy morning in June, Grandpa Flannery was working to untangle the line on an old Shakespeare fishing reel that was Matt's to use later, if Grandpa could ever get the line unknotted.

This was always Matt's rod and reel when he and Grandpa went fishing and he loved how it felt in his hands as he practiced casting his line out into the water and reeling it back in. He had gotten pretty good at it, too!

They were sitting inside the old weathered barn on Grandpa's small farm, the Flannery Homestead. Not that Bill Flannery had ever really been a farmer or even pretended to be one. He just liked a little space around him. He had completed a stint in the Navy, a family tradition, serving with distinction in the South Pacific aboard a couple different warships during World War II. He had seen serious action and had occupied a front row seat to bravery and cowardice, death and dying, and common men thrust into uncommon circumstances. Men just trying to get home in one piece to see their families again. But willing to serve their country without much complaint. It was a war they believed in.

After the war, he used the GI Bill to pursue a college education at the University of Florida, also a family tradition, where he graduated with Honors in History. He soon added a Master's Degree in Education and later completed his Doctorate in The History of Native Peoples of the Americas while working as an Associate Professor of History at the University.

Bill "Irish" Flannery, "Irish" being the nickname his friends bestowed on him as a nod to his Irish Heritage, was a born leader. He wrote and lectured his way to the position of History Department Chair at the University.

He made the daily commute to work from his comfortable residence in nearby Hawthorne which was just the right distance from Gainesville. Far enough to escape the hustle and bustle of university life but near enough to still be a short drive, only twenty minutes or so.

Matt cherished his time with Grandpa Flannery and never got his fill of it. The stories he told Matt about his Navy days and his university exploration trips were more exciting than anything he read in books or saw at the movies. It was even more thrilling, and sometimes scary, because Matt knew that Grandpa had really lived these life and death adventures and survived to tell about them.

Matt looked at the aging man with deep affection. He watched his grandfather bend over the tailgate of his old pickup truck, working with great patience to untangle the last knot in the fishing line. Grandpa was getting older, but he still had a youthful sparkle in his eyes and possessed a special something that was hard to define, but everyone knew he had it.

Perhaps it was his unbridled love of life and the passion with which he lived that drew everyone to him like a stick pen to a magnet. He made everyone around him feel a little more alive and a bit more special.

How lucky I am to have him for my Grandpa, Matt thought.

Suddenly, Grandpa Flannery raised up and stated with a triumphant yell "Got it!" as he pulled out the last piece of tangled line and reeled it all back in without a hitch. He then fixed the sharp hook into an eye on the rod for safe transport.

"Are we going to our secret fishing spot today, Grandpa?" Matt queried.

"You bet!" came the answer.

They gathered up their fishing gear, tackle box, and a small Gators sport cooler that contained plenty of ice and cold drinks as well as a couple of Grandma Flannery's special extra-crunchy peanut butter sandwiches with butter and honey that she had packed especially for their trip to the fishing hole. The two happy anglers tossed all of it into the back of the faded-red Ford F-150 and climbed in.

This was going to be a good day!

CHAPTER 19

Holden Pond

"My worst day fishin' is better than my best day workin'…"
-Unknown

THE SECRET FISHING HOLE was near 526-acre Little Orange Lake and was known as Holden Pond. Most people did their boating and fishing on the much larger Little Orange. That suited Grandpa and Matt just fine. They preferred the relative sanctuary of their quiet cove on Holden Pond.

The banks of Holden Pond were lined with a mixture of evergreen trees and tropical foliage, a place where two worlds collided. The part sand, part dirt embankments worked their way down to the water in a nice, gradual slope, perfect for sitting, fishing, talking, eating, or doing nothing at all. The scenic little cove that Grandpa and Matt frequented even had the added convenience of a couple of tree stumps to sit on. Years earlier, some enterprising angler had used a chain saw to shape them into nice sitting stumps. Some days, the two of them brought folding chairs. Other days were stump days. Today was a stump day.

Holden Pond had the same crappie, bass, catfish, sunfish, bluegill, and various other types of local fish that Little Orange had. What it did not have was noisy speedboats, loud revelers, and constant boat wakes creating havoc with fishing lines. Not to mention the effect it had on the fish.

Professor and grandson had their best talks sitting on the banks of Holden Pond.

CHAPTER 20

Holden Pond

IT WAS STILL EARLY in the day and the heat had not yet built to an uncomfortable level. Matt rigged his fishing line with a brand new, bright red, plastic wiggler/hook combo that Grandpa Flannery had picked up in the fishing section of Walmart. It was Matt's job to give it a tryout today.

With the wiggler securely attached to his line and his bobber fastened about six inches above it, Matt slowly hoisted the rod up, swung it back over his shoulder, paused, and then lashed it forward while releasing the lock on the reel with his thumb. The wiggler, line, and bobber flew straight and true about twenty feet out into the water, right where he had aimed. Nothing to do now but sit back on his stump and keep an eye on that bobber for any sign of a nibble.

Bill Flannery chewed on a thin stalk of grass and studied his grandson who was keeping a sharp eye on his floater and slapping away a fly. He saw something strong, durable, and trustworthy in the boy even though he was only ten years of age.

Was he the One? Would he do the right thing when the time came? Would he be strong enough to see it through? Would I be ruining Matt's life or protecting the life of millions?

Bill Flannery had decided that he was too old to begin this fateful journey, though he wished he weren't. Matt's father, Bradley

Flannery, was a good man with a wife, son, and daughter and he was working hard to move up through the ranks at NASA. Bill couldn't be prouder, but Bradley was in a political job and was beholden to a lot of people that had helped him along the way at NASA.

Whomever I entrust this to cannot be owing to anyone and must always be willing to follow his own path and listen to his own conscience. No matter what.

Bill looked hard at Matt.

So focused, so calm for a boy his age. Never needy. Independent. Balanced nicely between book smart and street smart. Many friends but true to himself and his family first. Hell of a baseball player, too.

It was in that moment that Bill decided for sure that Matt would be the one he would trust with a discovery that had the potential to either solve many of mankind's challenges or end the world as we know it.

CHAPTER 21

Atlantis

THE NON-MILITARY COMPONENT OF the Atlantis strategy involved the creation of a highly-trained cadre of Emissaries who would be in place at every nation's capital city prior to the military deployment. They would already be engaged in a dialogue with the heads of state and government leaders for each respective country under the guise of offering humanitarian aid, which was the light in which Atlanteans preferred to view their plan.

It was their hope that by creating relationships with these countries well in advance of the appearance of the military, the resistance could be kept to a minimum.

The decision had been made to build the new Special Weapons Research Center near the Life Source to enable easy access to its core and controls. This location was also in close proximity to the many underground tunnels and deep vertical shafts that had been excavated by the Ancients in creating the power grids for Atlantis. The engineers favored this site, situated on a thick rock shelf, as the ideal place to build the SWRC.

The race to build "superweapons of peace" was on.

CHAPTER 22

Holden Pond

THE DAY AT HOLDEN Pond had flown by and Matt caught two good size bass and several sunfish. They always threw their catches back because Grandpa said he was concerned about chemical runoff that was polluting the lakes these days and he didn't want to eat poison fish.

Grandpa Flannery had seemed rather distracted and deep in thought most of the morning, but that didn't matter. Matt's worst day with Grandpa was better than his best day most anywhere else.

The intensifying sun had driven them into the shade by early afternoon and they had devoured the last of the extra-crunchy peanut butter and honey sandwiches that Grandma had sent with them. Grandpa had rinsed his sandwich down with a bottle of cola and Matt had finished off a small thermos of cold, home-made lemonade that Grandma Flannery had packed. Her special lemonade was Matt's favorite drink when he came to visit. She always kept a fresh pitcher of it in the fridge.

"Well Matt, the sun's gettin' hot and I think it's about time to head back to the farm. What do you think?"

"Can we stop at the Dairy Barn and get a strawberry cone on the way?" the boy asked hopefully.

Grandpa chuckled and nodded in the affirmative.

"Two scoops?" Matt ventured, his eyes wide with anticipation.

Grandpa laughed out loud and said it would be OK as long as he didn't tell Grandma. She wouldn't approve of ice cream so close to dinner.

Not to worry. Matt could keep a secret.

CHAPTER 23

Atlantis

CONTINENTAL COMMANDER MISHON WAS the highest-ranking military officer in Atlantis and had been placed in charge of the military planning and build-up that would serve as the cornerstone of the global initiative.

He was a tough, inscrutable officer who did not reveal his inner thoughts to anyone. He was inwardly ecstatic about this new military plan he had been entrusted with but did not allow that to show to the outside world. He took care to maintain the façade of just being a good soldier doing his job in a workmanlike fashion. He understood that a show of ambition would not play well with his superiors.

Mishon had secretly fought frustration for years. Destined it seemed, to only commanding military units in a peaceful country that did not have natural enemies or a need to engage in live combat.

Foreign armies knew they were no match for Atlantis and would have had to traverse large bodies of water to threaten the continent. Mishon always kept his forces trained and ready to repel any such enemy incursion but knew the likelihood of it happening was remote. With their many trading ships traversing the globe, Mishon would have known about an invasion force coming his way long before it arrived.

He had always speculated how he would fare should he find himself pitted against another commander in glorious battle. He had presided over endless military drills and exercises but experienced no real opportunity to prove himself or his battle units. He felt certain that this new global deployment strategy would give him the answers he had sought for so long.

No matter what strategies the Assembly employed to keep the transition non-violent, Mishon knew it would not work out that way. It was human nature to put up a fight when challenged by a foreign army. No matter what the stated reason or cause might be.

His day was coming, and he would be ready…and more than willing.

CHAPTER 24

Hawthorne Farm

IT WAS LATE AFTERNOON and the sun was losing its ferocity as it slipped lower into the western horizon, saying farewell for another day with spreading shades of gold, mauve, and orange painting the sky.

Matt was hurriedly crunching down the last of his ice cream cone so Grandma Flannery would not see him eating it as Grandpa pulled the trusty old Ford truck into the barn where he kept the stuff that mattered.

Rows of tools hung neatly on the wall above an old workbench that ran about twenty feet along the back side of the barn. Above the rows of tools, there were windows that provided light to work by during the day. Fluorescent work lights floated over the bench at even intervals allowing for night work. Grandpa also had woodworking saws and a lathe and other things that Matt didn't know the names of yet, let alone their purpose. There was an old grey and blue Ford tractor with rusty fenders and wheels, an orange finish mower still hooked to the PTO shaft of the tractor, and a red bush hog parked in a corner of the barn.

Sometimes, when Grandpa was mowing with the tractor, he let Matt drive in the open field areas. That made Matt feel all grown up.

Well-used camping and hiking gear huddled under a tarpaulin in another musty corner. This was the equipment Grandpa used when he went on exploratory field trips for the university.

Grandpa Flannery had told Matt fascinating stories of going on archaeological expeditions with some of the professors from the university to look for fossils and artifacts. They would then bring their discoveries back to the Florida Museum of Natural History for further study and classification.

Once, Grandpa had taken Matt to the Museum to show him some of the items they had found on their trips and explained in simple language what the discoveries were and their significance.

Grandpa always made it interesting. He intuitively understood who his audience was and how to communicate with them, which made him a popular lecturer, always in demand. That and he told lots of funny jokes and stories.

The two anglers unpacked the fishing gear and put it in the proper places. Rods were always to be hung on the wall and the tackle box lived on a shelf under the workbench.

Grandpa dumped the ice from the Grinning Gators cooler, then turned it upside down over a couple sawhorses so it would dry thoroughly and not mildew. He threw the empty soda containers and sandwich wrappers into an antique, rusting, white milk bucket that served as a trash can for the barn.

He now turned his attention fully to Matt who had ended up with dried drabs of strawberry ice cream sticking to the corners of his mouth and crusting his upper lip. He made a mental note to have Matt wipe his mouth before they went into the house so Grandma would not discover the covert stop at the Dairy Barn.

Grandpa Flannery had found a vintage 1950's style dinette in good shape at a yard sale a few years earlier. He purchased it to keep in the barn for sitting, eating, talking, drinking, or playing cards. The chairs were covered with a marbled, deep red vinyl and trimmed with lots of shiny chrome with a few rusty spots trying to gain a foothold around the screws and joints. The table followed the same color scheme but with a durable surface that had held up well over the years. He also had an antiquated cream-chrome-rust-colored Frigidaire refrigerator sitting at the left end of the workbench. It had stayed cold years longer than anyone had a right to expect. He had collected magnets and bumper stickers from his many travels and displayed the entire collection on the old fridge. So many that the whole front and sides were covered. Grandma wouldn't allow them on her nice clean kitchen refrigerator as she considered them junky and unsightly. The barn refrigerator is also where Grandpa kept the cold beer he shared with his buddies from the university when they stopped by to swap tales and jokes or play a few hands of poker.

Matt noticed that Grandpa Flannery was now standing still and looking at him a little more seriously than was the norm. Grandpa seemed to be trying to make a decision about something.

"Matt, why don't we pull up a couple of chairs and sit down at the table for a bit. I have something I'd like to talk to you about."

The energy in the barn now shifted from the light-hearted mood of a lazy-afternoon-gone-fishing and ice-creaming to something more serious. Matt was starting to feel a little uneasy. He wondered if he had done something wrong and was in trouble.

Maybe it was that second scoop of strawberry ice cream I asked for…

CHAPTER 25

Science Minister Dr. Rona Sarontin marveled at the frenzied pace of the workers as they pushed to get the new SWRC built and functioning in record time.

The construction crews had erected the structure ahead of schedule and now the technicians were crawling over the interior like ants on a honey jar. They were installing computer consoles and pulling miles of special cabling that would connect the SWRC to the entire continent's data and information systems.

The SWRC was not an architectural work of art like many of Aquatica's structures but there was no time for that. It's design was functional and practical. Rona was quite pleased with the overall layout, functionality, and appearance of the facility.

There would be high-speed data and communications systems bringing updates from all parts of Atlantis as well as from the waterships and airships waiting to be deployed around the world. All that information would be available in near real time thanks to the light beam technology the Ancients had left for them to utilize. The whole network would be coordinated right here in the SWRC. It would be an amazing place.

Then why these nagging doubts?

Dr. Sarontin's face became clouded, her brows wrinkled. She was an attractive woman with intelligent brown eyes who carried herself with grace and authority. She was considered a superstar in scientific circles. But in spite of the great accomplishments she was witnessing daily, she was plagued by concerns over the development of superweapons and her role in it.

Her researchers were tasked with creating energy weapons that could wield destructive force on a scale only witnessed during natural disasters. The Assembly had repeatedly assured her the weapons were only for show and would lead to a peaceful transition worldwide once the other nations beheld the unprecedented power of these weapons. The more daunting the weapons, the less chance of a military response from other countries. That was what they told her. She was guaranteed the armaments would never actually be used on other populations. They told her these weapons would prevent wars from continuing among other nations. The Assembly had gone so far as to proclaim these were weapons of peace and she would receive the highest government honor as a peacemaker once the transition to the Atlantean New World Age was underway.

But she had reservations. She had always worked on projects intended for non-destructive purposes. Inventions to make life better for the people of Atlantis.

And what about her own family? She had a husband who worked in medical research and two grown sons who were completing their higher learning certifications. They had decided to follow in their mother's footsteps and work in physics and energy research. She was proud of them all. Her life was perfect in so many ways. Dr. Sarontin realized she was contributing to events that would change the world her sons and grandchildren would grow up in.

The nagging question remained: *will this change be for the better, or for the worse?*

She often thought of the Ancient Ones and the great wisdom they must have possessed—wisdom that matched the awesome capabilities of their technology. She felt certain had their societal wisdom not grown as quickly as their technological genius, they would have destroyed themselves at some point. And, they would not have left such a peaceful legacy for the future inhabitants of Atlantis.

This question begged for an answer in Dr. Sarontin's mind:

Did the leaders of Atlantis possess sufficient wisdom to ethically manage this awesome technology and its impact on the world?

CHAPTER 26

Hawthorne Farm

"MATT, DID YOU HAVE a good time today?"

"Yes."

Matt still did not have a good feel for where this conversation was headed.

"That's good. I want you to know that I'm proud of you and I think of you as another son."

Well, this doesn't sound too bad so far, Matt reasoned.

"We always have a lot of fun together, don't we?" Grandpa questioned with a smile and a look down at his shoes.

Matt just nodded his head up and down. He was still a little anxious about what this might be leading up to so he chewed on his lower lip.

"You're ten years old now. You think you're ready to handle some grownup responsibilities?"

Now, this was much better as far as Matt was concerned. *Instead of being in trouble for something, Grandpa was going to trust him with some adult stuff!*

Matt looked into his Grandpa's serious yet kind eyes and noticed something he was not used to seeing there. It looked like… *fear?* This was unsettling to Matt. Everyone knew Bill Flannery was fearless. So, what could be so scary that even Bill Flannery was afraid of it? Matt knew it was time to step to the plate, so to speak.

"You bet, Grandpa. I'm ready for whatever you want me to do. Just tell me what."

"Well Matt, it's not so much what I want you to do, as it is what I want to trust you with. Do you understand?"

Matt was unsure how to respond.

"Uh, not really."

"What I mean is, that I need to be able to trust you to keep a secret for me and keep something safe for a long time if it is necessary. Does that sound like something you can do?"

He let out the breath he had been holding, smiled, and said "You can *always* trust me, Grandpa!"

Bill Flannery thought to himself, *the poor boy has no idea what I'm asking of him.*

"I know that, Matt. I know that."

CHAPTER 27

Aquatica
Atlantic Industrial Complex

Commander Mishon surveyed the herculean construction effort unfolding in front of him. The sprawling shipyards had been expanded to include the building of airships as well as waterships. There were dozens of mammoth metal skeletons being energy fused together and outfitted on the fly with the latest technological breakthroughs, even as they developed. This truly was a golden age of discovery and innovation for Atlantis.

The decision had been made by the Military Council to build a smaller armada of large capital ships rather than a greater number of smaller craft. The rationale was that the massive dreadnought-class air and water ships would be more intimidating and act as a more effective deterrent against foreign military resistance. Truly, the world had never witnessed machines of this scale and sheer destructive power. The largest seafaring dreadnoughts would be floating cities with a crew of over 3,000 each and would carry devastating weaponry.

How long had he waited for a moment such as this? His whole professional life, that was how long. How difficult it had now become to hide his seething ambition and contain his excitement over this massive war machine that he alone would command. Would the weapons development and testing ever be complete?

Although it had only been months since the research had begun, it felt like years to Mishon. He longed to see the instruments of power and destruction integrated into the beautiful ships in front of him.

He wondered if he would be able to show restraint should he be challenged by the primitive military forces of other nations? Or would he make a proper example of them and unleash terrible retribution upon their cities and towns? He smiled, and his hands broke out in a light sweat at the very thought of it.

CHAPTER 28

Hawthorne Farm

Bill Flannery rose from his dinette chair and moved toward the end of the workbench where the Frigidaire was parked, looking as if he was still unsure if he was doing the right thing. Matt was watching him intently and observed that Grandpa looked older than he did a few minutes ago. A little more stooped over. As if there was a heavy weight pushing down on his back and shoulders.

"Matt, can you come over here and give me a hand?"

Grandpa had placed himself on the left side of the refrigerator which was farthest away from the workbench and motioned for Matt to take up a position on the right side, closer to the bench. There was less space to work with on the bench side and Matt could fit in there more easily. Grandpa had enjoyed Sue Flannery's cooking for enough years that it was starting to show around his middle.

He indicated he wanted Matt to help him wiggle the refrigerator away from the wall by working it back and forth and side to side. After an awkward start, the two of them soon got into a rhythm of working in harmony instead of opposing each other, gradually moving the refrigerator away from the wall and workbench. *Boy, they used to build this stuff a lot heavier than they do now,* Matt realized. Grandpa then signaled with his open palm that they could stop.

Grandpa Flannery knelt by the spot that had just been vacated by the refrigerator. He was squinting at the dirt floor, looking for something. He used his hand to whisk away some dirt, stopped, and looked closer. Matt could see something shiny peeking through the dust. It looked like a metal ring about two inches in diameter. Grandpa Flannery inserted a couple of fingers through the metal loop, stood halfway up, set his feet, and gave the loop a strong yank upwards.

Dust flew into the air, forming thin clouds that whirled around in front of the streaming window light. The metal hinged top had come swinging up and out towards Grandpa, causing him to lose his balance and almost land on his rear. If Matt had not been so intrigued by the box in the floor, he would have burst out laughing. But he could see from the look on Bill Flannery's face that this was no laughing matter.

Grandpa straightened all the way up, took a couple deep breaths, brushed the dust off his shirt and pants, and asked Matt if he would bring him the big flashlight that was always charging on the workbench.

As Matt moved to retrieve the flashlight, he thought, *what is Grandpa hiding and protecting so much he had to bury it in the barn floor? Is there treasure in that box? Antique guns? Shrunken heads? Ancient jewelry and coins worth a fortune? Pirate booty? And whatever it is, why didn't Grandpa take it to the Natural History Museum like he did all of his other finds? Was Grandpa hiding something illegal?*

Matt had no answers yet but as he handed the flashlight to his grandfather, he was sure anxious to discover the secrets hidden in that box.

CHAPTER 29

Aquatica
Special Weapons Research Center

Dr. Sarontin listened and watched as cheers and congratulations rang out in the SWRC.

Atlantis's best and brightest had reverse-engineered the Ancients' technology well enough to create a viable template for an energy weapon.

Of more importance, they had learned to duplicate the Life Source power storage and make it portable. This achievement was key to all their other projects. If they were not able to replicate the technology of the Life Source and make it portable enough to install on the large vessels currently under construction, the war machines would never leave the shipyard.

Now it all seemed possible, inevitable, unstoppable.

The Life Source was powered by gravitational field manipulation which had provided clean, limitless energy for Atlantis over thousands of years. Graviton generators would now power their fleets around the world and beyond if they so desired. After all, "beyond" is where the Founders had come from in the first place.

A new universe of options was opening wide to the Nation of Atlantis.

The destructive force of the weaponry would be created by the harnessing of light energy and molecular manipulation. This breakthrough would also take communication to another level. Communication at the speed of light. What a legacy and treasure trove of knowledge the Ancient Ones had left them.

Why do I not feel as good about all this as I should?

Dr. Sarontin stood quietly watching, a forced smile stretched across her countenance, masking her anxiety.

CHAPTER 30

MATT EDGED CLOSER TO his grandfather's side, trying to get a glimpse of the secret treasure hiding in the steel box buried in the floor. Bill Flannery was kneeling in the dirt and pointing the flashlight into the box, attempting to retrieve whatever was concealed there. As the object came into Matt's view, it appeared to be wrapped in yellowed cloth and about the size of the shoebox that Matt's size eleven tennis shoes came in.

After extracting the mystery object from inside the metal floor vault, Bill Flannery moved to the dinette table and placed the item in the middle, brushing aside the palm tree salt and pepper shakers to make some room to work.

As Grandpa removed the yellowed protective cloth with care, a black plastic, airtight storage container was revealed. The Professor carefully pulled up on the corners of the container, one by one, until the lid came off with a pop. He set the lid aside and stared at the contents of the container as if he were Superman confronting Kryptonite in one of Matt's comic books.

Bill Flannery paused for a moment, still considering his actions of this day, and looked sideways at Matt with a grimness in his eyes. His lips were drawn in a tight line as if he were facing something he had been dreading for a long time. He then looked back into the plastic box and reached for the cloth bundle inside.

CHAPTER 31

GRANDPA FLANNERY BEGAN TO slowly unroll the aging cloth that had protected the secrets within. Matt was becoming more apprehensive and was chewing on the inside of his left lip again. He had no idea if what he was about to witness was an unfathomable monstrosity or maybe something that a boy his age should never be allowed to see.

The elderly man pulled back the last layer of cloth only to reveal a roll of cushiony foam that had been used to further protect the contents. It seemed to Matt that Grandpa was taking way too long to unwrap the mystery item. Curiosity was eating him alive.

As if he could read Matt's mind, Bill Flannery glanced up at the anticipation on Matt's face and assured him with an uneasy grin, "Almost there."

Finally, Grandpa laid open the foam insulation to reveal what was inside. Matt could not help but feel let down at what he saw.

There was only three small, dark gold, triangular shaped objects and a piece of rolled up, yellowed paper with a string tied around it. This seemed to be an awful lot of hoopla about nothing as far as Matt was concerned. No shrunken heads. No illegal jewels that Grandpa had stolen. No pirate treasure. Nothing forbidden or exciting it seemed.

Grandpa Flannery could see the disappointment in Matt's face and thought, *if only he understood the magnitude of what he was looking at right now.*

CHAPTER 32

Dr. Sarontin surveyed the detailed plans of the energy cannon prototype presented to her by the weapons development team. They had produced remarkable work over the last few weeks. Small scale testing had been successful using this design and Sarontin's approval was needed for the go-ahead to build the full-scale prototype—the most powerful weapon ever known to have been constructed on this planet.

The power supply had already been fabricated and was ready to go. It could produce enough pure power to supply a small city. Yet, it was no larger than her computer console and desk combined.

She looked at the power supply and thought about its dual potential for good and evil. The thought made her shudder inside.

She pushed aside her fears and signed off on the plans for the full-scale prototype weapon. Once the energy cannon was ready to test, the next big decision would be where to safely test it.

Dr. Sarontin sent a message to Dr. Sagrin, the Lead Geologist on the Council of Science, requesting that he meet with her at the earliest opportunity to begin site selection for heavy weapons testing.

CHAPTER 33

Hawthorne Farm

BILL FLANNERY LET MATT'S eyes take in the objects on the table for a few silent moments, then resumed their conversation in a low, calm voice.

"Matt, I know these objects don't look important to you right now and you have no idea what they are. But you must believe me when I tell you that they are extremely valuable. Why don't you pick up one of the little pyramids and tell me what you feel?"

Matt did as his Grandpa requested and noticed that the pyramid felt warm in his hand, as if it were glowing from the inside out somehow. He looked closer and saw strange markings on the small objects, imprinted in a shiny gold color.

"It feels warm in my hand, almost like its vibrating or something", Matt offered.

Bill Flannery nodded and replied, "These little pyramids are always warm like this and seem to have their own energy source of some kind. They are part of a puzzle that you will have an opportunity to solve at some point in the future."

He then proceeded to untie the string that bound the rolled-up paper. He spread it out on the table next to the mysterious objects.

"This is half of a map that shows a set of coordinates where the other parts of the puzzle can be found and it's my hope that you will be the one to finish solving the puzzle someday. The other half of the map, as well as three more little pyramids, are in the possession of my colleague at the university, Professor James Bart. We discovered these artifacts during one of our archaeological expeditions to the Bahamas about five years ago. Professor Bart and I had conducted a lot of research in that area and we came upon some very revealing historical artifacts. Due to the important nature of these artifacts, we felt we could not trust them to fall into the hands of governments or people who would use them for their own selfish gain."

Bill Flannery paused to let his words sink in, then continued.

"So, we made the decision that we would take a few of the artifacts with us and leave the rest where we found them. Someday, we would entrust them to someone younger to investigate this in more detail. There are many more items waiting at the site marked on the map. I have decided to trust you with my half of the artifacts. Professor Bart will also select someone whom he trusts to give his artifacts to. He will instruct that person to contact you when the time is right."

"But what makes you afraid to let anyone know about them?"

"Because Matt, they have the power to change the world for better or worse. You must promise me with your most solemn oath that you will not tell a soul about these relics and you will not show them to anyone. Not even your mother or father. You must swear to keep them secret until you're contacted in the future by the person of Professor Bart's choosing. Will you make that promise to me?"

Matt nodded his head to the affirmative and replied, "I promise".

Matt thought for a moment and asked, "Does Grandma or anyone else know about this?"

Grandpa Flannery shook his head from side to side. "No. Nobody but you and I and Professor Bart. Now, let's put this back in the vault and I will give them to you to keep once you are older and on your own. I just wanted to make sure you knew about them and where I kept them in case something happened to me before I gave them to you."

With that, Grandpa Flannery wrapped the objects back up in their protective coverings, sealed them in the container, and placed them back inside the floor vault. They wriggled and maneuvered the Frigidaire back into its original place where it could resume standing guard over the secrets hidden below.

Grandma was now calling out the kitchen door for them to come eat dinner and they started toward the inviting, two-story country house.

Grandpa suddenly stopped and looked at Matt.

"Better go over to the water hose and wash that ice cream off your mouth before we get in the house."

CHAPTER 34

Present Day
Anna Maria Island

MATT'S BUNGALOW WAS A beehive of activity. Evidence technicians, police photographers, questioning detectives, Anna Maria and Sarasota County squad cars, a coroner's truck for the lifeless body that was being removed from the hallway floor, and curious neighbors and tourists watching from the street and beach.

A couple of hours had passed since the arrival, and final departure, of Matt's uninvited guest. The whole incident retained an otherworldly, surreal quality. Matt was deeply perplexed by it all.

Who was this guy? What was he looking for? What were these "codes" or "keys" that he kept asking for? Why would he think that I had them? Who sent this hit man to my house? What was so important he was willing to kill me for it? Could it all have been a mistake? But the dead guy insisted he had the right man and the right address, and he knew my name.

Matt needed to clear his mind and think. Needed someone to talk to about this day's events. Someone he could trust.

Matt pulled the cell phone out of his pocket and pushed the icon displaying Kelli's smiling face. He heard the ring repeat five times with no answer and then her cheerful voicemail greeting came on and it caused Matt's heart to sink.

He really needed to talk to her.

The fear and shock had subsided and a new urgency was building inside of him, threatening to blossom into full blown rage. He felt violated and angry. He also felt vulnerable. He had been attacked inside his own home. Would he feel safe anywhere again?

Many of the people who lived in Matt's neighborhood didn't bother locking their doors most of the time. That might change after today. He left a short, tense message at the beep asking Kelli to call him as soon as she could.

The police investigators were wrapping up their work and would be leaving soon which was welcome news to Matt. He needed to make some sense of this senseless day and it was hard to think with all this commotion going on. The lead detective approached Matt with a mixed look of concern, curiosity, and sympathy.

Detective John Riker had been dispatched from the Florida State Police to assist in the investigation. The Anna Maria Island Police Department did not see a lot of cases like this and had minimal crime scene resources at their disposal.

Detective Riker found the situation almost as troubling and puzzling as did the intended victim. Matt Flannery had no police record other than a speeding ticket a couple of years earlier and had no known associations that would offer a clue as to who might be behind this assassination attempt. Matt's service record in the Navy was exemplary and his reputation spotless in the community where he lived and worked as a charter boat captain.

Riker looked into Matt's bewildered eyes.

"Don't worry, Mr. Flannery. We'll do everything in our power to get to the bottom of this. We'll examine the body and the few items he had in his possession to see where they lead us. We don't know how he got here. He didn't have any car keys on him. He might have been dropped off or came by taxi or took the Island Trolley here from another location. Had a wallet with some cash in it but nothing else other than his knife."

"Our men have already started questioning everyone on your street and the surrounding area about any suspicious vehicles or people being near your house today. This being a popular tourist area doesn't help much. Lots of new people and out of town vehicles coming and going all the time. Is there anything else you can think of that might give us a clue as to who this guy was and what he wanted?"

Matt considered the question for a moment.

"No, Detective. I'm sorry to say, I can't. I'm as stumped as you are and quite honestly, I feel lucky just to be alive. But if I think of something that might help, I'll call you right away."

Detective Riker thanked him and left his card with a number he could call anytime, day or night.

The Police Chief of the Anna Maria PD informed Matt that police patrols would be increased in this neighborhood for the foreseeable future.

As the police crime scene units finished packing their gear and loading their vehicles, Matt's phone rang. It was Kelli.

"Kelli, when can you come over?"

She detected something unusual in Matt's voice.

"Matt is something wrong?"

"I'm fine. We'll talk about it when you get here."

Now, Kelli was concerned.

"Okay, let me finish up here at the office and I'll be right over. No more than an hour."

CHAPTER 35

Aquatica
Special Weapons Research Center

Dr. Sagrin, a renowned geologist, huddled over topographical and geological maps with Dr. Sarontin. After several minutes of examining them in close detail, Sagrin nodded a couple times and made an affirmative grunting noise in his throat. He then straightened and looked at Dr. Sarontin with a triumphant twinkle in his eyes.

"Dr. Sarontin, it seems good fortune has smiled on you for this next stage in the project. Since you chose to build the SWRC near the Life Source, you now have close access to the continental power conduit tunnels and shafts. Of course, you cannot do testing in any of the ones that contain actual power nodes and conduits, but for some unknown reason, the Ancients dug several large, deep shafts nearby and did not place any active systems inside them. Maybe they excavated more tunnels than they needed. I don't know for sure. But the good news is, the larger shafts would make excellent test ranges for the new energy weapon you are building. These tunnels extend for great distances into the earth's crust and with all the bedrock surrounding them, they should provide a safe and stable test environment, without you having to leave the vicinity of the SWRC. This would expedite your testing and analysis if I understand the situation correctly?"

"Yes, Dr. Sagrin, you are correct in your assumptions. This would simplify and accelerate our testing tremendously. Other than finding an easily accessible test site, my secondary concern was that it would be safe and secure. You seemed to have concluded that this site would be both?"

"Dr. Sarontin, as you know, one of the reasons we chose to build the SWRC in this location was due to the deep layers of bedrock and the strong foundational properties of the surrounding area. Additionally, this is a preferred location in Aquatica that can be accessed from all areas of the continent due to the nearby transportation lines, airship terminal, and watership dockage. It has proven to be an ideal location in every way and I believe it will serve you well in your weapons development program."

Dr. Sarontin felt a sense of relief flow through her mind and body after hearing the evaluation from Dr. Sagrin. This would be a very convenient and efficient location for the testing program. Every phase of the project would be centrally located allowing for optimum communication between all the scientific departments and disciplines involved.

Yet, another nagging thought bedeviled her.

I hope Dr. Sagrin and his team fully understand the tremendous forces that this weapon will unleash during testing…

CHAPTER 36

Matt's Bungalow
Anna Maria Island

MATT PACED BACK AND forth between the front windows of his house, waiting for Kelli's arrival and trying to calm his mind and emotions.

The minutes crept by and it seemed like an eternity before he saw her white, short-bed, four-wheel drive pick-up truck come into view. Yellow, orange, and black graphics covered the truck, spelling out "The Dive Station Siesta Key, FL". Matt always kidded Kelli about the truck looking too tacky, but on this day, it was a welcome sight.

She parked directly in front of the house and Matt was relieved that all the police vehicles had left so she would not be freaked out by the sight of them.

Matt watched Kelli slide out of the driver's seat, shut and lock the truck door, and walk around the back of the truck. She was wearing a pair of white stretchy short shorts, turquoise flip flops, and a turquoise tank top with the same loud logo and colors that were displayed on her truck.

Always the promoter.

Kelli Renner was in her early thirties. Her shoulder length light-brown hair was sun-lightened and streaked blond from working outside on the waters of the Gulf and Sarasota Bay. She kept it in a ponytail most of the time, except when she dressed up for an occasion or was trying to get Matt's attention. She was average in height, thin and rather petite, but extremely fit and surprisingly strong.

Lean and mean Matt liked to say.

She had a cute upturned nose, a golden tan, and kind blue-green eyes that reminded Matt of the Gulf waters on a calm, sunny day.

Never had she looked more beautiful to Matt than she did at this moment.

Kelli bounded to the front door and Matt opened it wide before she could manage to knock. She was a little startled but Matt motioned for her to come inside. She stepped through the open door and Matt quickly closed and locked it behind her. She nervously looked into Matt's eyes for clues to his strange behavior.

"What's going on, Matt?"

Instead of answering her question, he pulled her to him, embracing her tightly, and did not let go of her in the amount of time that he normally would.

Now she was really worried.

"Matt, please tell me what is wrong?"

He managed a weak smile and chewed the inside of his left lip.

"Okay, I tell you what. Let me fix us a drink and we'll go sit on the lanai. There's a lot to tell you and we might as well get comfortable. And…thank you for coming over right away."

Without waiting for a response, Matt took her hand and headed toward the kitchen with a bewildered Kelli in tow.

CHAPTER 37

As Matt led Kelli down the hallway from the front door to the kitchen area, the scene from the earlier struggle lay dead ahead. As Kelli reached the threshold separating the hallway and kitchen, she saw it. She stopped as if suddenly flash frozen, pulling Matt backwards a bit as he still had hold of her hand. He had tried to hurry past the spot where he had taken the intruder's life, but now they stood squarely in the midst of it.

A look of horror and confusion spread over Kelli's face and she put her hands up in front of her as if to shield herself from the awful reality of what lay before her. Her eyes took in the broken table, the shattered glass tabletop, the buckled floor lamp, the ship picture that had fallen off the wall and broken, and the unmistakable spatter of wide-ranging blood stains still visible on the floor and wall. Matt had made a half-hearted effort to clean things up after the police left but did not have the strength or inclination to finish the job.

Kelli's large eyes searched Matt's face for answers, but the only thing she could see was the still-present disbelief reflected in his eyes. Matt knew it would take a while to bring Kelli up to speed on the day's events and he did not want to do it while standing in the middle of this bloody wreckage.

He let go Kelli's hand, stepped on into the kitchen, and forged ahead with mixing a batch of margaritas. He felt it important to accomplish this small act of defiance since he didn't get to drink the first one he had made. Hell, he didn't even know who won the football game. It didn't seem quite as important as it did earlier.

He prepared the cocktails in a silent, workmanlike fashion. He poured Kelli's drink into her favorite tall-stemmed margarita glass with colorful palm trees and flamingos hand-painted all the way around it. He had bought it for her while on a romantic trip to the Caribbean they had taken on his boat. Matt washed and rinsed his Jimmy Buffett tumbler and filled it with ice and perfect margarita, the same way he had earlier before all this happened. The sturdy glass had survived the battle and was now back to being what it was meant to be, a drink glass instead of a weapon. He looked down at the smiling visage of Buffett in sunglasses and grinned back at him. Matt and Jimmy had fought well together, and both had survived to live another day.

He led Kelli outside through the sliding door to his small patio facing the peaceful panorama of the Gulf. The water was calm today, unaffected by the day's trials. This was the proper place to do their talking. Kelli was desperate to know what had happened, but knew it was best to let Matt tell it in his own time. She could sense he was unsettled by being inside the house. Mother Ocean's waters had the power to heal and calm the troubled spirit. Kelli understood it was time for Mother to do her thing for Matt now.

After a few sips of his cocktail and several minutes of being calmed by the eternal movement of the peaceful waters, he told her everything in detail; including the fate of his Louisville Slugger bat which the police had retained as evidence. For some reason unknown to him, they had not confiscated the Jimmy Buffet glass. That was fortuitous. He needed it more than they did right now.

Kelli watched Matt through wide, watery eyes as he recounted the day's harrowing attack. It was numbing to hear Matt describe what he had just survived, and her heart pounded violently in her chest as he spoke. She was terrified by the revelation that she might have lost him today and would never have had the chance to sit by the water with him, hold his hand, or hear his voice again, ever.

She could not bear these thoughts another moment as they filled her with so much pain as to paralyze her nervous system and send her into a state of shock, so she squeezed her eyes tightly shut in an effort to force those thoughts out of her mind. She then reopened her eyes, took a deep breath, and returned her focus to Matt and his incredible, terrible tale. He had noticed her reaction and offered to stop talking about it. But she knew it was as important for him to get it out as it was for her to hear it. She squeezed his hand and urged him to continue.

When Matt had said all he had to say, they sat looking toward the ever-shifting colors and restless motion of the Gulf of Mexico.

There was no more talking. Didn't need to. They held hands. Finished a couple more drinks. Watched another spellbinding Anna Maria sunset. Went upstairs. Made love like it was their first time. Fell asleep entangled in each other's arms and legs. Held each other tighter than they had for a long time, maybe ever.

Both profoundly aware of how fragile, fleeting, and precious life and love can be.

CHAPTER 38

Aquatica
Special Weapons Research Center

SO, THERE IT WAS. The gleaming energy weapon prototype that the military was eagerly waiting to install on board their fleet of air and waterships. A culmination of the technology of the Ancients and ideas from the best scientists and researchers in Atlantis. First of its kind in known Earth history. A hybrid borne of alien technology and human imagination.

It was constructed of a refined, cutting edge metal alloy that was not only stronger than any metal they had forged before, but with an extraordinary ability to shed and tolerate heat as well. The gunmetal grey barrel gleamed under the bright lights of the assembly area. It had a menacing beauty about it that was spellbinding. Its destructive power formidable.

The design team projected it to be capable of taking off the top of a small mountain with a single discharge at maximum power. It worked by disrupting the molecular cohesion of its target while simultaneously delivering a high energy shock wave to the same spot. Nothing known on the planet could remain intact when engaged by those two forces acting in concert. In fact, the design team would only be testing the shock wave capability in the early trials because they were not sure what effects the anti-cohesion component might have on the test range itself. They would have to find a remote, exterior area for that simulation. Even then, it would have to carefully controlled as they were not sure how far the anti-cohesion wave might travel before stopping.

Dr. Sarontin looked upon it in wonder and apprehension. A mixture of pride and dread.

Commander Mishon stared at it with wide-eyed amazement in anticipation of its promise. A young child presented with a coveted new toy.

Dr. Sarontin had received an urgent message from Minister Tiborus of the Guardians Assembly. He had pleaded with her to assist him in stopping this headlong rush to world dominance. She knew it was far too late for that. The Assembly as well as the entire citizenry of Atlantis had charted this course and there was no turning back. The opposition voices were become weaker and fewer in number with each passing day. The entire nation was consumed with a fervor unmatched in its history. Atlanteans were going to change the world and show it a better way. The New Age of Atlantis was at hand!

Dr. Sarontin had sent Tiborus a polite but dismissive reply stating she could not be of assistance to him. The matter was out of her hands.

His reply was to let the record show he had washed his hands of the whole affair and the deed had been done over his deepest protestations.

Dr. Sarontin directed the technicians to begin installing the energy cannon on its base which was waiting at the opening to Test Shaft Alpha. Testing would commence as soon as the weapon was fully wired to the control panels, monitors, and power supply.

CHAPTER 39

Anna Maria Island
The Arrival

WHEN MATT AND KELLI awakened the next morning, the light coming through the bedroom window was subdued and dull. The weather was changing. A storm front was moving in. They reluctantly untangled from one another, threw on shorts and shirts, and headed downstairs.

After a couple cups of coffee and more discussion of the previous day's events, they decided to clean up the broken items in the living area and to scrub the blood stains off the floor, wall, and hopefully, Matt's mind.

Kelli canceled her dive sessions for the day, much to the disappointment of her devoted students. She knew Matt needed her more than they did right now and there was nowhere she would rather be than by his side, seeing him through this traumatic event. With the weather kicking up, she would have had to cancel dive classes for a couple of days anyway until things calmed down in the Gulf.

As the morning passed, the cleanup succeeded in putting things back to an acceptable state. An altered form of normal. As they worked, they could hear the Gulf start to churn while the wind and waves gathered energy and momentum. The water had morphed from a soft blue-green to an angry blackish-green.

Matt monitored the Coast Guard weather reports by means of a marine radio in his kitchen. The forecast warned of at least twelve hours of active tropical storm activity coming in off the Gulf.

Nothing serious unless you were unfortunate enough to be on a small boat in the middle of it.

Morning gave way to afternoon and the waves became more persistent. They boomed and rolled, insisting on having their way with mortal men. The wind coming onshore had transitioned from occasional gusts into a constant howling force. Awesome and spellbinding as it built to a beautiful fury.

As Kelli and Matt were putting away the last of the cleaning supplies and pitching the remnants of the damaged goods into the outside garbage container, they heard a commotion stirring on the beach. Matt peered through the kitchen window, that he had yet to clean, to see what the clamor was. It appeared that a sailboat was floundering about twenty yards offshore and the owner was battling to keep it from running aground.

The boat's captain was tacking along the coastline, attempting to make it into a safe harbor, but was in obvious distress. Every time he maneuvered away from shore, the incessant wind and waves pushed him closer to it again. He was losing ground with each wave that battered his boat. People were gathering on the beach to watch this valiant struggle between man and the stubborn elements.

Matt and Kelli walked out onto the beach and joined the gathering of curious onlookers. They reminded Matt of race car fans waiting to see a dangerous crash. Torn between wanting to see it and not wanting it to happen, both at the same time.

The boat's owner finally conceded sail power was not working, so he dropped the sail and hastily lashed it to the lower boom of the L-shaped mast. He staggered and lurched his way to the rear of the boat in an attempt to use the outboard motor and rudder to control the vessel. It soon became apparent the boat was being pushed closer and closer to the beach with every wave and gust of wind that it absorbed, and the motor was not powerful enough to stop the momentum. It was only slightly delaying the inevitable.

Then the motor stalled and stopped working completely. The ill-fated sailor had no sail, no motor, and no hope of avoiding being beached or sunk.

In desperation, the man threw out the anchor. It bounced and dragged along the bottom like a kid's fishhook, powerless against the weather. The captain threw himself into the foaming, frothing water on the landward side of the boat and attempted to push the boat away from the beach with the strength of his arms. The sailor was thin of build and his wet clothes hung on him like drapes. The tactic he was employing was not only futile, but extremely dangerous. The powerful forces of nature drove the boat relentlessly to the shore and the embattled sailor was now being buffeted by the boat and the boiling water and the grey, howling wind. Matt could see the man had put himself in serious physical danger at this point. He felt it was time to get involved.

Matt yanked his tee shirt over his head, kicked out of his Reefs, pitched his wallet to Kelli, and waded out to where the man and the boat were struggling, now only a few yards from shore.

Matt screamed at the man above the noise of the wind and waves, imploring him to listen to reason. He told the captain if they worked together, they might be able to save the boat from serious damage.

The man was desperate, wild-eyed, half-drowned, his long, wet brown hair whipping across his face and eyes, all while being tossed around like a rag doll in a tempest. He nodded his head agreeing to work with Matt.

Matt instructed the captain to get back into the boat. Matt gave him a boost up as the exhausted man dragged himself over the lurching side of the boat. He was then instructed to get a rope…a long rope.

The beleaguered sailor pulled a coiled rope out of a storage locker on board. Between waves, Matt gestured and shouted for him to tie off his end of the rope to a cleat on the front of the boat and throw Matt the other end. The captain laid down on his stomach and crawled out onto the front of the rolling, pitching boat where he managed to secure one end to a rope cleat near the bow. He then tossed the rest of the coiled rope out to Matt who walked his end of the line out of the water and tied it off to a mature palm tree on the shore. After several years in the Navy and more years as a working charter fishing boat Captain, Matt could tie a strong seaman's knot of any configuration and it would hold.

Matt directed the tired and fading sailor to untie the line that ran through a pulley at the top of the main mast and throw both ends of the rope down to him in the water. This left the line still attached to the pulley at the top of the main mast, but both ends free at the bottom.

Matt enlisted some of the onlookers to give him a hand with the next task. Together, they pulled on the main mast lines with all they had. In effect, they were pulling the line attached to the pulley at the top of the mast toward the beach. This heeled the boat itself over sideways, exposing the keel to the open water and the heavy waves pounding onshore. These lines were not as long as the first one, so Matt had to tie them off to a metal park bench that was anchored into concrete on a stretch of beach nearer to the boat. The three secured lines prevented the bow from moving violently about and the boat from rolling back and forth as the waves hit it. By pulling the boat over by the mast, it allowed the bottom of the boat to remain exposed to the open water and absorb most of the punishment being meted out by the crashing waves.

Matt sloshed and fought his way back to the sailboat and signaled the owner, who was hanging on to the main mast, to jump down into the water with him. The man did not question or hesitate. He just nodded and grabbed a waterproof duffle from a locker near the wheel as he stumbled toward the side of the boat. He fell, more than jumped, over the side and the two men waded ashore together, Matt supporting him and half dragging him out of the churning water. With some help and cheers of encouragement from the crowd of people on the beach, they worked to further tighten the shorelines as the waves pushed the boat further onshore, slackening the ropes.

Once the boat had become fully beached and secured by the tightening of the tether lines, the crowd trickled away, rather disappointed that the show was over, but convinced they had been properly entertained and the ending was appropriate.

The weary sailor cracked an exhausted and relieved smile at Matt and extended his trembling hand.

"My name's Lucien Bart."

"Matt Flannery".

The shipwrecked castaway took a quick step back and shot Matt a disbelieving look as if seeing a ghost, then shook his head, water flying out of his hair as he did so.

"Well, I'll be damned! If that don't beat all. That's just too frickin' weird. The very person I was coming here to find when this storm got hold of me and the *Windchaser*, ends up pulling me out of the water and saving me and my boat. Man, I can't thank you enough for savin' my ass out there…literally. I was losin' it pretty bad 'til you showed up. What's the odds of you bein' the very one to bail me out?"

Matt was beginning to feel like he had fallen down the Rabbit Hole in Alice in Wonderland.

"Well, after all, you washed up on *my* beach, but I'm glad I could help. Why are you looking for me?"

Lucien looked at him for a moment, grinned, winked, and asked, "Ever hear of a man named James Bart?"

Matt thought for a moment then recalled that James Bart was the colleague and friend of his grandfather's that he had heard so much about in his younger years.

He looked at the newcomer and nodded.

"I believe I have."

"Well, I'm his grandson and before he died a couple years ago, he asked me to look you up. Seems there's some business that our grandfathers started together and you and me are supposed to see it through."

Matt scratched his head and chewed on his lip as he tried to connect the dots. In an effort to buy time to think, he sidestepped the subject.

"What do you say we go up to the house and get you into some dry clothes, mix up something to drink, and then we'll talk about it? What's your favorite poison, Lucien?"

Lucien did not hesitate with his answer.

"Margaritas, my friend! And I could sure use a stiff one or two after all that."

Matt looked at Kelli and they both burst out laughing as they turned and headed toward the bungalow with Lucien wearily trailing just behind them.

Matt spoke over his shoulder toward Lucien. "Yeah, I think I can round us up a margarita or three."

CHAPTER 40

THE INAUGURAL TEST OF the new energy cannon was about to commence. It was fully functional and hooked to monitors which would record all the data needed to analyze the results of the test firing.

The weapon was situated on the rim of Test Shaft Alpha and the cradle that held the cannon was firmly secured into the bedrock.

The cannon could be discharged at varying levels of potency just by adjusting the level of energy being sent into the beam generator. The test would start with the lowest energy setting and be gradually increased as long as the test data remained positive.

The suspense in the room was palpable and intense. There was a lot riding on these trials and everyone felt the pressure. All the data from the preliminary tests looked good going into today, but the proof would be found in the actual firing exercises that were about to commence.

Dr. Sarontin looked around the room at the department leaders who represented the greatest scientific minds in Atlantis and had to stifle a laugh. They looked like expectant fathers and mothers about to witness a birth. Some were chewing their fingernails and others were pacing the floor. Some sat at their computer stations staring anxiously at their screens while their knees bounced up and down. The rest were just fidgeting and eager to proceed.

Science Minister Sarontin then uttered the fateful words…

"Commence low energy testing on my mark…"

CHAPTER 41

"HOW IN THE WORLD am I going to get my *Windchaser* off the beach in one piece?" worried Lucien as they sat down with their gold margaritas fresh out of the blender.

Lucien had changed into a dry pair of khaki cargo shorts and a wrinkled navy-blue tee shirt that had a white imprint on the front proclaiming "Its Better in the Bahamas". He had pulled them both from his waterproof bag.

"When the weather calms down, maybe tomorrow at high tide, we'll see if we can get some water back under your boat so we don't do any more damage by pulling it out of there. I can use my boat to tow it off the beach and into the marina. I'll have Jake check it out for damage if you want. He's a good friend of mine who owns the nearest marina and he does good work at an honest price".

"Cool." replied Lucien, "I appreciate it, man."

"Spent any time in the Bahamas?" Kelli inquired, pointing to Lucien's tee shirt.

"Not too much…a week here and a week there. Just sightseeing mostly and doing a little sailing. I'd like to spend more time there, though. The water was frickin' unreal! Like sailin' on a big swimmin' pool when the weather's calm. How 'bout you?"

Kelli smiled as she visualized Lucien's word picture of the sailboat on a swimming pool.

"Yeah, Matt and I vacationed there once on his boat. Did some diving and fishing and drinking. More drinking than anything." Kelli flashed a mischievous smile and added, "Yeah, some things *were* better in the Bahamas as I remember!"

Matt turned a little red and they all enjoyed a good belly laugh. It felt damn good to laugh after all that had happened over the last thirty-six hours.

After more light conversation about life on the water, Matt opened the subject of why Lucien had come looking for him.

"So Lucien, what did your grandfather tell you about this mysterious business that he and my grandpa stumbled into?"

"Not much. Just gave me part of a map and some little triangle like things with weird writing or something on them. Made me promise not to tell anyone about them or show them to anybody, no matter what. Then he told me about you and said I was to look you up and then we could figure it out together and that it was very important. Do you know anything more than I do?"

Matt chewed on his lip, squinted a little, swirled his margarita in circles around his Buffet glass, then looked directly into Lucien's eyes, trying to get a read on this stranger who had washed up on the beach in front of his house.

"When did you say your grandfather passed away?" Matt asked.

"A couple years ago. So, I figured it was about time to look you up. Is your grandfather still around?"

The question pained Matt a little as he still winced at the knowledge that Grandpa Flannery was no longer there to talk to about things that mattered in life.

"He passed about five years ago. He was one of a kind. The best."

"Yeah, so was Grandpa Bart", Lucien replied with a wistful look on his face. "I guess that's why the two of 'em got along so well for so many years. Cut from the same cloth, I reckon."

Matt nodded in agreement.

"Well, all I know is that we're supposed to finish what they started. I feel like we owe them that. Grandpa Flannery always told me this day would come and someone would come looking for me with the other clues to the puzzle. That would appear to be you."

Lucien just looked down at the floor, shook his head from side to side, and chuckled.

"Yeah, that appears to be me."

CHAPTER 42

Matt's Bungalow
The Three Musketeers

THE GLASSES WERE RUNNING low, prompting Matt to make a trip to the refrigerator to get the partially full pitcher so he could refresh the drinks.

"So Lucien, did you bring the map and relics?" Matt asked.

Lucien paused for a few moments.

"Hey guys, I don't want to be rude or anything and I really appreciate what you did for me today. But Matt, I've got to ask this question. Should we be discussing this stuff in front of Kelli? I mean…our grandfathers swore us to secrecy and all and I'm just tryin' to be careful, if you get my drift?"

Kelli immediately spoke up.

"I totally get it, Lucien. Matt has not really discussed this much with me other than he mentioned his grandfather had left him some old relics that might mean something someday. I'll be more than happy to leave you two alone to work on this and get to know each other…"

Matt interceded as he filled the glasses.

"Hold on, Kelli. Lucien, that was a real important question and it was not rude or inappropriate. In fact, it shows me that you take your pledge to your grandfather as seriously as I do mine and I'm glad you spoke up. However, I hope you will believe me when I tell you that I would trust Kelli with my life, and not only will she keep this information private, she could be a big help in figuring all this out. She is probably smarter than either one of us, she can handle a boat, and is one hell of a diver. Will you trust me on this one?"

Lucien shrugged and thought it over for a few seconds, looked at them both with a serious expression, then broke out in his trademark grin.

"Oh, what the hell! If she's okay by you, then I guess she's okay by me. This is probably just a big fuss about nothin' anyway."

Matt looked at Kelli and then back at Lucien, extended his hand, and took Lucien's in a firm grip.

"Thanks for going with me on this. I guess it's the Three Musketeers now. What do you say we all turn in and get some rest and we'll pick it up again in the morning? Lucien, I have a spare bedroom and I insist you stay here for the time being."

"No argument from me, mate. I'm exhausted after that battle to save the *Windchaser* and I could definitely use some shut eye."

With that pronouncement, all three turned up their margarita glasses, drained them to the last drop, set the empties on the kitchen bar, and dragged their weary bodies upstairs to their waiting beds.

CHAPTER 43

Special Weapons Research Center
Aquatica, Atlantis

THE SIGNAL WAS GIVEN by Dr. Sarontin. Everyone assembled at the test site had donned hearing protection and tinted eyewear. The firing sequence control technician commenced the countdown which was displayed on a large wall-mounted telescreen.

The imposing weapon was pointed into a deep shaft measuring about twenty feet across and thousands of feet deep. No one was sure why the Ancients dug it or why they chose not to use it. The shaft did not go straight down but rather at an angle. This made it easier to mount the cannon at the rim. If the tunnel had ran straight down, it would have required them to rig a suspension system out over the shaft that would have had to be strong enough to support the cannon and its recoil when firing. The slope of the shaft was ideal for their purposes.

The countdown initiated at ten and worked its way down to zero. The deep boom and concussion wave that followed was felt as much as heard by the test observers. The air crackled around them as the energy pulse erupted out of the barrel of the cannon and disappeared in a blinding flash down the shaft. They held their collective breath and waited for the data results.

All eyes swung toward the technicians who were scanning the test monitors and interpreting the data as it flowed into their computer stations.

There was a wait of about two minutes as the technicians compared the test data they had received. For those waiting, it seemed like two hours.

The Director of Weapons Testing, Dr. Brota, turned to the anxious group of onlookers and pronounced that the weapon had fired successfully. He further explained that power had been delivered at optimum levels and the weapon had performed well within safety parameters.

A spontaneous cheer went up from the group of scientists and technicians who had poured their sweat and tears into this project for months now. They had sacrificed time with their families and abandoned their hobbies in tenacious pursuit of this joint goal.

And on this day, at this moment, it seemed to be worth it.

CHAPTER 44

Matt's Bungalow
Anna Maria Island

MORNING SUNLIGHT BROKE OVER Anna Maria Island like a golden flood, slipping through windows like a happy thief, driving away the night's darkness and shadows. The storm had run its course and moved on overnight.

The new day's arrival held a sense of adventure tinged with foreboding for Matt and his two companions. Too much had happened too quickly for Matt to feel at ease and he was unsure what his next step should be. Sometimes it helps to do something mundane and routine to bring a sense of normalcy back into one's life, so this was the path Matt chose to follow today. Get Lucien's sailboat off the beach and safely into the marina. That was something Matt could wrap his head around and it felt familiar and safe.

Kelli had risen from bed to use the bathroom and had not returned, but Matt could smell fresh coffee brewing downstairs.

As Matt approached the stairs to go down and join her, he could hear voices coming from the kitchen area and realized Lucien had already made his way to the source of the alluring coffee aroma wafting through the house.

Matt paused to listen to their lowered conversation as they evidently did not want to disturb his sleep. Kelli was filling Lucien in on Matt's encounter with the strange intruder and the ensuing events while expressing her deep concern for Matt's safety. He heard Lucien emit a low whistle, then an incredulous "Christ!" as he listened to the story.

Matt was pulling his tee shirt over his head as he shuffled down the stairs, interrupting their conversation.

"Mornin'."

He traded a kiss on Kelli's soft, cool cheek for a steaming mug of coffee, strong and black. An acquired taste from his Navy days. Kelli had learned to doctor her coffee with a little cream to temper the bite. She managed a weak smile as she handed him the mug, but it did little to mask her anxiety.

Matt stole a quick glance toward the corner where the intruder had fallen and died. The memory was so surreal, he questioned if it had really happened at all or if it was just a bad dream. But the dark stain on the wall confirmed it to be very real indeed. He needed to keep moving forward. No time to dwell on it.

"Lucien, you ready to get that tub of yours off the beach today?" Matt asked with a small grin in an effort to refocus his thoughts on matters at hand.

"Hell, yeah!" Lucien countered. "Some pirate might try to steal her and that would really piss me off. She's the closest thing to a girlfriend I've got. Me and that boat, we're a lot alike. We both like to drift with the wind and the tide and the ladies seem to prefer a guy who's a little more, uh, predictable, you might say. So, women come and women go, but the *Windchaser's* always there for me. Always ready for the next adventure. She's also my home right now. I don't have a permanent base anywhere else at the moment. She's all I've got and we take good care of one another. Oh, and she's a sensitive girl. I would appreciate it if you wouldn't call her a tub where she might hear it."

Lucien's face had taken on a somewhat worn and tired expression as he spoke, as if he had fought a lot of battles in his personal life and was reviewing some of them in his mind's eye.

The look disappeared as he snapped back to the present and flashed his high-wattage smile.

"Is anybody else hungry?" Lucien asked.

Kelli responded by grabbing a skillet out of the lower kitchen cabinet, slapping it on the front burner of the stove, and declaring that the other two musketeers were going to be treated to a man-size breakfast replete with crispy bacon, eggs over easy, toast, real butter, grape jelly, and hash browns.

Lucien's face lit up like a kid on Christmas morning.

"Now that's what I'm talkin' about! Quite a girl you got here, Matt."

To which Matt replied, "Yes, she is."

Something was causing a ball to form in Matt's stomach though he could not discern its origin.

A feeling of foreboding. Dread. Storms on the horizon.

CHAPTER 45

Anna Maria Island
The Boats

THE THREE MUSKETEERS ate every morsel of the big breakfast and they felt better with their stomachs full. Matt and Lucien took care of the cleanup since Kelli did the cooking.

Matt checked the marine report and confirmed high tide should occur around midday. It was now a little after 9:00 AM, so there was ample time to bring Matt's boat around to the *Windchaser* while the water was at its highest point. It would be the best way to get the sailboat off the beach with minimal effort and damage.

After the kitchen was squared away, they climbed into Kelli's truck and headed to the marina where Matt kept his boat. The marina was simply named "Jake's Marina" as it was owned by a man named Jake. After a quick ten-minute trip down the island, they pulled into the parking lot in front of the marina office.

Jake's Marina sits on a canal that provides direct access to Sarasota Bay and the Gulf of Mexico. The distance from the marina to the Bay is roughly 150 yards. From the bayside, you can follow the inside coastline up to the northern tip of Anna Maria Island where the Gulf meets the Bay. This is a large junction where Tampa Bay flows out into the Gulf under the majestic canopy of the Sunshine Skyway Bridge.

If you plan to head south, you proceed down the Bay until you reach Longboat Pass which allows quick passage to the Gulf. It is a popular gathering place for weekend boaters and partiers. They anchor or beach their boats on the small sand bars found in the shallow green waters of the Pass, creating a floating party often lasting all day and well into the evening, especially on holiday weekends.

Jake's Marina is strategically positioned. Being on the Bay side, the boats are better sheltered from the big Gulf storms. Yet, you can get out to the big water quickly when needed. Best of both worlds.

Matt led the way into the office of the marina where he found Jake standing at the counter, poring over paperwork.

Jake Preston was a local legend of sorts. Tall, fit, greying, and weathered, he knew the local waters, and people, like the back of his hand. He held few friends close, but for those he did, there was nothing he would not do. Matt was one of those few.

Jake looked up as the door swung open and in his usual smart-ass manner, hailed the trio.

"Damn, I would've locked the door if I had known *you* were comin', Captain Flannery. And Kelli darlin', I still can't believe you hang around with this bum. You know you can do better."

Kelli laughed, scampered around the counter, and gave Jake a big hug while playing along with his sarcastic banter.

"I know, Jake. But he has grown on me like a bad habit and I just can't seem to shake it."

Jake chuckled, shook his head, and replied, "Yeah, me too."

Matt stood with his arms folded in front of him, smiling patiently, and nodding through the whole exchange. It was the usual greeting he received from his good friend. He had learned long ago it was best to just let it play out.

Now it was his turn.

"How you doin', you old buzzard? Fleeced any snow-birds today?"

"Not as bad as you do with those overpriced charters of yours!"

Rich.

Jake nodded toward Lucien standing quietly behind Matt and inquired, "Who's this fellow you brought with you?"

"Jake, meet my new friend and partner in crime, Lucien Bart. His grandfather and mine were best friends and they worked as a team for years at the University of Florida. They went on a lot of adventures together. Lucien came down here looking for me, but he and his sailboat ended up on the beach in front of my house during the storm yesterday. We tied her off best we could and let her ride it out. He spent the night at my place but now we need to get his boat off the sand and into your marina to see what damage his old girl suffered. Her name is *Windchaser*."

CHAPTER 46

Jake's Marina
Anna Maria Island

"So, I guess you want me to help salvage your prize, Lucien?" Jake said with a stone face, sizing Lucien up.

"Matt says you're the man for the job, Jake."

Jake's features relaxed just a little.

"He's right about that. Sometimes, Matt's a pretty smart fellow. Don't worry, we'll make the old girl as good as new. What kind of boat is she?"

Lucien beamed. He liked talking about his boat…as most boat owners do.

"She's a 40-foot Hunter Legend and she's in real good condition…or at least she was."

Jake looked at Matt and said, "I'll get someone in the shop to watch the front and we'll go get her. Your boat or mine?"

"We'll take mine. I haven't had her out in a couple days and I know she misses me."

Jake said, "Alright then, let's get movin' while we have high tide and plenty of daylight."

The four of them walked out of the office and made their way to the end of the longest line of slips. Matt's boat was tied off at the very end of the walkway—the biggest slip for the biggest ship.

The *Nice Catch* was a 55-foot Viking offshore cruising/fishing yacht with a fully functional flying bridge and a tall observation tower above it. It was loaded with the latest electronics including a 3D GPS chart-plotter, 3D radar, 96 mile "bird" radar, dual GPS units, forward-looking and side-scan sonars, satellite radio and TV system, dual VHF radios, satellite phone, and autopilot.

The *Catch* was also outfitted with high-end deep-sea fishing tackle as well as a generous complement of scuba and diving gear. The *Catch* boasted three staterooms, each with their own head and shower. She also featured a full galley and salon with all the comforts of home, including its own freshwater conversion plant capable of making up to 600 gallons of freshwater per day.

Marine power was supplied by a pair of MAN 1,300 horse-power diesel engines with upgraded drive and control systems designed to take the boat anywhere her owner wanted to go.

The *Nice Catch* was stunning as it shone in the midday sun. The hull was a faint mint green and the deck structures were bright white. Lots of chrome and stainless steel completed the upscale look and feel of the beautiful craft.

Lucien stopped and stared at the *Catch*, turned to Matt with bugged-out eyes and said, "Is that yours, like for real?"

"For real."

"Damn, did you win the lottery or somethin'?"

"No such luck. Ten years of saving my Navy pay, investing it, and good credit. That's why I run a lot of charter trips. Have to take care of the monthly payment, insurance, and upkeep."

"I bet you get a pretty penny to charter *that* boat?"

Jake broke in.

"Steals 'em blind I tell you. But if they want the best boat, the best fish, and the best captain, the *Catch* is where they end up. Now, that's enough boat worship for today. Matt, fire up those gas guzzlers of yours and let's get under way."

CHAPTER 47

Anna Maria Island
The Windchaser

MATT MANEUVERED THE *CATCH* as close to shore as he dared, being careful not to run aground or foul the props in the sandy bottom of the Gulf. While carefully monitoring his depth finder and sonar, he kept his stern and propellers turned out toward the open water so he could nose the bow closer to the shoreline.

Kelli and Lucien had driven the truck back to Matt's house and joined the effort from the beach. Kelli was busy untying the lines holding the *Windchaser* lashed to the palm tree and metal park bench.

Lucien waded through seaweed and shallow water over to the sailboat to check its condition and ready it for the salvage attempt. The *Windchaser* had water under her from the rising tide and her hull was now partially submerged. It was a matter of gently tugging her off the beach until she was fully afloat. The boat was not leaking or taking on water and the battery-operated bilge pumps had done their job, emptying the worst of the storm water out of the hull. She appeared to be seaworthy.

Kelli finished untying the lines from the sailboat to the shore moorings, walked them out into the water, and tossed them back to Lucien. He stowed the longer line back in the deck locker and reattached the shorter one to the main mast rigging.

Jake had brought along one of his favorite toys, a device called a line thrower. Essentially, it was a rope gun using compressed air. It could "throw" a rope to another vessel at a distance up to 400 feet.

Jake yelled over for Lucien to make ready to receive the tow rope and Lucien gave the go ahead sign by motioning toward himself. Jake aimed the line thrower towards Lucien and then elevated the front end a little. He adjusted the pneumatic pressure setting on the gun to match the approximate distance needed and squeezed the trigger.

The front tip of the line was housed in a weighted plastic bullet so it could cut through the air and be guided to its target. The orange bullet tip arrowed straight and true but slightly over the *Windchaser*, splashing into the water on the far side. Lucien quickly fished the line out of the water and tied it off to a cleat on the bow of his boat. Jake secured the line on his end to a cleat on the stern of the *Nice Catch*.

Jake signaled a thumbs-up to Lucien asking if he was ready and Lucien poked the air with his thumb indicating he was good to go. Jake turned, peered up at Matt on the bridge, and pushed against the air with his hand, gesturing for Matt to back her out.

The powerful diesel engines were barely throttled above idle speed yet they effortlessly eased the *Windchaser* off the sand. Once the two boats were safely out in deeper water, Matt slowed to a stop and skillfully employed his bow thrusters and opposing engine throttles to execute a slow, precise turn. He pivoted the big cruiser completely around with Jake making sure the tow line did not get caught on anything. The *Catch* was now in proper position with the bow heading south toward the marina and the *Windchaser* securely in tow to the rear.

Kelli saw everything was good and headed back to her truck to meet up with them at the marina. Lucien remained on board the *Windchaser* to steer.

Jake climbed the steps to the bridge and took a seat in a captain's chair alongside Matt. Matt reached down into the refrigerator located by his right leg, pulled out a couple cold ones, and handed them off to Jake. Jake twisted open the beers, inserted them into a couple of can coolers with the logo of the *Nice Catch* and her profile printed on them, held one out to Matt, and they both took a long pull. They had accomplished the salvage without a hiccup.

Jake looked at his beer, then squinted sideways at Matt, hesitated, then just came out with it as he was apt to do.

"Matt, what did you mean when you said Lucien was your new partner in crime? You taking on a business partner? Hell, I thought you were doing alright. And there's always plenty of good deckhands willing to work charters with you, so I know you're not shorthanded."

Matt started laughing and almost choked on his beer.

"No, I'm not taking on a business partner. I didn't mean it that way. It's a personal thing I have to do. Lucien and I both promised our grandfathers we would do something and we feel we need to see it through, even if it turns out to be a wild goose chase. Kind of hard to explain."

"Try me."

"Listen Jake, it's not that I don't trust you. You know I do. But Lucien and I were sworn to secrecy about this thing a long time ago by our grandfathers. We have taken that oath pretty seriously so far."

"Have you told Kelli?"

"I won't lie to you. Yes I did, last night with Lucien's permission. I felt she could be a big help and Lucien agreed."

"What kind of mission are you going on that might require Kelli's help?"

Matt could see that Jake was not going to let go of this easily.

"Not sure yet. It would involve taking the *Catch* on a trip and looking for some stuff our grandfathers wanted us to find."

"I see. You think it might be dangerous?"

"The truth is, a week ago I would have said no. But things have gotten a little strange."

"Does this have anything to do with that man they hauled out of your house, deader than a doornail, a couple of days ago?"

"You know about that?"

"Oh come on, Matt. You know that I know everything that happens on our little slice of paradise."

CHAPTER 48

Bridge of the Nice Catch
Gulf of Mexico

"Wʜᴀᴛ ᴇʟsᴇ ᴅɪᴅ ʏᴏᴜ hear, Jake?"

"Not too much. I don't think the locals really know what went down. All they heard was some guy broke into your house, and for whatever reason, left with a sheet over his face. You want to tell me what happened?"

Matt took another sip of his beer, looked out from the bridge at the peaceful green water, and chewed absentmindedly on his lower lip, reconnecting with those disturbing memories of a couple days ago.

"Okay, here's the quick version. I was getting ready to watch the Gators and 'Noles play and had just fixed a drink. Then this big ass giant was suddenly standing in the doorway to my kitchen. He demanded that I give him some codes or keys or something or he was gonna gut me with the switchblade he pulled. I told him he was in the wrong house, but he knew my name. I'm tellin' you the truth, Jake, he was going to kill me if I didn't do something fast. He even admitted he was a professional hit man."

Jake's eyebrows raised into twin arches and his eyes opened a little wider.

"What did you do then?"

"Well, he had a knife and I had a margarita, so I improvised. I threw the margarita into his eyes and while he couldn't see, I took my Buffett glass and slammed the bottom into his nose. Made a real mess when his nose blew up and pissed him off royally."

"Well hell Matt, that might have slowed him down, but it wouldn't have killed him."

"You're right, it didn't. He was rubbing his eyes and yelling and trying to filet me, so, I grabbed my old baseball bat out of the corner and put a big swing on his bald head."

"And that's what killed him?"

"Not even close. Can you believe that? Put him down on the floor though."

"It didn't even knock him out?"

"No! This guy was a like a bull on steroids. It just stunned him a little and caused him to fall on his ass. He started telling me what he was going to do to me with that knife of his and I knew that one of us was not going to get out of there alive. And if I let him get back on his feet, I was pretty sure that would be it for me."

"How in hell's blazes did you put him away?"

"When I hit him upside the head with the bat, I hit him good and the bat snapped off at the handle. I still had the handle in my hands and it had a sharp tip left on it. He was swinging that knife around like crazy trying to get in a lucky cut on me because he still couldn't see very well, but I ran to his other side away from the knife, got behind him a little, and severed his jugular and windpipe with the tip of the bat handle."

Jake's eyes were now as big as silver dollars and he let out a low whistle.

"Are you shittin' me? You took him out with a broken bat handle?"

Matt was now wearing a sheepish look and appeared a little embarrassed.

"Yeah, I did."

"And that was the end of it?"

"Yep."

"Damn! You're a dangerous man, compadre! I have a new-found respect for your crazy ass. So, what in God's green earth do you think he was after?"

"That, my friend, is the million-dollar question." Matt slowed the engines, preparing to enter Longboat Pass. "But as weird as it sounds, the more I think about it, the more I believe it might have something to do with this little trip that Lucien and I are planning. That dead guy had a tattoo on his neck that reminded me of something Grandpa had given me."

"Is this thing your Grandpa gave you got something to do with the trip you and Lucien and Kelli are going on?"

"Bingo."

"So, the two might be connected?"

"Could be."

"I'm thinkin' you might need a little backup on this trip? You know, just to make sure your boat don't break down. Don't want to see you end up getting cheated by a crooked boat mechanic somewhere."

"I couldn't ask you to do that, Jake."

"You didn't. Anyway, I could use a little vacation."

CHAPTER 49

DR. SARONTIN PORED OVER the test results from the new pulse cannon and concluded that it was performing beyond their expectations.

It was time to increase the power levels to determine if it could continue to perform at optimum levels under a heavier load.

Up to this point, they had only tested it at power level 1 on a scale of 1 to 10. The technicians had installed a transparent viewing wall between the staff and the weapon to minimize the noise and shockwave they would experience as the intensity of the testing was dialed up. The viewing wall was heavily tinted to protect their eyes from the blinding flash of the energy pulse. Monitoring screens and data feedback stations were installed near the viewing area to allow quick assessment of the tests as they occurred.

Sarontin gave the signal to move ahead with Level 2 testing. Dr. Broda acknowledged and activated the alarms that preceded a test firing. The countdown was initiated from his command console and it started at sixty seconds counting down to zero. The countdown screen arrived at ten seconds and Dr. Broda pushed the red button that armed the weapon. The countdown continued to zero and Dr. Broda depressed the green button that commenced firing.

The flash from the cannon muzzle was immediate and intense. The viewing wall kept the flash at a comfortable level and protected them from the concussion wave. The pure energy of the pulse was awe inspiring and the staff looked at each other with a sense of wonder at what they had accomplished.

The test data came back clean and Dr. Sarontin gave the order to commence testing at Level 3.

CHAPTER 50

Jake's Marina
Anna Maria Island

MATT CAREFULLY MANEUVERED THE *Nice Catch* alongside the service dock at Jake's Marina, allowing the *Windchaser* to slowly drift toward the pilings. Jake had radioed ahead and a couple of his marine mechanics were waiting with ropes and boat hooks to capture the sailboat. With the *Windchaser* secured, the marina employees loosed the tow rope that bound it to the *Nice Catch* and threw it over to Jake. He put the rope back in the case with the rope gun so it would be ready to use another day.

Matt guided the *Nice Catch* alongside the fuel pumps, brought it to a stop, topped the tanks off with diesel fuel as he always did, and skillfully coaxed it into its berth. Mission accomplished.

Jake and Matt headed for the marina office where they found Lucien and Kelli waiting. Lucien was standing at a window overlooking the marina. He was gazing at his cherished boat, now safely secured. He looked visibly relieved.

"I can't tell you guys how much I appreciate your help." Lucien said.

"Not a problem, Lucien. I'll have the guys haul your old girl out of the water and give her a good once over. We'll find out why your outboard shut down, too. Probably just flooded with all that water flying around. I'll do everything I can to keep the cost down, but if you really want to show me your appreciation, then pay the bill when the work's completed." Jake said with a straight face.

Lucien was taken aback by the directness of the remark.

"Uh…well…you can count on that." Lucien replied.

"I am." Jake deadpanned.

Lucien looked around and saw that Matt and Kelli were suppressing grins and it dawned on him this was Jake's dry sense of humor on full display.

Lucien ignored the jab and continued.

"Anywhere around here to get some decent food and a cold beer?"

"Several places." Matt said. "My pick would be the Bridgetender Inn down by the Cortez Bridge."

"Fine by me. I'm buyin' everyone dinner tonight. You too, Jake. I'll have them fix you up a fresh grilled plate of hardass!"

The room went silent for a moment as everyone turned to see Jake's reaction. Jake narrowed his eyes at Lucien, shot him a steely look, then broke into a wide grin.

"You might be alright after all, Mr. Bart!"

CHAPTER 51

Bridgetender Inn
Bradenton Beach, Florida

IT WAS NOW LATE afternoon and the sun was diving toward the western horizon where the sky meets the water, blessing all it touched with a soft, golden hue. The golden time of day.

Kelli pulled her truck into the parking lot at the Bridgetender Inn and the four of them spilled out. It was a mild evening and Matt suggested they eat at the outside dining and bar area across the street from the main restaurant building.

The outdoor dining area features a spacious, rectangular bar situated under a large tree shading the entire area, including most of the tables. Small strings of lights, some colored and some white, are strung throughout the tree's branches and they are switched on every night at dusk. There is usually live music to complete the mood.

The tables and chairs are brightly painted works of red, green, yellow, and blue wrought iron. Some have a Green Bay Packers logo painted on them as the owner is an avid fan. They are informally arranged and sit loosely on a groundcover of crushed seashells that crunch under your feet as you walk. It is a come-as-you-are sort of place with an interesting mixture of locals and tourists hanging out together. There is a small boat dock nearby as well where boaters are welcome to tie off and tie one on.

Some evenings, a pirate ship on wheels parades past with a gang of partying swashbucklers throwing beads to the ladies who yell the loudest or are willing to bribe them in other ways.

The colorful tables are all waterside and offer picturesque views of Sarasota Bay to the south, the newly renovated Cortez Pier, the Cortez Drawbridge, and lots of boats.

About twenty sailboats as well as an assortment of power cruisers are typically anchored in the bay. In the late afternoon light, it is a scene lifted straight from a travel brochure. Pelicans diving and dolphins frolicking…don't get much better.

On this calm, clear evening, a solo guitarist was playing and singing a nice selection of beach songs and love ballads. It was a great way to end the day and celebrate new and old friendships. A gentle bay breeze came onshore to cool everyone.

The owner, Fred, came by the table and shook everyone's hand, thanking them for stopping in. Matt and Jake were long time regulars and had thrown back more than a few frosty ones with Fred.

Fred insisted the first round was on the house, and it was not long before ice cold beer was being enjoyed by all.

A debate ensued over what food to order. Matt and Jake went with the fresh grouper platter, Kelli opted for glazed salmon, and the newcomer Lucien followed the waiter's recommendation and decided to try the house specialty, Roast Duck.

After everyone had enjoyed a few swallows of beer and settled into their surroundings, Matt felt it was time to take care of some pressing business.

"Hey guys, I don't want to ruin our fun, but I need to talk to you about some things that are on my mind. I've been doing a lot of thinking about what happened in my house a couple days ago. I don't believe it was a case of mistaken identity and whatever the guy was after, he meant business. He believed it was worth killing me over. Then Lucien washes up on my beach the very next day. Seems like an awfully big coincidence to me. The more I think about it, the more I'm convinced there's a connection."

Matt looked around for their reactions, saw only blank faces, so he forged on.

"Kelli, Lucien, please hear me out. I haven't told Jake any details about our little adventure, but Jake being Jake, he could tell something was up. He also asked me if what we were about to do would be dangerous? I wasn't sure how to answer his question, but the fact is, if the guy that came looking for me was after the stuff that Grandpa Flannery and Mr. Bart left us, then it could be dangerous...real dangerous."

Matt let that statement sink in and continued.

"While we were on the way to the marina with the *Windchaser*, Jake asked me to let him help. He doesn't know the details of what's going on, but he's worried about our safety and wants to go with us to watch our backs."

"Lucien, this is twice I've had to ask you this and I apologize. I realize that it's hard to know what to do since we know so little. And you've only known Kelli and me for two days and Jake for part of one, so I'll let you choose and I will honor your decision. But first, let me say this about Jake."

"Jake is aware we were sworn to secrecy by our grandfathers, but still wants to pitch in with us. That's the kind of friend he is. There's nothing he can't do around a boat or the water and I suspect he can do a lot more than I know about. But in the end, I will respect our pact and I will abide by your decision."

Lucien pondered the situation for a moment while rubbing the reddish-brown scruff on his chin. He took a long pull on his beer, shook his long, curly, sun-streaked hair away from his face, waved at the waiter and ordered another round, whispered something in the waiter's ear, then looked hard at Matt.

"Matt, you really think what happened at your house is connected to our relics?"

"Well Lucien, without saying too much, I can tell you this. The man said he'd been waiting a long time to get his hands on whatever he was after and our grandfathers had this stuff for years before passing it on. But this is the crazy part. After he died, I got a good look at his neck. He had a tattoo that was a dead ringer for those little pyramid-looking things we have. There was three of them in a triangular grouping on his neck. Took a day for me to put the two things together, but there it is."

"So, Matt, what you're sayin' is somebody could have been watchin' me and knew we both had some of these things and planned to catch us together and get a two for one deal?"

"Could be. You were a little late showing up due to the storm and maybe messed up their plan, but it makes sense."

Fresh brews showed up and they traded in their empties for cold replacements. The waiter assured them the food would be out shortly.

"What in the hell are we gettin' ourselves into?" Lucien wondered aloud.

"Don't know, but our grandfathers chose us to see it through. Evidently, they believed we could handle it."

Lucien considered Matt's words for a moment and brightened.

"We've got a lot more questions than answers at this point. I don't like the idea of us being sittin' ducks. Seems those old codgers knew we would finish their dirty work, so I guess we should prove 'em right. Jake, tell me again, why are you willing to put yourself at risk with nothin' to gain and everything to lose?"

Jake looked Lucien dead in the eyes and said in a low, calm voice, "Because Matt and Kelli are my friends, and that's what friends do."

Lucien held Jake's stare for a few more moments, his face flushed a little, he looked down, shook his head from side to side, and broke out his trademark grin.

"I'll be damned. If this group don't beat anything I've ever seen. Jake, if you're crazy enough to put your ass on the line, I'm crazy enough to let you. So welcome aboard you crazy bastard!" Lucien stood and offered his hand to Jake and Jake rose to meet his gesture.

Matt could see the waiter bringing the food, so he said, "Kelli, you good with all this?"

Kelli smiled and nodded in affirmation. "We could use Jake's help if things get complicated, and it sounds like they might."

"Alright then, it's settled." Matt stated. "Let's meet at my place tomorrow morning for breakfast. Eight bells. Time to make some plans and figure out what this is all about."

Everyone nodded in agreement.

The waiter placed a shot of tequila in front of each of them that Lucien had secretly ordered. Lucien lifted his shot glass and said, "To the Four Musketeers!" They all threw back their shots to seal the new alliance. The food was being distributed around the table and it was time to eat and relax.

Relaxation would be harder to come by in the days ahead.

CHAPTER 52

Dr. Broda confirmed the test results on the pulse cannon had remained stable and within acceptable safety parameters all the way through power level 10.

"Outstanding! Great work everybody." Sarontin exclaimed to the team of fifty or so technicians and researchers within hearing range of her voice.

The new weapon had performed beyond their wildest dreams and was a testament to the commitment and genius of the men and women who had built it on such a short timeline.

Dr. Broda now appeared in front of Dr. Sarontin, staring at her with a look of excited anticipation.

"What is next, Dr. Sarontin?"

"The military wants the weapon to not only be powerful, but to be able to fire in rapid succession should the need arise. The only obstacle I see to that is the power supply. The single power unit we are currently using has a recharge time of about one minute before it can support another full pulse. They want a faster recovery time."

"Makes sense in a tactical situation. Do we have a plan to accomplish this?"

"Yes, I believe we do, Dr. Broda. I already have a team working on a dual power source system with auto-switching capability. The cannon would automatically switch power sources immediately after a discharge. The second power source would come online immediately after a weapon discharge and be available to support another full pulse. Even if rapid firing is called for, this method would serve to double the number of firings in the same period of time. Commander Mishon has affirmed this would be an acceptable rate of fire and he will support the implementation of this new system."

"Dr. Sarontin, how many consecutive pulses does the military want the cannon to be able to perform before allowing a cool down?"

"Their desired number is twenty. That is pushing it, but I believe it still falls within our safety and performance parameters. I have asked the technicians to strengthen the cooling system on the cannon to enhance this capability."

"Well Doctor, I hope the military will never need to employ that level of firing. At power level 10, combined with the molecular disruptor, this thing could destroy an entire city with twenty pulses."

"Yes, I know. The military leaders, as well as the Assembly leaders, have assured me the more power we can display, the less resistance will be offered, and the less violence will be encountered. Their line of thinking makes sense in a way, but I will admit to experiencing horrific night visions about it all. I pray that our powers of compassion and wisdom has grown to match our power of destruction."

Dr. Broda's eyes grew wide and his face a little pale as he considered the possibilities—both good and bad.

"And I as well."

Dr. Sarontin looked quickly at the test supervisors in an attempt to quell the doubts arising once more in her mind.

She spoke with authority.

"The dual power system for the cannon should be ready within 48 hours. Let's begin preparations. The stated goal will be 20 consecutive pulses with no more than a 30-second interval between each pulse. Dr. Broda, will you check on the cooling system upgrades as well?"

CHAPTER 53

Matt's Bungalow
Anna Maria Island

THE FOUR MUSKETEERS MET for breakfast at Matt's house at 8:00 AM the next morning as planned. Lucien volunteered to be the short order breakfast cook this time. He claimed to have spent considerable time as a cook on a couple of the different jobs he had worked while supporting his vagabond lifestyle.

This morning's fare consisted of waffles made from scratch, fresh strawberries and cantaloupe, maple syrup, fluffy scrambled eggs with Colby cheese blended in, spicy sausage patties, orange juice, and plenty of strong coffee.

There were no complaints from the diners and they wasted no time cleaning their plates. Now, it was time to get down to business.

Matt spoke first.

"I think we should begin by examining these artifacts we inherited. Lucien, I'm assuming you have yours tucked away in that bag you carry?"

"You assumed right, sir!"

Lucien proceeded to dig into his duffle and brought out a small waterproof bag with a locking zipper. He put his hand inside his shirt collar and pulled out a key hanging around his neck on a silver chain. He held the bag's locking zipper up to the key and unlocked it. He then dropped the key back under his shirt and unzipped the bag, spilling its contents onto the kitchen table.

Matt went to his upstairs bedroom and opened a small combination safe. He reached inside and extracted the same black plastic airtight container his grandfather had shown him more than twenty years earlier. Grandpa Flannery had transferred possession of them after Matt's tour of duty in the Navy had ended.

The four of them gathered around the kitchen table where Matt and Lucien cautiously unwrapped their mysterious inheritances. They each produced an identical set of three little brown pyramids with strange, gold symbols inscribed on the sides. There was also the two yellowing, rolled up papers bound by string.

Everyone at the table took turns examining the little pyramids and puzzling at the vibrant, warm energy emanating from them. Then the papers were unbound and rolled out side by side, completing a crude map. Matt opened a kitchen drawer and found some clear scotch tape which he used to join the two map halves together.

Each of the four were experienced boaters and knew their way around maps and charts. They pored over the completed map and began to decipher in their own minds what they thought was being displayed.

After a minute of mutual staring at the map and tracing lines with their fingers, they looked at each other to see what the consensus would be.

Matt looked at the other three.

"What do you think its showing?"

Kelli spoke first. "This looks like the outline of the Bahamas to me."

Lucien spoke next. "Yeah, I agree. I spent some time sailing in and out of lots of little coves in those islands and it looks like the area they marked would be near Bimini Island—the northern section. There's some coordinates on here so we could check it out?"

"Yeah, my grandfather had mentioned to me once that the two of them had spent quite a bit of time exploring the Bahamas. So, it makes sense." Matt added.

Matt walked over to his old desk in the corner of the living room and produced boating charts showing the Bahamas and the positions of the islands there. He compared the coordinates on their pieced together map to the coordinates on the charts and confirmed it was North Bimini Island where they would be headed.

"Bimini Island, huh?" Jake questioned. "Lots of legends about that place."

"I didn't know you were a history buff, Jake?" Matt jabbed.

"There's a lot of things you don't know that I know, Pardner. Just because I'm good lookin' doesn't mean I'm not smart!"

"Okay Mr. Good Lookin', what kind of legends are you referring to?" Matt inquired.

Jake shifted his weight to his other foot and turned his attention back to the map.

"There's a strange thing there called the Bimini Road. An underwater stone road that seems to come from nowhere and lead to nowhere. Nobody's been able to come up with a good explanation for it yet."

"Yeah, I saw it on a TV documentary about unexplained mysteries." Lucien added.

Jake nodded and continued.

"Some say it was part of the lost continent of Atlantis."

"Isn't that just an old sea story or ancient myth?" Matt asked.

"Legends and myths usually have some basis in fact, from what I've read." Jake replied. "Some believe Atlantis existed about three thousand years ago as a big island continent in the middle of the ocean. Sort of like Australia. There are arguments over which ocean it was. Some say the Mediterranean, some the Caribbean, and some say the middle of the Atlantic. Legend says it was a highly-developed civilization with advanced technology. The most popular theory says it was destroyed by a big volcano and sunk into the ocean, but nobody knows for sure."

"Well, let's see if we can solve *our* little mystery before we take on Atlantis." Matt replied with a grin.

"How we gettin' to the Bahamas?" Lucien asked.

"We'll take the *Nice Catch*." Matt offered. "She's built for trips like this. There's plenty of sleeping space, full galley, freshwater system, and two big ass diesels! Might as well go in comfort. Any objections?"

"Not from me." Lucien replied. "I was hopin' you'd volunteer that yacht of yours. I love the *Windchaser*, but she does get a little cramped after a few days."

Matt looked around the table.

"Here's what I'm thinking. We spend the rest of the day getting food and provisions on board the *Catch*. She has full fuel tanks and is ready to go."

"Kelli, you'll have to get someone to cover your students and I'll have to cancel my scheduled charters for the next couple weeks. I know good captains I can refer them to."

"Jake, you and I can check out the engines to make sure there's no maintenance needed before we leave."

"Kelli, I would like for you to inspect the dive gear and the air compressor. There are plenty of dive suits and tanks for the four of us."

"Lucien, I want you to enter our destination into the chart-plotter on the bridge and get the long-range weather forecasts for the areas we'll pass through."

"It might be a good idea to stop at the marina in Cape Coral to top off the tanks again before making the run to the Keys. If you guys don't mind, I want to overnight at the Coast Guard Station in Key West to let my brother-in-law know where we're going in case there's any trouble. He's the Base Commander there and I'll feel better if someone knows we're out on the water. We'll top off with fuel again at Key West and should be good to go for the final run to Bimini. Any questions?"

Jake asked the tough one.

"I know this might not be a question you want to hear, but do we have weapons?"

Matt replied, "I always have my Sig Sauer stowed on the boat. It's the P226 9mm I trained on in the Navy. Never know when somebody will try to rob you on the open water."

"To be honest, I have no experience with handguns." Kelli confessed. "But I'm hell on wheels with a knife and a spear gun!"

"Fair enough." Jake laughed.

"I carry a little .22 caliber for personal protection." Lucien said. "Not real experienced with it though, other than shooting at junk on the water."

"No problem." Jake stated. "Lucien, I'll upgrade your firepower before we leave and Kelli, I'll fix you up with a simple handgun that you'll be comfortable with. I've got a few toys in my collection that might prove useful if some shit breaks out. We'll have some downtime on the way and if you all agree, I'd like to put it to good use. I'll do some weapons refresher training with each of you and we'll do some target practice when we can. I'll take care of getting extra ammo and other fun stuff. We won't be SEALs when I'm done, but it might keep us from shooting each other."

"Alright." Matt said with an air of expectancy. "It's settled. We leave at daylight tomorrow."

CHAPTER 54

Test Shaft Alpha
Special Weapons Research Center

THE TECHNICIANS WERE ABSORBED with monitoring the data pouring into their display consoles from the latest testing of the pulse cannon. Other than a couple of minor synchronization glitches, the new cooling system and the dual power packs had performed well in tandem. The weapon had been able to fire with maximum thirty second recovery times and had reached the twenty consecutive firings mark the Military Council had requested as its basic requirement.

This first series of tests were conducted at power levels 1 through 5. The next step would be to increase the output into the 6 to 10 range to confirm the cannon would perform as well at maximum power discharges.

The Fire Control Supervisor looked at Dr. Sarontin, waiting for the go ahead. After another review of the data displayed on her systems monitor, she gave the signal to proceed.

Dr. Broda set the controls to level 6 and initiated firing. So far, so good. Level 7. All systems nominal. Level 8. Green lights across the board. Level 9. Cooling systems operating within safe parameters.

Dr. Sarontin now instructed Fire Control to move to maximum power level 10 and initiate a full sequence of 20 pulses at 30 second intervals.

This would be the ultimate test to determine the weapon's readiness for deployment.

All lights in the control room changed to red announcing firing was about to commence. Everyone in the room held their breath...

CHAPTER 55

Aboard the Nice Catch
Southwest Coast of Florida

DAYLIGHT WAS BREAKING OVER the mainland to the east as the *Nice Catch* made its way through Longboat Pass, into the Gulf of Mexico, and now on a southerly heading.

The course had been laid in for the first leg of the trip which included a stopover at Tarpon Point Marina in Cape Coral to top off the fuel tanks before heading on to Key West. They should arrive at Tarpon Point around noon.

The skies were clear, the weather forecast favorable. This being the fall of the year, storms were fewer, humidity lower, and seas calm most of the time. Perfect conditions to be out on the big water.

Matt guided the boat well offshore into deeper waters and away from shore traffic, then eased the throttles forward to cruising speed. Most boats this size could cruise at no more than 25 knots, but the powerful engines of the *Catch* could reach speeds of up to 40 knots which was rare for a boat of that length and weight.

Matt leveled the throttles once a comfortable cruising speed had been attained and adjusted the controls to bring the boat up on optimum plane. The *Catch* was now running comfortably at about 25 knots and the ride was as smooth as sitting on a living room sofa. Matt engaged the autopilot, checked the gauges, radar, and sonar one more time, and relaxed a little.

Everyone on board was sipping their morning coffee, taking in the scenery, and basking in the spreading scarlet and gold sunrise. A pair of smiling grey dolphins jumped back and forth across their wake like small children at play. Snowy-white long-necked egrets, chattering seagulls, and swooping pelicans were emerging from the mangroves where they made their beds at night. Searching for food starts early in the day for coastal wildlife.

Lucien was sitting cross-legged on the bow of the boat, lost in the sea breeze and the million-dollar view. Jake and Kelli shared the bridge with Matt. The adventurers were quiet as they pondered what the coming days held for them.

It would prove to be the calm before the storm.

CHAPTER 56

Test Shaft Alpha
Special Weapons Research Center

THE PULSE CANNON, NOW at maximum power level 10, efficiently delivered potent concussive waves into the test shaft. The gleaming new weapon was outperforming all expectations and the staff gathered at the SWRC viewing platform were awestruck by the sheer power and efficiency of this machine they had created.

The pride of accomplishment was somewhat tempered by nagging back-of-mind thoughts of how it would feel to be on the receiving end of those Godhammer blows.

They comforted themselves by remembering what the Assembly and the Military had told them. It was only for show and would never be unleashed on the defenseless populations of the world.

It was a fearsome and unsettling sight just the same.

Dr. Sagrin, the Lead Geologist, approached Dr. Sarontin and asked to speak with her.

"Dr. Sarontin, I have detected slight seismic activity in the vicinity of Test Shaft Alpha. I am not sure if it holds any significance, but I thought it would be prudent to bring it to your attention."

"Dr. Sagrin, do you think the seismic activity is significant enough that we should suspend testing?"

"It is only minor at this time and I am not sure it is indicative of anything at all. After all, we did build this center on a strong shelf of bedrock and it could be that the rock itself is simply picking up the energy waves and transmitting them along to our sensors which is then being recorded on our seismic monitoring instruments."

"I see, Dr. Sagrin. Nevertheless, I am going to inform the Assembly of your findings and ask their guidance. Thank you for keeping me up to informed."

Rona Sarontin halted the weapon testing and proceeded to place a call to Minister Leturis himself to address the issue.

"Minister Leturis, we are experiencing tremendous success with the pulse cannon testing so far and are currently operating at the maximum power level. However, we have picked up slight seismic disturbances in the vicinity of the test shaft. Do you suggest we proceed or suspend testing until we investigate further?"

"Thank you for the update, Dr. Sarontin. I will consult with the Assembly and Military Leaders and give you an answer shortly."

CHAPTER 57

Special Weapons Research Center
Aquatica, Atlantis

"Dr. Sarontin, I have consulted with my colleagues in the Assembly as well as the Military Council concerning the seismic activity you brought to my attention. We appreciate your vigilance and professionalism. After reviewing the level of the activity, we believe it to be background noise, if you will, and nothing to be concerned about. Certainly, nothing that would warrant the suspension of weapons testing. We are on a very tight and accelerated construction schedule and must get the pulse cannon certified and ready to install at the earliest moment possible. We have an armada of airships and waterships in final construction phase and awaiting armaments. Therefore, unless or until we have something firm and verifiable indicating these small tremors are somehow connected to our weapons program, we cannot suspend testing. Are we clear on this directive?"

Dr. Sarontin replied, "Yes, Minister. Perfectly clear. Testing will resume immediately. We will commence the final phase of testing which will involve not only the 20 continuous pulse cycles, but a series of back to back 20 pulse cycles with only the minimum cooling time in between to test the durability of the system under heavy and consistent demand. I am confident that once this battery of tests is successfully completed, we will be able to certify the pulse cannon as fully operational and begin outfitting the ships of the fleet."

"Thank you, Dr. Sarontin. I cannot express the depth of the Assembly's gratitude and admiration for what you and your team have accomplished in so little time. You have made history and are national heroes. Of that, there is no doubt. Please express our sentiments to all of your team members."

"I certainly will, Minister. Thank you for the kind words."

CHAPTER 58

Tarpon Point Marina
Cape Coral, Florida

THE CREW ON BOARD the *Catch* had enjoyed a scenic and uneventful journey so far. They had cruised south along the coast past Sarasota, Siesta Key, Venice, Manasota Key, Boca Grande, Cayo Costa, Captiva Island, Pine Island, and Sanibel Island. They swung around the southern tip of Sanibel, past the Lighthouse, and under the Sanibel Causeway Bridge. From there it took only a few more minutes to pass the southern tip of Pine Island at St. James City and move on into the mouth of the Caloosahatchee River. Tarpon Point Marina was located on the north side of the river at the southwestern tip of Cape Coral.

Matt noticed Jake had been peering through his binoculars for quite a while now, focused on something in the distance. As Matt slowed the boat to No Wake speed and prepared his approach to the marina, he inquired as to what Jake was looking at.

"Jake, you looking for mermaids?"

"Nope."

"What's so interesting out there? A boat babe lose her bikini top?"

"Maybe nothin'. Did you notice that boat shadowing us starting back around the time we passed Cayo Costa?"

"No, I was watching the instruments a lot during that time. There were some shallows and sand bars I had to keep an eye on. What kind of boat is it?"

"Looks like one of those competition fishing boats that have three or four big outboards on them."

"That's not an unusual sight in these waters. Lots of fishing tournaments are held here and people come from all over the world to fish for tarpon at Boca Grande. I've done several of those charters myself."

"Yeah, I know. But this one hasn't slowed down or done any fishing. It has stayed back and matched our course and speed for the last half hour or so."

"Probably thinks I know where a good fishing spot is and decided to hang around and get in on it later."

"Maybe. Well, now it looks like they disappeared when we rounded Pine Island and headed toward the marina. Maybe I'm just being paranoid."

Matt was now maneuvering the big boat into the entry channel to the marina and executing a wide turn that would bring him alongside the fuel pumps. He deftly manipulated his dual engines and bow thrusters to lay it in, nice and easy. A couple members of the marina staff moved quickly to accept the mooring lines that Kelli was offering to them and tied the *Catch* off to the padded pilings in front of the pumps. Kelli unlocked the cap to the fuel tanks and the attendants inserted the fill hose to top off the boat for the next leg of the journey. Matt monitored the activity from the bridge and was satisfied that the refueling was going smoothly. He turned his attention back to Jake.

"Well, that's a good thing, Jake. I need you to go on being paranoid."

The fuel tanks were quickly filled and Matt paid the fuel attendant. He then turned and addressed his shipmates.

"You guys want to stretch your sea legs for a while and have a sandwich and a beer over there at the Nauti Mermaid before we leave?"

He saw two heads smiling and bobbing affirmatively while Jake was once again staring through his binoculars in the direction of

Pine Island. The pump attendants loosened the ropes from the pilings and tossed them back to Lucien and Kelli who stowed them away. Matt eased the *Catch* away from the pumps and out into the channel. He maneuvered alongside an empty stretch of dock space across the marina and they secured the ropes to the pilings again. Matt shut down the engines, they all hopped off the boat onto a long boardwalk and headed to their destination.

The Nauti Mermaid is a classy waterside bar and grill and is part of the Westin Hotel complex. All the seating is outside. You can sit around the large circular covered bar or choose one of the many tables that sit out in the open. Anywhere you sit offers a great view of the marina and the Caloosahatchee River with Pine Island, Sanibel Island, and the Causeway Bridge in the distance.

Matt looked at Kelli and grinned. She had ditched her sport glasses and put on her movie star sunglasses, as he called them. She had made a trip to her condo and packed some fresh clothes before leaving on the trip. She decided to look a little more fashionable for their lunch date…and that she did. She had changed into a crisp pair of canary yellow shorts and a white midriff top along with her designer shades and some matching bling. A white pair of raised platform sandals showed off her toned legs. She usually tried to be just one of the guys, but today, nobody would be mistaking her for a guy. Sometimes, a girl just needs to be a girl.

She noticed she had Matt's full attention and shot him a sly, knowing smile. The kind of smile that promised, *later big boy*.

They chose a table near the outside railing close to the water and hailed a waiter. He took their drink orders and left them each a lunch menu. Matt leaned back in his chair and began the conversation.

"Last stop before Key West. I don't think we'll get there in time to catch my brother-in-law at the Coast Guard Station, so we'll have to either drop anchor somewhere close by or find a marina with an open slip. I'll call him and let him know we're headed his way and see if he can meet with me in the morning. Jake thought he saw a boat shadowing us the last hour or so before we got here. Anyone else see it or notice anything unusual?"

"I saw it, too." Kelli said. "I got a good look at it through the binoculars and I could see a couple guys on it. It looked like a high-end fishing boat, but the strange thing was, it didn't have any fishing gear that I could see. Maybe they were out sightseeing, but it's unusual to see a boat like that with no gear showing."

"I want to emphasize again", Matt added, "That we need to be on the lookout for anything out of place or that doesn't make sense, no matter how little it may seem. We don't know who or what we may be up against and until we do, we need to have our heads on a swivel and our eyes peeled."

Lucien spoke next. His mind was on food and drink as usual.

"What's good, Matt? You've eaten here, right?"

"I have, a couple of times. I know we're sittin' in the middle of snapper and grouper heaven, but they have a great burger here and awesome sweet potato fries."

Everyone seemed inclined to find out if Matt's burger evaluation was sound, so when the waiter came by with their beers, they ordered burgers all around with sweet potato fries on the side.

Lucien raised his beer for a toast and said, "Here's to the Four Musketeers. May we have a safe journey with the wind at our backs and clear skies ahead!"

They replied in unison "Hear, Hear!" and all took big swigs of cold beer. As they were putting their bottles down on the table, Kelli said, "Hey guys, there's that boat again."

While they had been talking and toasting, the suspicious fishing boat had slipped around the outside of the marina back into a little cove off to the east side. It anchored in a position allowing them a good view of the Nauti Mermaid and the *Catch*.

The two men on the boat were trying to look inconspicuous, but they were failing badly at it. It was obvious they were keeping an eye on the *Catch* and its crew.

Jake and Matt locked eyes.

"What do you think, Jake?"

"I think we wait and see what they do. See if they continue to follow us after we leave. Until then, I suggest we enjoy our burgers and beer. Might just be a weird coincidence, or they could be watching us. Either way, we'll know soon enough."

CHAPTER 59

Special Weapons Research Center
Aquatica, Atlantis

THE MIGHTY CANNON WAS now being pushed through repetitions at a blistering pace. Level 10 energy pulses were being released into the test shaft in an endless stream. The weapon continued to perform flawlessly and Dr. Sarontin and her test team were astounded at the results and could sense victory at hand.

Rona could wind down the test firing soon and certification would be finalized. It had been a hectic few months. A great deal of anxiety and pressure had been placed on the shoulders of her team and on the Council of Science in general. She had hardly seen her family in days and the stress was beginning to show on the faces of everyone who worked in the SWRC.

But now the end of their long marathon was in sight—the final goal almost in their grasp.

Dr. Sarontin turned toward the Fire Control Officer to recheck the test data a final time before giving the signal to discontinue the firing sequence. As she raised her hand to initiate the cease fire command, she felt a strange sensation under her feet…

The Earth was moving.

CHAPTER 60

Onboard the Catch
South of Fort Myers Beach, Florida

EVERYONE ENJOYED LUNCH AT the Nauti Mermaid and managed a few laughs, even with the ominous watchers nearby. The group decided Matt knew a good burger when he met one and the sweet potato fries were a hit.

They were now underway again and following the coastline south toward the Keys, the southerly current pushing them along. The mystery boat had pulled anchor and followed them out of the marina but remained well behind the *Catch*. The jury was still out on whether they posed a threat.

Matt checked his phone and saw that he still had good cell coverage this close to the mainland and used his cellphone to call his brother-in-law, Ken Spader. Ken was a career military officer with ten years served in the Navy and another fifteen in the Coast Guard where he had risen through the ranks to Commander of Coast Guard Station Key West. Ken was married to Matt's older sister, Cindy, who worked as an elementary school teacher in the local school system. They had strong, athletic twin sons named Gage and Gavin. The boys were in their teens and approaching college age.

After a few rings, Ken came on the line.

"Well, hello Matt! Good to hear from you! How're you doing you old fish chaser?"

"I'm doing fine, Ken. If I were any better, I'd have to be twins. Speaking of twins, how's my sister and crazy nephews these days?"

"Cindy is awesome as always. And the boys, well, they're teenage boys. So, I'll just leave it at that. Between school, sports, and girls, I don't see much of them these days."

"Good to hear everyone's fine, Ken. Listen, the reason I called is to let you know I'll be arriving in Key West on the *Catch* later this evening and I would like to meet with you in the morning if possible?

"Not a problem. Something wrong?"

"Not sure yet, but I have Kelli and a couple of buddies with me and we're making a run to North Bimini Island. I wanted to let you know where I'm headed. Nobody else knows."

"But you're not sure if something's wrong?"

"No, but I'll fill you in on the details in the morning."

"You want me to wait around till you get here, Matt? I could try to get Cindy and the boys down here as well?"

"Thanks Ken, but you go on home to your family this evening. Not the best time for a visit. We're on a tight schedule."

"Alright then. Where you dropping anchor?"

"Don't know that either. Any suggestions?"

"I've got a spot open here at the Station. I'll have the night watch keep an eye out for you and they'll get the *Catch* tied off and hooked up to shore power."

"That'd be perfect, Ken. Much appreciated. I'll see you in the morning for some government coffee."

"Roger that, Matt. I get to the Station no later than seven bells. Come on over when you're up and at 'em."

"Will do."

CHAPTER 61

Special Weapons Research Center
Aquatica, Atlantis

EVERYONE IN THE SWRC froze as the floor trembled underneath their feet. Then, it abated.

Dr. Sarontin looked over at Dr. Sagrin with a wide-eyed, questioning stare.

"Dr. Sagrin, any idea what that was about?

Sagrin glanced up at Sarontin and then back to his seismic monitors.

"I am not sure, but the readings were widespread this time and not strictly localized."

"Could this have anything to do with our weapons testing?"

"Too soon to say. There is not enough data to formulate a theory yet and there is activity being recorded in locations other than here."

"You need to pinpoint the source of the tremors, Dr. Sagrin. I see the communication stations from around the continent are already checking in to see what we know."

"I agree, Dr. Sarontin. We will review the seismic readings right away and try to confirm the source of the disturbance."

One of the technicians stationed at the bank of telescreens displaying live telefeeds from all over the continent, sprang to her feet knocking her chair over in the process. "Look!" she screamed in horror, pointing at one of the large monitors above them.

The telefeed she was pointing to originated from the Regional Capital City of Lemurus.

The images moving across the monitor screen were surreal, similar to one of the computer-generated simulations that were so popular with the citizens. Except this was not a simulation. This was real time, a live feed.

The control room personnel watched in stunned silence and shock. Tall, graceful spires in the city center were toppling like building blocks being kicked over by an out-of-control toddler. Throngs of people were screaming and running out into the street only to be crushed beneath collapsing towers or swallowed up by one of the gaping cracks in the earth opening wide to claim them. Camera angles switched occasionally as the feed was lost and another cued in from a different part of the city.

Fires and explosions were erupting everywhere. It appeared there was no safe place to hide in that beautiful city. Wholesale destruction and death were running rampant through the streets and showing no mercy.

The techs brought up multiple transmissions from many locations in Lemurus and the surrounding region. The story was the same everywhere. It looked like a giant animal had snatched Lemurus up in its teeth and was shaking it about with great violence. Learning academies, homes, theaters, commerce zones, shopping areas, office buildings, government centers, were disintegrating before their eyes and taking with them all the inhabitants of the city. Over three million souls called Lemurus home.

Dr. Sarontin shook herself out of the trance she was in and shouted to Dr. Sagrin.

"Where did this catastrophe start and what is causing it?"

Dr. Sagrin was staring at the data analysis that had just finished running on his computer. He looked at Sarontin with wide, disbelieving eyes and pointed with a trembling finger toward the floor where he stood.

"It started here."

CHAPTER 62

Onboard the Catch
South of Marco Island, Florida

"THAT BOAT STILL TAILING us, Kelli?" Matt asked.

"Not since we passed Naples. They stayed in sight from Fort Myers all the way to Naples and then fell back."

"I guess that's good news. Now that we're on the south side of Marco Island, there isn't much to see until we get to the Keys. Just the Ten Thousand Islands and there's nothing there."

Lucien was listening and asked, "Ever do any fishin' around the Ten Thousand Islands, Matt?"

"Now and then. Took some charters down there. A million little coves and back bays to explore and nobody much to bother you. We fished in places so shallow that only the dinghy could get in and out. It was a lot of fun and something different than just lookin' for trophy fish out in the big water."

Jake was listening to the conversation and his mental wheels were turning.

"You know, these islands you're talkin' about would be ideal to hide in, would they not?"

Matt considered the question.

"Yeah, I guess they would."

Jake replied, "We're running by them late in the day and I think we should be on our toes. Everybody check your weapons and remember what we practiced a few minutes ago."

The *Catch* was running strong and close to shore to shorten the trip around to the Keys. The Ten Thousand Islands now lay off to the east side of the *Catch*. A glint of something reflecting the late afternoon sun caught Jake's eye. Jake raised his binoculars and observed a couple boats coming out fast from behind one of the small islands.

Jake already knew. Trouble had arrived. Serious trouble.

CHAPTER 63

Special Weapons Research Center
Aquatica, Atlantis

"Dr. Sagrin, what do you mean when you say it started here? Here in Aquatica or here in the SWRC?" Dr. Sarontin inquired with fear building in her heart and voice.

Dr. Sagrin, still watching data stream in from the seismic monitors around the continent, replied, "Here in the vicinity of the SWRC. The monitors we installed near Test Shaft Alpha are showing activity at the highest level they can record."

"Are you saying that we might have caused this event with our weapons testing?"

" I suppose it is possible."

"How could that happen, Dr. Sagrin? You said this was a stable location to conduct the testing?"

"On the surface and upper levels of earth's strata, it is. This location was as strong as any on the continent. However, I am beginning to suspect a major fault line was located at the end of that test shaft. One that was too deep for our instruments to detect. Perhaps, it is why the Ancients did not finish that particular shaft or use it for any purpose."

Dr. Sarontin felt the blood drain from her face and her palms popped a sweat. Her legs and hands began to shake and she felt unsteady. But she could see that all eyes in the SWRC were upon her and Dr. Sagrin.

As she considered what to do next, more gasps were heard from somewhere in the room. All heads swung in the direction of the alarming sound. A young woman monitoring the telefeed from the Regional Capital City of Solus, had switched the feed to the larger overhead monitors for all to see. She was bent over her console, heaving and sobbing.

Another sweeping vista of catastrophic ruin was playing out in real time on the big screens. Solus, another magnificent city of over four million inhabitants, was suffering the same fate Lemurus had just minutes earlier.

These images were particularly telling.

One of the remote cameras transmitted a view of a giant fault line opening wide as far as the camera lens could cover. Other feeds were now following it as the fault line seemed to be racing across the entire landscape of the Solus Region. Off the main fault line ran newly opened crevices, spidering out in every direction, toppling or swallowing everything in its path like a growing army of hungry mouths forming in the ground. People were being consumed before they could even try to escape the certain death that was spreading everywhere. The terrifying truth was…there was no escape. No safe haven.

The emergency telecoms began to light up.

Commander Mishon was nearby and on his way to the Control Center. Minister Leturis was asking for an explanation on the telecom, but events were unfolding so quickly that Dr. Sarontin was struggling to provide a coherent answer.

She desperately turned to Dr. Sagrin for more information.

He noticed her pleading eyes reaching out to him as she patched him into the telecom link with Minister Leturis and herself.

"Dr. Sarontin, Minister Leturis, the best analysis I can offer at this moment is there was a critical geological fault at the bottom of Test Shaft Alpha. This fault line appears to span our entire continental shelf at extreme depths. Unaware of the existence of the fault, we fired a large number of high energy pulses into it which had the effect of cracking the continent open like a giant walnut, for want of a better analogy. The fault withstood our initial low energy testing, but that final barrage at maximum levels and frequency must have destabilized it completely."

Minister Leturis exclaimed in disbelief and shock, "This cannot be! Not our beloved Atlantis! Not when we stand so close to our destiny. Is there nothing we can do?"

The feed from Minister Leturis went dead.

CHAPTER 64

Onboard the Catch
Ten Thousand Islands, Florida

JAKE DROPPED THE BINOCULARS from his eyes, turned towards his shipmates and yelled, "Get ready people! These are not likely to be friendlies coming toward us. Check your weapons and ammo. Kick it, Matt! See how fast you can get us out of here. Kelli, grab your binoculars and see how many people are on those boats and what kind of boats they are. Lucien, come back here to the stern and stand by to give me a hand if something starts. I'm going below to get my goody bag. I'll be right back."

Matt pushed the powerful twin diesels to full acceleration and the *Catch* responded like a thoroughbred racehorse breaking out of the starting gate. They were soon approaching 40 knots. The water was calm and they were riding the southerly current which added to their ability to run at a high rate of speed.

"Kelli, are we pullin' away from them?" Matt shouted.

"Don't believe so. No, they're gaining on us, but not as fast. I see three men on each boat and they're not dressed for fishing. Looks like military-style clothing. There's a driver and two passengers on each boat. The passengers have weapons. Rifles of some sort. They have two of those "go fast" boats with three outboards and high-performance hulls."

Jake was back on the stern deck where he was busy opening his large kit bag. He reached inside and pulled out a set of high-tech field glasses. The glasses were complete with range finder and night vision. He turned his ball cap around backwards and brought the glasses to his eyes.

Matt hailed him from the bridge.

"Jake, how far back are they?"

Jake adjusted the glasses a couple of times.

"About 150 yards. I don't know what kind of weapons they're carrying, but I figure we'll find out about the 100-yard mark."

Jake signaled Lucien over to take the field glasses and instructed him to keep an eye on the pursuers. He then pulled a long, protective case out of his duffle bag and laid it on the deck. He opened the case and began to assemble a powerful looking rifle. He quickly and expertly completed the assembly and checked the action, then opened another section of the case. He extracted a high-tech scope which he clicked into mounting brackets on top of the weapon.

Lucien was staring at Jake with his mouth hanging open.

"Damn Jake, what the hell is that thing?"

"Sniper rifle. Accurate up to a mile or more. Long range scope with night vision."

Matt was alternately watching the horizon, the bridge gauges, and the scene unfolding on the stern deck behind and below him. So far, the engines were running strong and temps were high but staying in an acceptable range. He was not sure how long that situation would hold at this speed.

After watching Jake adjust the scope in the direction of the pursuing boats, Matt chewed on his lower lip, smiled tightly, and yelled down to the stern, "Jake, I believe there's some things from your past you haven't shared with me. I'm a little hurt."

Jake shouted back, never taking his eyes off the pursuers.

"Need to know basis Matt, and you didn't need to know. But when we get on the other side of this current situation, I might tell you my dirty little secrets—well some of 'em anyway."

"Fair enough." Matt replied.

"Lucien, range!" Jake barked.

Lucien snapped out of his fascination with Jake's arsenal and sighted the pursuing boats through the combat field glasses.

"120 yards!"

Jake sat cross legged on the deck behind the back wall of the stern and unfolded a bipod from underneath the sniper rifle. He positioned it on the top of the half wall, pointing the weapon toward the two boats. He continued to adjust the large scope in an attempt to achieve perfect accuracy.

"110 yards." Lucien called out.

Jake checked the ammo clip again, clicked it back into the body of the rifle, and chambered a round—a big round.

"Closing on 100 yards." Lucien yelled.

As Lucien's words faded on the wind, a couple puffs of smoke appeared above one of the chase boats and whizzing noises zipped past the *Catch*.

"The shit has officially started!" Jake exclaimed. "Lucien, get down behind this wall with me but try to keep the glasses on those damn boats. Kelli, either get down behind this wall, or better yet, go inside."

"If it's all the same to you, Jake, I would rather stay out here." Kelli said with an indignant tone. She then crab-walked to the stern wall with the others.

"Suit yourself." Jake replied with a half grin. "Just keep your head down."

Kelli ducked behind the wall and more gunfire erupted from the trailing boats. All four gunmen had fired at near the same moment. A couple bullets lodged into the stern just above the waterline and one clanged off the observation tower above the bridge.

It seemed to Jake that the gunmen were randomly firing toward them more as warning shots rather than attempting to actually hit someone. The bad guys likely assumed the *Catch* would slow down and surrender in the face of overwhelming firepower and they could board her and take whatever they wanted.

If the pursuers were to succeed, Jake had no doubt they would execute the four of them and leave no witnesses. They would either sell the *Catch* on the black market in Mexico or burn it with the bodies on board. Jake could now see the attackers with more clarity and they were carrying automatic weapons but had chosen only to fire a few single pops with the intention of intimidating the crew of the *Catch*. The one thing they had not counted on was Jake being on board.

Jake shouted up to Matt on the bridge.

"If I were you, I'd put that thing on autopilot and get low right now!"

Matt took Jake's advice and set the autopilot to keep the boat on the plotted course to Key West. He then crouched low behind a built-in cooler/locker where he was still able to view the instruments and gauges but had some degree of protection. He worried about the engines running wide open for an extended length of time. He would have to cut the throttle back at some point to let them cool down. At least they had plenty of fuel. Matt always insisted on topping off his fuel tanks whenever he could. Just in case.

"Jake, I can't keep these engines at full throttle forever. We need to make a plan before I'm forced to slow down. They'll be on us in a heartbeat once I do that."

"Yeah, I know." Jake growled. "I'm workin' on it. Lucien, pop up and give me a range."

"95 yards."

Lucien ducked back down.

Jake leaned into his weapon. The late afternoon sun backlit his targets with a nice golden glow. He took a deep breath. Relaxed. Exhaled. Adjusted for the rise and fall of the boat. Gently squeezed the trigger.

Boom! Pause. Eject and rechamber. Acquire next target. Boom!

The two gunmen on the boat running to their right had been removed from the fight. One was lifted overboard from the impact of Jake's round. The other flipped backwards over a seat. Both drivers took immediate evasive action.

Jake just glared. As if the enemy could hear him, he muttered, "Welcome to your nightmare, boys…"

CHAPTER 65

THERE WAS SIMMERING PANIC in the Control Room as images from all around the continent continued to pour in. Sirius City, the third Regional Capital City, was imploding inward upon itself, just like the others. Many remote cameras had battery backups and were still operating but occasionally one blinked out, never to return.

It seemed that Aquatica, with it's millions of inhabitants, would be the last metropolis to fall due to the enduring rock shelf foundation that lay under it. But everyone realized, without it being said aloud, that it would be a short reprieve. The entire underpinnings of the continent were breaking apart. They had felt several strong tremors in the SWRC, but so far it had maintained structural integrity.

Many of the technicians, scientists, and team leaders were nervous and in various stages of shock and disbelief; looking around wild-eyed, feeling as if they should be doing something to help their loved ones.

Dr. Sarontin could see the terror on their faces and knew she needed to address them. She was still their leader and they needed her more than ever.

Using the microphone and intercom system, she spoke.

"My friends and colleagues, I feel the same shock that you feel. I know you have families and desperately want to help them, as do I. But you also know the reality of the situation. There is nothing left to go home to. Here in Aquatica, much of the population has already perished and the rest soon will."

As if to punctuate the finality of it all, the telescreen images from Solus, Lemurus, and Sirius City suddenly displayed a new horror to which all their eyes were drawn.

Mammoth sections of Atlantis, encompassing hundreds of square miles, were shearing off the main landmass and sliding sideways into the ocean or simply sinking beneath the water. Towering tsunamis were being generated, annihilating everything in their path. Smoke and fire filled the skies. The fault line that ran through the middle of the continent was ripping asunder the entire landmass. Quadrant after quadrant of fractured and bleeding Atlantis was submerging into a watery grave.

Then another heartrending image appeared on the Control Center monitors.

The Great Hall of the Ancients and the Royal Residence were being lifted and dashed to pieces. Gaping chasms were opening in the earth, claiming the beautiful palaces, pillar by pillar, spire by spire. A sure ending for King Lemurius XV and his wife, Queen Alshura. No shelters had ever been constructed for a disaster such as this. It did not matter. None would have survived.

Dr. Sarontin began speaking again in a quivering voice.

"It appears our beloved Atlantis will not survive this day. Is there anything we should do at this late hour? Something that would give this tragedy some meaning?"

Commander Mishon had quietly entered the Control Center as Dr. Sarontin addressed the souls still alive there. He stepped forward and cleared his throat. All eyes turned blankly toward him. He looked at the solemn faces scattered about the room. Pale faces awaiting their fate. He gathered his courage and spoke.

"I have an idea."

CHAPTER 66

Onboard the Catch
Ten Thousand Islands, Florida

THE GUNFIRE FROM THE pursuing boats intensified as they now realized they were in a firefight.

The two gunmen in the boat to the left had hunkered down behind the windshield and were sticking their weapons above the glass, firing random bursts toward the *Catch*. Jake chuckled under his breath at their misguided belief that windshield glass would offer any protection against his high-powered rounds.

The boat that had lost its gunmen, was falling back behind the other boat for protection. Jake peered through his scope at the two gunmen on the lead boat and squeezed off two quick shots. One gunman fell sideways and down but the boat had veered just a little after the first shot causing the second bullet to take out the driver instead.

The lead boat was careening sideways, and the remaining gunman was struggling to move the deceased driver out of the way and grab the controls.

Perfect, Jake thought.

The meandering boat was now sideways to Jake, presenting a clear profile of his targets. He proceeded to take down the new driver and put another round into the drive units connected to the outboard engines. The boats were close enough that Jake could make out every detail through his high-tech scope. The hobbled boat was slowing down and would soon be dead in the water, just like its inhabitants.

The second boat, with the only survivor aboard, turned tail and ran away at full throttle. Jake took aim at the escaping boat's drive system, now completely exposed to him, and put two well placed rounds into it. The second boat sputtered and slowed immediately as the engines lost their link to the propulsion system. Jake's powerful rounds struck the targets at such high velocity, they had an explosive effect at this close range. The potent metal slugs had mangled the stern drive units, rendering them useless.

Jake signaled the "all clear" to everyone which allowed Matt to throttle the *Catch*'s engines down and circle back to capture the lone survivor. They could take him to the Coast Guard Station and try to sweat some information out of him. Maybe then, they could find out who was behind all this.

Matt slowed the *Catch* and brought her around in a big circle approaching the disabled pursuit boat. Jake kept his rifle trained on the driver in case he reached for a weapon or tried any tricks.

As the *Catch* slowly approached from the side, Matt grabbed the microphone on the bridge and engaged the ship's PA horn.

"Keep your hands up and prepare to be boarded. Do not move."

Suddenly the man collapsed. Matt hurried to bring the *Catch* alongside. Jake set the rifle down, jumped across to the smaller boat, and trained his handgun on the fallen assailant.

Jake looked closely at the man and picked up something small laying on the deck beside his still body. It was a wrapper. He took a sniff of it and threw it down in disgust.

"Damn it! He's a goner. Took a cyanide pill once he knew we were about to take him prisoner. This is some crazy shit going on here, guys. This bunch would rather die than be captured. Whatever those things are that your grandfathers left you must be real important to somebody. I don't think this is the end of it. I expect there's more assholes where these came from."

"Those bastards shot holes in the *Catch*!" Matt exclaimed as he surveyed the bullet holes in his boat.

"Well, that sucks canal water, Matt." Jake replied with a hint of sarcasm. "But at least they didn't shoot holes in us."

Matt took a deep breath and tried to push down his adrenaline a bit.

"Yeah, thanks to you." Matt said in a lowering voice. "And they didn't hit any critical systems. It could be a lot worse. So, what the hell do we do with these boats and bodies?"

Lucien and Kelli were starting to come down off their adrenalin highs as well and the reality of what had just happened was sinking in. Lucien turned his back to the dead boats and deader bodies. Kelli stared blankly at Jake and Matt, then looked off in the distance. Her hands were shaking but she was hanging tough.

Jake replied to Matt's question.

"The way I see it, we've got several options. We can call the Coast Guard and tell them what happened and get detained for hours or days while they investigate. Or…we can sink the boats and the bodies with them and move on. But that's breaking the law and would carry felony charges for us all. Probably not the best option, just the easiest. The other thing we can do is round up that floater wearing a life jacket over there, put him back on one of their boats, tie both boats to the *Catch*, and tow them to Key West. Maybe Ken can cut through some of the red tape and get us out of there a little faster."

"I like the last option best." Matt said. "Everyone agree?"

Kelli and Lucien, with grim faces, nodded their agreement.

"Then, that's what we'll do. Kelli, pull some extra ropes out of the locker. Lucien, you help Jake tie off the boats once I get us in position. Then, I'll circle around beside the floater and somebody will have to pull him out."

Lucien and Kelli both looked up with reluctant eyes, but neither refused.

Jake noticed their repulsion to the idea and quickly took the lead on this one.

"Don't worry, guys, I got it. This ain't my first rodeo as you might have figured by now. Let's just keep movin'. Best way to keep your mind off what you just went through is to stay busy. Kelli, throw me that rope. Lucien, let's lasso that first boat and get it secured to the second one. We'll lash them together and then run a tow line to the *Catch*. They will tow easier that way."

Matt looked down at the scene below from his lofty perch on the bridge. As he watched everyone swing into action, he could not help wondering what he had gotten them into.

Jake and Kelli are volunteers and made no vow to a dead relative. Should I even allow this trip to go forward? Maybe, I should just call it off before one of them gets hurt…or worse.

Jake paused what he was doing and was watching Matt's face. The *Catch* had not yet moved and the hesitation flagged Jake's attention. He knew that look and what Matt was thinking. As if to answer Matt's inner questions, Jake walked over to a position just beneath the bridge and looked him straight in the eyes.

"Don't even think about it, compadre. I'm in it to the end."

Kelli joined in on the interaction as she handed Jake a rope.

"You're not going to the islands without me, Mr. Flannery. I'm not about to let some island girl steal your heart when I'm not around to protect you."

Matt just looked at them. Lucien was displaying a subdued version of his shit-eating grin by this time.

"Okay. I hear you. I'm coming about. Let's finish up and get the hell out of here."

CHAPTER 67

*Special Weapons Research Center
Aquatica, Atlantis*

AN EERIE, LOUD SILENCE hung over the Control Room of the SWRC. The realization of inevitable, impending doom permeated the space like a dark wraith, slowly extinguishing hope from the hearts and minds of the human spirits within.

A couple of staff members snapped and ran screaming into the streets, hoping against hope to find their families. Others huddled in corners or wept at their workstations. Most were just gazing into the distance, the ten-mile stare had set in, already dead to themselves and the world. The scope and finality of the situation was starting to overwhelm them. Especially them. The best and brightest of Atlantis. They fully understood their role in this tragic play unfolding in front of their eyes.

A scattered few of the technicians continued to dutifully attend their stations because they did not know what else to do and felt a need to be doing something. Some looked inquiringly at Dr. Sarontin and Commander Mishon, waiting for instructions or ideas.

Commander Mishon saw the mournful eyes fixed upon him. He could not prevent thoughts of frustration and missed opportunity from searing his mind.

This is how it ends? With me never fulfilling my dreams any more than Atlantis will fulfill its destiny? I was close, so close. Never will I see our mighty armada take to the air and seas. Never will I get to see the world's people watch in awe as I demonstrate our mighty new weapons, the likes of which they never dreamed of. Never will I hear the roar of the people hailing me as their hero. Never will I get the chance to lead my forces into battle against the rebellious armies that would have risen to test me. Now…all I have is a little time…a small army of survivors…and a chance to leave a legacy. Perhaps, I can still do this last thing.

Commander Mishon addressed the group in a strong, clear voice.

"All we have left, is a little time and each other. Nothing here will survive this day. You know that and I know that. I propose we gather what we can of our historical record and send it to a distant location away from the continent. Something of us must survive! History cannot pretend Atlantis never existed."

The room's occupants listened with rapt attention as they considered the Commander's proposal. Their faces animated and their eyes brightened just a bit at the sound of his stirring words.

Dr. Sarontin spoke next.

"Commander, even if we can gather the records in the short time we have left, how do you propose we get them off the continent? There is no time to prepare a ship to transport them, even if a ship still exists."

Commander Mishon relished the idea that everyone was looking to him, even in this final hour. That he was the one with a plan. He was born to lead. Even until the end.

"Excellent question, Doctor. While you and your staff were developing the energy cannon, there was another group designing and testing short to medium range rockets as an additional weapon to have in our arsenal. They completed their testing about a week ago and were quite successful, just as you were. There are a couple of working prototypes stored in the building adjacent to this one. They were designed to carry explosive payloads, but the warhead compartments are still empty and have enough space to hold quite a few items such as our records. They were kept fueled and ready for continued testing as needed."

"If we are able to successfully launch one of these rockets Commander, where could we send it that would be within the rocket's range but far enough away to prevent it from being destroyed along with the continent?"

Dr. Sagrin, the geologist, spoke up.

"I would like to research those options if you will permit me to do so. I may have the clearest understanding of how far this destruction will spread and where our legacy rocket would be safest to land."

Dr. Sarontin looked quickly at Commander Mishon who nodded his approval.

"There may not be much time Dr. Sagrin, so your selection must be made quickly." Dr. Sarontin said.

"I understand what is at stake. I will start immediately." Sagrin replied.

Dr. Sarontin moved on to the next task.

"What items will we include in the legacy rocket?"

Dr. Brota was the next to speak up.

"In my role as a member of the Weapons Design and Testing Team, I have been deeply involved in gathering all the records from the Ancients, deciphering them, and recording our progress. We have also been monitoring and recording all major news reporting from all over Atlantis as we carried out the testing. We were always conscious of the reactions from the citizens as we moved forward. These news reports will show much of our way of life and culture."

"Very good, Dr. Brota. Can you condense all this information so it will fit into the limited space available on the rocket?"

"Yes, I believe I can. The records from the Ancients are all contained on compact storage crystals. We have been recording on similar crystals recently. We emulated that technology as well."

"Can you gather the crystals quickly enough?" Dr. Sarontin inquired.

"All the storage crystals are here in the SWRC as we were constantly deciphering them or making new ones. I can gather them very quickly."

Dr. Sarontin and Commander Mishon nodded in unison.

"Make it so." Sarontin instructed.

Commander Mishon asked for volunteers to help prepare the legacy rocket for its momentous journey.

Many hands and voices lifted.

Even with the pallor of death hanging over the SWRC like a suffocating cloud, a sense of purpose rekindled. A spark. Something that would give meaning to the little time that remained.

The SWRC was now a beehive of activity as the staff who had worked so well together to achieve so many great things, had one more task to complete.

It was a race against time and their own destruction.

CHAPTER 68

DARKNESS WAS FALLING HARD on the weary occupants of the *Nice Catch* as Matt Flannery guided her into the channel leading to the Station's private docks. They had been slowed by having to tow the two damaged boats into port with them.

Matt had called the Night Watch Supervisor on his marine radio and informed him of their impending arrival. The Supervisor heartily welcomed them to the station as he had been alerted by the Commander to be expecting them.

Matt then broke the news of the deadly encounter, outlining the situation to the Supervisor.

The Supervisor went silent for a moment as he considered the new information, then recovered and said he would have a team ready to secure the boats and bodies. The response would have been more forceful had this not been the station Commander's brother-in-law. He was well known to the staff from previous visits. Regardless, this remained an unexpected and troublesome turn of events and would require answers and an investigation.

It occurred to Matt, as he idled through the channel, that most of the boat traffic coming into the Keys through this passage, did so for pleasure and diversion.

Diving, fishing, nightlife, cruising, and relaxing was why most people passed this way. The Key West Express from Fort Myers brought boat loads of fun seekers into this channel every week.

But this trip had been anything but fun for the Four Musketeers.

Matt skillfully maneuvered the 55-foot *Catch* alongside the Coast Guard docks as the station crew stood by to assist. Dockside crewmembers were throwing ropes to Jake, Kelli, and Lucien while others were already on the water in one of the 24' SPC rubber-sided boats that the Coast Guard uses extensively. The crew of the SPC was busy untying the two trailing boats and towing them into a secure location further up the dockside facility. They were throwing curious glances toward the crew of the *Catch* after seeing the six dead bodies aboard the smaller boats. They had been instructed by the Supervisor not to react or ask questions. They were to perform their tasks in a business-as-usual manner.

Kelli twist-locked the shore power cord to a receptacle on the *Catch* and threw the other end to a crewman who plugged it into a dockside power station. This enabled Matt to shut down the engines and the generator. The deep thrumming of the diesels ceased and the ship felt unnaturally quiet.

Matt gave the Night Supervisor an expanded version of the incident at Ten Thousand Islands. The Supervisor asked if Matt knew who the assailants were or why they attacked. Matt said no. The Supervisor surmised they could have been pirates looking to steal a prize boat and informed the four of them that he would post armed security details around the dock for the rest of the night and also put the Station personnel on high alert, just in case.

Matt expressed his appreciation to the Supervisor and took note of what time it was. 10:30 PM. Enough time to grab a sandwich from the galley and drink a beer or two, or three, before they turned in for the night. It had been a full day and then some.

Extra security lights were switched on around the docks and pairs of armed sentries were already deployed. Matt invited the other three Musketeers to join him in the galley for some well-deserved food and drink.

As usual, Lucien was the first to get to the galley and was busy pulling out sandwich fixings and twisting caps off cold beers. He handed a frosty beverage to each of them as they filed into the galley area.

Lucien chugged his entire beer without stopping to take a breath, wiped his mouth with the back of his hand, and exclaimed, "I have to tell ya, that might be the best beer I've ever had!"

Everyone laughed a little. It felt good to break the tension even if just for a few moments.

Jake spoke next.

"Matt, I want to tell you what I saw on one of the dead guys. The one that poisoned himself had a triangle tattoo on the back of his hand, like the one on the neck of the guy who broke into your house."

"I'll be damned." Matt replied, shaking his head. "We need to look at those other five guys, too. See if they have that tattoo. This must be some kind of cult or something. This is gettin' weirder by the minute."

The four of them devoured their cold meat and cheese sandwiches, chips, pickles, and cold beers. They fell silent as fatigue set in.

"C'mon Matt, let's turn in." Kelli said with a tired smile. It was not the same *come hither* smile she had flashed at Matt earlier in the day at the Nauti Mermaid. That ship had sailed and the mood was now heavy and dense.

At that, everyone started shuffling toward their respective staterooms.

Jake turned to them and warned, "I know we have patrols out there, but I'd feel better if all of you kept your handguns close by, just to be on the safe side. We still don't know what we're dealing with here."

Matt replied, "Good idea, Jake. But when things calm down, I still want to hear more about the secret life of Jake Preston."

Jake just smiled and headed to his cabin.

"Later pardner, later."

CHAPTER 69

Special Weapons Research Center
Aquatica, Atlantis

COMMANDER MISHON AND HIS volunteers rolled the brightly-painted legacy rocket through the large overhead doors and onto the outdoor staging area. The red and white rocket was mounted on a mobile launcher and carried a full load of fuel.

Mishon returned to the Control Room where he noticed most of the remote viewscreens had blinked out. The screens still operating revealed the rolling, pitching, all-encompassing nightmare moving into its final death throes. Atlantis continued to cave inward and slide into the massive fault line…piece by piece…person by person…horror by horror. No signs of life could be seen on the monitors any longer.

Mishon quickly looked away from the apocryphal images and directed his attention to the staff in the Control Room.

"Dr. Broda, how are you progressing with the gathering of records?"

"Finishing now, Commander. We are putting them in crash-proof containers for loading into the rocket."

"Very good, Broda. Sagrin, have you selected an optimum landing site for our rocket?"

"Yes Commander, I have. The Sandora Islands. They are within the rocket's range but far enough away that I am confident the records will survive there. Ironically, the Sandora Islands are also known among our people as the Islands of Hope."

Commander Mishon urged the volunteers to begin loading the records into the empty warhead space on the rocket as soon as the protective containers were sealed. He directed the technicians to determine the coordinates of one of the Sandora Islands and to program them into the guidance system of the waiting rocket.

Time was running out—for everyone.

CHAPTER 70

Coast Guard Station Key West
Key West, Florida

Coast Guard Station Key West is located at the southern tip of Key West and the crew is known as the "Southernmost Lifesavers". They take that title seriously and do their jobs with great pride and professionalism.

The mission of Station Key West is large and multi-faceted. It is responsible for an area in excess of 2,500 square miles. With a complement of five boats of varying configurations, the crew men and women are charged with carrying out search and rescue, boating safety, environmental and fishing regulation, counter-narcotics/drug interdiction, immigration control, plus other duties too numerous to mention. Overseeing this hub of endless activity is Commander Ken Spader, Chief Warrant Officer. It is a job he loves and spent his entire professional life preparing for.

Commander Spader was already at his desk at 7:00 AM when he looked up and noticed Matt standing in his office doorway.

"Mornin', Ken. Can a man get some hot sludge around here?"

"Good Morning, Matt! Come on in and have a seat. I'll grab you a mug and we'll talk."

Commander Spader walked out to the ready room and poured some government-issue coffee into a large mug displaying the

Coast Guard Key West logo on one side and "Southernmost Lifesavers" on the other.

He returned to his office and handed the mug of strong coffee to Matt. "Keep that mug for your boat. Just got some new ones in."

Spader slid around behind his desk and settled into his high-back, executive style chair.

Ken Spader was a military man through and through. He was squared away at all times with close-cut hair and a well-pressed uniform. Somehow, he had always managed to make time for his wife and sons even as he juggled a demanding career. Matt admired Ken's character and felt fortunate to have him as a brother-in-law. He was tough but fair. Dependable and honest. Always ready to do what needed to be done. He loved God, loved his family, loved his country, and loved the Coast Guard. A good man. Salt of the earth.

Ken Spader looked intently across his desk at Matt.

"What kind of hornet's nest did you get into yesterday? I got here about an hour ago and debriefed the Night Supervisor. Six dead bodies and a firefight? Who did you piss off?"

"I wish I knew, Ken. They came out from behind an island at full speed and started shooting. If it hadn't been for Jake, I wouldn't be talking to you right now."

"I know Kelli, of course. But who's this Jake and the other guy that's with you?"

"Jake's a good friend that owns the marina on Anna Maria where I keep my boat. But I have to tell you, after the way he handled that situation yesterday, I suspect there's a lot more to Jake than what I know. He took those guys out like clockwork with that sniper rifle he brought with him. He nailed five of them without a miss while we were running at top speed. Then he shot up their drive units so they couldn't maneuver. The one that was still alive took a cyanide pill before we could get to him. Lucien Bart is the other guy with me. Our grandfathers worked together at the University of Florida and went on a lot of archaeological expeditions together. Those two found some things they entrusted to Lucien and I and that's the reason we are on this trip to begin with."

Matt proceeded to fill Ken in on the intruder that broke into his house and how Lucien had washed up on his beachfront the next day. Without going into too much detail, Matt outlined the reasons he and Lucien were headed to North Bimini Island.

"Holy Crap, Matt! That's one hell of a story. And you believe there's a link between these attacks and the relics Grandpa Bill left you?"

"It's the only thing I can come up with so far that makes any sense."

Ken sat back in his chair, looking off into the distance for a few moments, then back at Matt. He rubbed his face and shook his head as if it were all too hard to believe.

"Well, no matter what, you know the drill. I have to take statements from all of you and try to determine who these dead guys are. We'll run their fingerprints and see if they have any ID's on them. I'll get all this done as quickly as possible so you can be on your way. That is, if you're still determined to go through with this trip?"

"Yeah Ken, I have to see it through. There's something important out there, important enough that somebody would kill over it. And Grandpa wanted me to be the one to find it. Same with Lucien. I couldn't talk Jake and Kelli into backing out, but I did try. So, there you have it. It seems we're all in it for the duration."

"I'll call in investigators from Station Miami to help expedite this thing as much as possible. Stay close by and if you go out somewhere, let us know your whereabouts. Fair enough?"

"Fair enough."

Ken paused and seemed to be considering something else.

"I know Cindy will make time to stop by and visit while you're here. She's always excited to see you. I'll try to keep things quiet about what happened, so she won't worry too much. You can tell her whatever you want her to know, but I have one more question. Does your father know about any of this?"

"No, he doesn't. I see no reason to worry him with it. I have no answers for him anyway and that's what he'll be looking for. You know he's always snowed under at NASA and this would just add to his list of things to worry about."

"I see." Ken said. "Well, it's your call Matt, but I can't help thinking he would want to know. I'll get my staff busy gathering evidence from the boats and bodies and taking statements from you and your guests. If there's anything you need while you're here, just let me or my people know. And don't wander too far without telling us."

"I won't. Thanks, Ken. Oh, one more thing. Could you check the bodies for something specific? The man who broke into my house had three little triangles tattooed on his neck. Jake noticed the same tattoo on the back of the guy's hand who poisoned himself. I would like to know if any of the other bodies have that tattoo."

"No problem. I'll have the investigators photograph all tattoos and distinguishing marks so you can see them."

"That would be great. I appreciate it."

Ken stood and moved around the desk, grabbing Matt's hand in a firm handshake while putting his other hand on Matt's shoulder. With a deep look of concern, he said, "Be careful, Matt."

CHAPTER 71

Atlantis
The Final Act

PREPARATIONS WERE COMPLETE. THE legacy rocket was positioned at the staging area in front of the SWRC. The tremors were increasing in frequency and severity. Time was about up. Everyone knew it. A desperate sense of urgency now coursed through the team like an electrical current.

Records containing the entire recorded history of Atlantis, the knowledge of the Ancients, and the story of the millions of inhabitants who had called this land their home, were now stowed aboard the rocket. The Sandora Islands' coordinates had been programmed into the rocket's guidance system and double-triple-checked for accuracy. There could be no mistakes in this last action they would take as a people. The ground was lurching as the remaining staff of the SWRC struggled to maintain their footing around the small rocket that would carry their story to the future. The chances that the rocket launcher would tip over and be damaged were increasing by the moment.

Dr. Brota had rigged a control box that would fire the rocket when the command was given.

Dr. Sarontin looked into the eyes of the souls that remained. Her heart broke even as she spoke in a shivering voice that was full of pride and overwhelming sadness at the same time.

"My friends, you have done a great thing today. Atlantis, and its people, will live on in the records we have preserved. I have the deepest respect and affection for every one of you and in no way should you blame yourselves for what happened. That no longer matters. We all love our homeland and that is what should be remembered."

Dr. Sarontin motioned for everyone to form a line off to one side of the rocket and they took the hands of the one on each side of them.

"Broda, are we ready?"

"Yes, Doctor. Green lights across the board."

"Good. Let's do the countdown together, backward from ten to zero. Commander Mishon, we would be honored if you would push the ignition button when the countdown reaches zero."

Commander Mishon mumbled his appreciation and positioned himself next to Broda and the launch panel.

Through eyes now brimming over with tears, Dr. Sarontin tightly squeezed the hands of those next to her. She took a last look up and down the line at those she had grown so close to, had accomplished so much with. Each of them understood the situation—the importance as well as the horror of it. There was not a dry eye to be found among the small group, not even Commander Mishon. She understood their tears were not so much from fear, but rather for what had been lost. Families. The limitless future of Atlantis. The legacy of a great people and nation left unfulfilled.

Dr. Sarontin straightened herself slightly and began, "Ten… Nine…Eight…"

Everyone now joined in and formed a single voice.

"Seven…Six…Five…"

Dr. Broda flipped open the arming switch cover and depressed the button beneath it.

"Four…Three…Two…"

Commander Mishon's finger was now poised over the firing switch that would send the rocket skyward.

"One…Zero!"

The firing control was engaged by Mishon and a small roar began in the rocket engine as it stirred to life.

The engine noise increased in intensity as it strained against the docking clamps. A blue orange flame now extended from the rear of the legacy rocket as it broke free from its restraints and began to move forward in the launcher. The ground beneath the portable launcher was shaking and lurching like a drunken sailor on a ship's deck during a boiling storm. The onlookers began to fear the rocket would not get away in time.

At least in this final moment, fortune smiled on the small gathering of doomed people.

The motor overpowered the force of gravity and pushed the rocket up and out of the launcher. The blast of the engine grew louder, and the flames grew brighter, extending further behind the rocket. The messenger that carried the whole of what Atlantis had been was safely away.

A subdued but thankful cheer went up from the small band of scientists, technicians, and leaders. Atlantis' legacy might live on— somewhere, somehow, sometime. At least the possibility now existed. That was important.

As the condemned group of Atlanteans continued to hold hands and follow the graceful rocket's rise into the grey, smoke-filled, billowing sky; the earth groaned, pitched, and fractured. The SWRC's metal structure was screeching and twisting and failing. Out here in the open, the thunderous noise of explosions and rumbling quakes could be heard more clearly.

Hollow wails now poured from the last survivors of the once-proud continent of Atlantis. They desperately clung to each other's hands in an attempt to stay united just a little longer. To not draw their last breath alone. These were truly the best and brightest, perhaps the noblest that Atlantis ever produced, and it was somehow fitting they should end their time on Earth much the way they had spent their lives. Together.

The ground where they stood opened its cruel maw and called for them—a great karmic justice demanding to be addressed by the injured planet beneath them.

The besieged band of souls continued to hang onto whatever they could grab of each other; hands, legs, clothing. Not wanting to see it all end. Please God! Not yet! Shrieks and cries born of terror and pain pierced and tore the heavy air, then waned as one by one, the number of the unclaimed dwindled. Not to be cheated out of a full measure of vengeance, the tortured, bruised fabric of Atlantis opened wider still—intent on claiming its final victims.

Dr. Sarontin relaxed into her fate, letting her arms hang loosely at her side, falling into the bowels of her cherished continent, accepting her demise without further struggle. She looked up even as she was taken in by the monster she helped unleash, seeking the sunlight one last time. None was to be found. Ashes and dust clouds covered the once bright azure sky of Aquatica. Time slowed for Rona. As she descended into the darkness below, she saw the lights of the SWRC blink off. She could no longer hear the travails of her countrymen. She was alone. She was conscious of her own stillness and the gnashing and grinding of the earth she was falling into. In her altered state of consciousness, she found she had time for final thoughts.

Rona watched as images of her life flickered across the screen of her mind like a nostalgic home video. Her carefree childhood spent going on imaginary adventures with her friends. The favorite beach where she spent so many warm days frolicking in the sun and water. The sound of her mother's voice calling her to the evening meal. The feel of her father's strong hand holding hers. The learning academies where she excelled at every level. The first kiss from the wonderful man who would become her life partner. The young faces of her two children as they looked up at her the way small ones do—with undiluted joy. The family trips and get-togethers. A life filled with good friends, a loving family, and great accomplishments. A nation filled with the same. All brought to an unexpected and tragic end.

Perhaps, it had to end this way. Did our reach exceed our grasp? Did our technology outpace our wisdom and judgment? If we had succeeded in carrying out our plans as a people, would we have brought even greater trouble and pain into this world instead of less? Would our blind ambition have continued to grow unchecked and spin completely out of control? Was this the only way we could be prevented from disrupting the natural order of the entire planet? I wonder…

Now wrapped and cocooned in darkness. Final peace. Debt repaid. Books balanced.

Atlantis was no more.

CHAPTER 72

Coast Guard Station Key West

MATT HAD RETURNED FROM Commander Spader's office and he and Kelli now sat side-by-side on the bridge of the *Nice Catch*, watching the Coast Guard investigators pore over the captured attack boats, taking pictures from every angle and of the most minute details. They checked every surface for fingerprints and clues that might reveal the identity of the assailants and where they came from.

A temporary morgue had been set up inside the station complex and a postmortem examination was being carried out on the bodies of the dead men who had gotten more than they bargained for.

Matt decided to see what was going on with the rest of the crew, so he and Kelli climbed down the ladder to the main deck. Lucien was already preparing breakfast. Jake was meticulously cleaning his rifle. He intended to be well-prepared should trouble break out again.

They ate their meal together with good humor and small talk. Everyone pitched in for cleanup and it was completed in short order.

Jake went back to cleaning his rifle and checking the condition of other mystery items he had stored in the kit bag in his stateroom. Nobody was quite sure what all he had in there and nobody asked.

Lucien headed to the long front deck of the boat and stretched out in the morning sun to catch some rays and work on his tan.

Matt and Kelli wandered back up to the bridge to watch all the activity going on at the Coast Guard station. It ran like a well-oiled machine with shifts changing and patrols coming and going with missions in hand. Ken ran a tight ship.

They had settled back into the comfortable twin captain's chairs, loosely holding hands, when Kelli looked at Matt with searching eyes.

"You okay?"

Matt met her look and nodded his head, affirming that he was. "And you?"

Kelli's face relaxed into a slight smile and she leaned into Matt's shoulder.

"Yeah, I'm good. A good night's sleep and bacon and eggs always makes things seem better. Sorry I was so tired. I had other intentions when the day began."

"No apology necessary. I was exhausted, too. Maybe when this is all over, we can spend a few days alone and make up for lost time." Matt winked and smiled at her as he said it.

Kelli replied, "I'll hold you to that."

Several quiet minutes passed as they remained connected by their fingers, then Matt straightened in his chair and turned to face her. A more serious look moving across his face.

"Kelli, I want you to know I'm really worried about your safety. If anything were to happen to you, well…"

"Matt, please don't." she interrupted. Kelli squeezed his arm with both her hands, swiveled around toward him, and looked him squarely in the eyes. Her voice was soft but resolute. "I know what you are trying to say and I appreciate how you worry about me. But what you have to understand is that I'm here because there's nowhere else I want to be. My place in this world, at this moment, is with you. No matter where that is or what happens. I know you don't run from a fight. I don't either. When something this important is happening in your life, I want to be a part of it. It's as simple as that. And there *is* that one other thing, too. I happen to be in love with you."

Matt stood and pulled her to her feet in front of him, put his arms around her and drew her closer as if to create a cloak of protection around her. He thought about Kelli's past and the things that had made her the tough yet loving person she had become.

Kelli Renner had grown up in West Palm Beach and enjoyed an idyllic childhood as a typical Florida girl. She had taken to the water like a fish and loved everything about it. She took a special interest in the creatures that lived in it or near it. She spent all her spare time swimming, fishing, diving, and interacting with the ocean creatures surrounding her.

Her perfect life was shattered at the age of twelve when her parents battled through a bitter breakup. The divorce proceedings lasted over two years but the war between the two of them never truly ended.

The parents attempted a shared custody arrangement, but no longer agreed on anything; including how to raise a teenage girl. Kelli grew tired of the squabbling and the trips back and forth between her parents who made her feel like a pawn on a chess board. Out of exasperation, she asked permission to live with her paternal grandmother who lived on Bird Key in Sarasota. She and her grandmother had always been close and she welcomed Kelli into her home with open arms. The parents did not put up much of a fight over it. They seemed relieved to no longer have to deal with each other where Kelli was concerned.

Kelli's grandmother, Isobel Renner, was a striking woman. Tall and elegant, yet tough as nails. Isobel was a widow but independent and well-to-do. She and her late husband, Frank, had moved from the Upper Peninsula of Michigan to Florida in the early sixties to escape the brutal northern winters. Over years of vacations to the area, they had fallen in love with the temperate climate and beautiful scenery that was Southwest Florida and decided to make it their home. Frank and Isobel believed that many more people would move to the area over the next few years, so they began a land investment company. Their hunch was correct and it paid off handsomely. Over the next thirty years, the Renners purchased key parcels of land in the area surrounding Sarasota. Some they sold at a profit, others they used to partner with developers to create new business centers and residential communities. The visionary couple made a lot of money and built their dream home on Bird Key; home to celebrities and the super wealthy.

This is the environment in which Kelli's father, Frank, Jr., had spent his youth. He had always felt a sense of entitlement, much to the chagrin of his parents who had tried to teach him self-reliance and a strong work ethic.

Now it was just Kelli and Isobel and Isobel insisted Kelli call her by her name only. She was not fond of being called Grandma or Mamaw or Mimi or any of those other names they foisted on matriarchs. She did not see herself in that light and did not want anyone else to either.

Kelli thrived in her new environment. Isobel's lively spirit and thirst for new experiences rubbed off on her. Kelli loved the long, animated talks with Isobel as they sat overlooking the waters of Sarasota Bay from the large lanai behind the house. Isobel shared a lifetime of stories and experiences with Kelli. Isobel taught her about discipline and hard work, but always with a twinkle in her blue-green eyes.

Kelli followed her passion and earned a degree in Marine Biology from the University of Miami, staying around as an adjunct instructor for a period of time following graduation. She had become a fixture around the Marine Biology program and they did not want to see her go. But after a while, she felt a tugging in her mind and heart to move back to Sarasota and be closer to Isobel. It was home.

Isobel was overjoyed to have her return but did not want Kelli to become complacent. She asked Kelli what she really wanted to do next and Kelli stated she wanted to open her own dive school. Isobel dispatched her to do the research necessary to open a dive business and then gifted her the seed money to do so. No time to waste when pursuing one's dream…that was Isobel's philosophy.

Kelli chose a location near Siesta Key and opened The Dive Station. She purchased the essential dive gear and a twin-engine dive boat with a small cabin and never looked back.

Kelli's enthusiasm for her chosen profession was infectious. She soon had a waiting list of students during the winter season when tourism was at its peak.

She met Matt about a year after she opened the Dive Station. He had taken a group of experienced divers on a charter and ended up doing a dive in the same spot where Kelli was conducting a class. The two of them compared information about the best diving spots in the area, discussed their boats, then exchanged phone numbers. They became an item soon after.

"Hey, Matt. Where'd you go?" Kelli asked with a laugh.

"I was just thinking about you and how we met and what we have together. I don't want anything to happen to that."

"As long as I'm alive, Matt, nothing will."

"Then, I will have to make sure to keep you alive…"

CHAPTER 73

Dominion Transglobal Headquarters
Dallas, Texas

JORDAN DOMINION TOOK THE call on his secure line.

"What do you mean, you failed?" he asked.

The caller frantically tried to explain what went wrong.

"I didn't build a global empire on excuses, Mr. Petrov."

"Yes I understand, Mr. Dominion. I apologize. It seems our field operatives underestimated our targets' capabilities."

"The reason I am more successful than my competitors is because I never underestimate my adversaries."

"Yes, Mr. Dominion. I know this to be true. I just need a little more time and manpower and you will have your answers."

"Time? You've been tracking these items for over two years! Manpower? How many men have you lost just in the last few days? Seven?"

"Yes, sir."

"Were these men imbeciles?"

"No, Mr. Dominion. They were highly-skilled Soviet ex-special forces and former KGB operatives."

"So you tell me, but they didn't perform like it. Were they all sworn to the Brotherhood?"

"Yes, sir. All wore the mark of the Brotherhood and gave their life for the cause. The last one to die took his own life by poisoning rather than risk being interrogated."

"I see. Where are the bodies of this group of miserable failures?"

"Six of them are at the Coast Guard Station in Key West and one is in a morgue in Sarasota."

"Did these men carry any identification or anything else that would allow them to be traced back to me?

"Absolutely not, Mr. Dominion. Only the tattoos. But that meaning is known only to us and the Brotherhood."

"Do you have any idea where our targets are planning to go next?"

"No, sir. But I believe they have a map that shows them where to find the relics and all we have to do is follow them. When they are in an exposed position, we will strike them again and claim the information and relics you seek."

"No mistakes this time, Petrov."

"No sir. We will prevail."

"How many men do you have on station in the area around the Keys?"

"Ten, sir. We also have boats on standby. But the targets are currently under the protection of the U.S. Coast Guard."

"Call for reinforcements, Mr. Petrov. Double your force. Do not underestimate your targets again, do you understand?"

"Yes, Mr. Dominion."

"I trust you do. If there is another failure, I will hold you personally responsible. Is that understood as well?"

"Understood."

"Very well. Make sure you personally supervise this mission. As soon as the targets are unprotected, eliminate them and secure the maps and relics."

"Yes, sir. They will not escape my men again, Mr. Dominion."

"For your sake, they better not."

Jordan Dominion slammed down the phone and began to pace the floor of his cavernous office.

CHAPTER 74

Coast Guard Station
Key West, Florida

Cindy Spader, Matt's older sister, approached the *Catch* which still sat dockside at the Coast Guard Station in Key West. It was now early evening of the first full day at the station.

Cindy was an affable, capable woman in her early forties. She had reddish brown hair with blond highlights and had worked to retain her athletic build. Easy laugh lines radiated from the corners of her hazel eyes. Today, she wore white capris, a tangerine tank top, and white sandals with slightly raised heels. The days were still warm in the Keys, even this late in the year, and the locals dressed appropriately.

Cindy spotted Matt checking out the damage his boat had suffered during the firefight. He was high atop the stainless-steel observation tower which gleamed like a mirror in the fading afternoon sunlight. A stray bullet from one of the gunmen had glanced off a tower support and left an ugly ding in it. Matt felt like it had put a ding in him instead. He prided himself on keeping his boat in perfect condition and took its appearance personally. After all, any captain worth his salt understood their boat was a direct reflection of himself or herself.

Cindy waved heartily, hailing her brother. "Ahoy, Captain! Permission to come aboard!"

"Friend or foe?"

"Depends. Climb on down from there and give your sister a big hug."

"Be right down." Matt replied as he scurried down the ladder leading to the deck below.

He ran to the side of the boat where she was standing on the dock and extended his hand out to help her aboard the *Catch*. She took his hand and jumped across to the deck where she was immediately swept up into a big bear hug by her younger brother. He twirled her around a couple times before he set her down.

"Welcome aboard!" Matt said through a big grin.

"Thanks, Captain!" She said as she returned his smile.

"How long's it been, Cindy?"

"Almost six months, little brother. The last time I saw you, you were running a charter down here with some guys wanting to do some diving and fishing. That was back around the Fourth of July if I remember correctly."

"Yeah, that sounds about right. Time just seems to get away from us. How are you and the boys?"

"We're just fine. I'm busy getting ready for the holidays at school and home, but I enjoy that. The boys are doing great. They are truly a combination of their unstoppable old man and mushy old mother. Not a bad combination though. They're tough but have big hearts. Ladies beware!"

They both had a good laugh and Matt invited her into the salon where Kelli and Lucien were preparing dinner and Jake was looking over maps of the Bahamas. Just as they were ready to open the sliding door from the deck into the salon, Cindy hesitated. She put her hand on Matt's arm and said, "Can we talk in private for a few minutes? I look forward to seeing Kelli and meeting your friends, but how about just you and me for a little bit?"

"Sure. Let's head up to the bridge."

Once they settled into the bridge lounge, Matt twisted open a couple of the beers that he always kept in the bridge fridge. He handed one to his sister and sat beside her on the cool, white bench seat.

"What's on your mind, Sis?"

"Well, Ken tried to keep me in the dark about what's going on here, but that just wasn't going to happen. So, I tortured and threatened my husband until he came clean."

"Uh oh, poor Ken. I know what that's like. You're tough to say no to. I remember when we were kids, I never could keep anything from you if you wanted to get it out of me bad enough."

Cindy laughed and said, "Ken had to learn that just like you did. He can't bring that "need to know basis" crap home and use it on me where my family is concerned. But you should know he did put up a valiant fight."

"So, how much did he tell you before you released him from the rack?"

"Pretty much everything. At least I think he did. He told me about you being attacked at your house and about the dead guys and boats you towed in here last night, and how they got dead. He told me about this Lucien fellow shipwrecking in front of your house and that the two of you were given some secret stuff by Grandpa Bill and his partner, Mr. Bart. Now, supposedly, all of you are off on some grand adventure to figure out what the two grandpas wanted you to find. Does that about cover it?"

"Yep."

"What the hell, Matt?"

"What do you mean?"

"I mean, what the hell are you guys getting into that would involve people trying to kill you? Did Grandpa leave you a treasure map to a sunken pirate ship full of gold or what?"

"No, I don't think it's anything like that. But whatever we're supposed to find must have a lot of value to somebody. When that guy broke into my house, I had no idea what he was after. But eventually I figured out that it had to do with the stuff Grandpa left me. I remember Grandpa would get real serious when he discussed these relics with me, like it was extremely important and he couldn't talk about it or let anyone know that he knew what he knew. I never saw that look in his eyes any other time that I can recall. When Lucien showed up with his half of the relics and the rest of the map, he said his grandfather had acted the same way and swore him to silence as well. So, I don't know what's waiting on the other end of this, but I promised Grandpa I would see it through when the time came, and that's exactly what I'm doing."

"Even if it gets you killed?"

"We're up 7-0 on the body count so far!"

"That's not funny, Matt. You no longer have the element of surprise working for you. Whoever's after you and your little treasures will be better prepared this time and you know it."

"Well, I'm kind of hoping that we've scared them all off by now."

"Oh, really? What are you doing to protect yourself?"

"You know Jake's with us, the friend of mine who owns the marina where I keep my boat? He insisted on coming. And I know, you're thinking that having an old friend along who runs a marina won't be much help. But there's a lot more to Jake than any of us knew. He hasn't told me about his previous background yet and he's in no hurry to talk about it, but he had another life before I knew him and I'm pretty sure it didn't involve fixing boats. He put down five of those six dead guys that are laying in the morgue before they knew what hit 'em. It would be safe to say that he's done that before. He brought a little arsenal on board with him, too. So, he's now my official Director of Security."

"Jesus, Matt. What a mess. Ken told me that you haven't said anything to Dad or Mom about all this?"

"No, Sis. I haven't. I don't know what good it would do. It would just worry him and Mom and there's nothing they can do to help. Anyway, you know how busy he is. Even if he wanted to do something, NASA keeps him tied up 24/7."

"I know. But if it were your son, wouldn't you want to know what's going on?"

"Yeah, that's what Ken said, too. I suppose…"

Matt looked down at his feet for a minute and then back at Cindy.

"Okay, yes I would. So, I'll think about it. I have a sat phone on the boat in addition to my cell if I decide to call him. Ken has my sat phone number and I will leave it with you, too. Now, if I promise not to get myself killed, can we go below and see everyone else before we get accused of being antisocial?"

Cindy threw her arms around Matt's neck and held him close in silence for a few moments. She released him, stepped back a step, looked at him with concern etched into her face and tears welling up in her eyes, and shook her head up and down.

"Alright then, but only if you promise."

CHAPTER 75

Coast Guard Station
Key West, Florida

THE SECOND NIGHT PASSED without incident. Commander Spader had maintained armed patrols around the clock and he would continue to do so as long as the *Nice Catch* was docked in his facility.

Matt was standing in Commander Spader's doorway again on this second morning. It was 0730 hours according to the clock in the ready room. The Commander had already been at his desk for an hour and a half studying the investigative reports coming in over the last twenty-four hours.

The door was open, Matt rapped on the wooden frame.

The Commander looked up from his paperwork and gestured for Matt to come in and take a seat.

"Up for some more of that Mississippi mud, Matt?"

"No thanks, Ken. I think I've finally lost my taste for it. I had coffee on the boat before coming over here, so I'm good."

"Can't say as I blame you. I'm sure your coffee's a hell of a lot better than this used motor oil, but I've gotten used to it."

"So, what have you found out about these guys so far?"

"Sad to say Matt, but nothing useful really. We ran their prints and got some interesting hits. Evidently, these guys were a mixture of ex-KGB and Soviet Special Forces before the Soviet Union broke up. We think they must have gone out on their own after the collapse. We had no further records on them until now. They had no ID's on them or anything else. Whoever they worked for made sure they could not be traced back up line. They were obviously part of a para-military organization of some kind and it functions at a high level. They know how to operate as individual cells that leave no link to the other cells or handlers. This is not an amateur group, Matt. You were in Navy Intelligence for quite a few years so you know how these things work without me telling you. The question remains, who's sending these guys after you? It either has to be a foreign government or a private organization with a lot of money and resources. My guess is the latter. If these ex-Soviet guys were involved with another government, we would have some intel on them. As it is, we've got zip. NSA, CIA, FBI, Interpol. They all drew a blank."

Spader opened a file folder, withdrew a stack of 8 X 10 color photos, and continued.

"However, you did ask me to look for those tattoos. Here are the pics we took of each of the dead guys you brought in. All of them had that same tattoo somewhere on their bodies. Either on the neck or on the back of one of their hands."

The Commander spread out the photos on the desk in front of Matt so he could see them for himself.

Matt leafed through the grim photos, chewed on his lower lip, squinted at the lifeless faces, and rubbed his face with his hands as if it would cleanse him of all of this.

"Damn it Ken, this whole thing is just strange. It's like a secret society or something."

"Yeah, maybe. But if it *is* a secret society, it's a damned serious one."

"Did you run those tattoos and symbols through all the databases as well?"

"You bet. Nada…nothing."

"So, I've got a paramilitary cult following me with symbols of my little relics tattooed on their bodies and they want to kill me and steal them. Does that pretty much sum up what we know so far?"

Ken could not help but smile a little at Matt's summary.

"Well, when you put it like that it sounds pretty crazy, but that's how it looks so far."

"I appreciate all your help, Ken. When can we get underway again?"

"We should have everything finished up today, so you can leave in the morning if you want."

"I think I should. The longer we stay in one place, the easier it is for them to track us and bring in reinforcements."

"I hate to see you go Matt, but I have to agree with your assessment of the situation. So, I don't guess I can talk you into staying a while longer to give us more time to investigate?"

"No, I don't believe so. I know you've got Cindy pressuring you to talk me out of it but if you think about it, they'll continue to come after me even if I go back home. Hell, that's where it all started! These guys won't stop coming at me until I finish this, one way or the other. I'll tell you this, I'm not going to walk around looking over my shoulder the rest of my life. I'm going to get to the bottom of this and put it to rest."

"I understand where you're coming from, Matt. Between you and me, I would feel the same way and probably do the same thing but I'll swear you're lying if you tell Cindy I said that. Let me know what else I can do for you while you're here. I'll have a cutter escort you out into open water as far as I can without getting my ass in a sling."

"Much appreciated, brother. I'll take all the help I can get at this point."

"Oh, and one other thing, Matt. We ran a background check on each of you as part of our investigation. Standard procedure you know during an incident like this. I got nothing remarkable on Lucien really and Kelli came back squeaky clean as expected. But I did find some interesting stuff on your buddy, Jake."

"Oh, really? What has that old buzzard been hiding from me?"

"Ready for this? That "old buzzard" is ex-CIA black ops. And I mean deep cover black ops."

"You gotta be shittin' me!" Matt exclaimed. "I worked with some of those guys when I was in Naval Intelligence. Sometimes we had to coordinate our intel with them and provide logistical support as part of their mission planning. They are some real bad asses. Remind me of a cross between a SEAL and a spy. They are beyond deep cover."

"The background report didn't give any specifics about his record because its top secret and the files are sealed, but I've heard a few things about them, too. They work so far undercover, the government won't even admit they exist and if they get caught, they're on their own."

"That's the deal they sign up for, Ken. They do the dirty work the government wants done behind the scenes."

"All I can say is, I'm glad he's on your side and not theirs."

"Yeah, me too."

CHAPTER 76

Coast Guard Station
Key West, Florida

THE *NICE CATCH* EASED back out through the same waterway that had led them into Station Key West a couple days earlier. Trailing a short distance to the rear was the Coast Guard cutter that Ken had promised would escort them out. It was highly unlikely anyone would start something as long as a well-armed cutter was nearby.

The dawn was spectacular. Just the right mixture of sun and clouds to create the magentas and golds that paint the morning sky in a masterpiece of colors and textures.

The soft rays of the morning sun reflected off the *Catch*, revealing the pale mint green of the hull while shooting golden glints and stars off the chrome and stainless fixtures of the boat. She stood tall and proud as she exited the Coast Guard compound and pointed toward open waters.

Matt was at the helm on the flying bridge sipping fresh, steaming coffee from his new Coast Guard souvenir mug, keeping a light hand on the wheel and taking in the sensual sights and smells of dawn breaking over tropical waters. The salt air, the brightening green of the waves, gulls and ospreys calling out for their mates and fishing buddies, and the warm morning glow pouring over his graceful boat.

Lucien was already sitting cross-legged in his favorite spot out on the bow. He was fittingly dressed in cut-offs and flip-flops and cupping his hands around a warm mug. Kelli was taking her morning java on the stern deck. She was relaxing in one of the fish-fighting chairs, sport sunglasses on, wearing a pair of navy short-shorts and a white and navy striped midriff tank top, bare legs stretched out, watching the security of the Coast Guard Station slowly diminish behind them. Matt glanced down at her and was quite sure the lookouts on the cutter were checking her out through their binoculars. Who could blame them. She was a naturally beautiful woman.

Jake climbed the steps to the bridge and took up a position next to Matt in the second captain's chair.

"Mornin', Captain." Jake said in his gravelly voice.

"Mornin' to you, Jake." Matt replied as he took another sip of his coffee, keeping his eyes fixed on the horizon. "Sleep good?"

"Good enough. Listen Matt, I think we need to talk about our situation before we go much further."

Jake was also focusing his eyes straight ahead and took a big swallow of his coffee.

"By situation, I assume you mean these people that are trying to kill us and what we're going to do about it?"

Matt allowed a slight grin while stealing a sideways glance at his friend.

"Yeah, that would be the situation I'm referring to."

Jake kept a stone face, still staring straight ahead.

"I think you know these guys are going to keep coming and next time, they'll come heavy after what we did to them. We could use a little more help, in my humble opinion."

"What kind of help?"

Matt slightly adjusted the wheel to stay inside the channel markers.

"Another good hand might help."

"And by "good hand", I assume you mean someone that has the same "skill sets" you do?"

Jake finally looked at Matt with raised eyebrows and slight amusement in his eyes.

"What "skills" do you assume me to have, compadre?"

Matt played along.

"Don't forget Jake, I worked Naval Intelligence for a long time. I saw how you handled yourself during that firefight. You've done that before, probably quite a few times. You didn't learn to do that by going boar huntin' in the woods twice a year. Hogs don't shoot back."

"Maybe I just got off some lucky shots?"

Jake was still deadpanning and had returned his gaze to the horizon.

"Maybe. But I ain't buyin' it. Ken informed me that when they ran your background check, your records were sealed up tighter than a drum. But they could see enough to know you're ex-CIA black ops."

Jake's eyes widened and he feigned a surprised smile.

"Matt, I'm shocked! You know I'm just a harmless boat mechanic."

"Sorry to blow your cover, Jake."

"Just as well, I guess. But could you keep it to yourself? It's not the sort of thing I talk about at parties."

"I worked with some of your fellow operatives when I was in the Navy and I know you need to stay on the down low. So tell me about this "good hand" you're proposing to add to our crew?"

"He would prefer to avoid using his real name since he's trying to live a quiet life these days like me. We called him "Ghost" when I worked with him. We did a lot of missions together and survived some real shit storms. He's as good as they come, Matt. He's currently spending time near Miami. I called him yesterday to see what he's up to and he's available."

"Why do you call him Ghost?"

"Cause that's how he operates. The guy can appear and disappear like a ghost. Never saw anything like it. He claims he's part Cherokee and that it comes natural."

"Why would he want to put his ass on the line with us?"

"Same reason I did. Friend needed it. That's all he needed to know."

Matt looked at Jake who was still staring out toward the open water.

"Jake, you're somethin' else. I don't know what to say…"

"Just say you know how to steer this oversized fishing boat to Miami and I'll tell Ghost we're on our way."

Matt chuckled and said, "Okay, you crazy bastard."

CHAPTER 77

JORDAN DOMINION DOMINATED THE large, round mahogany table before him. He was impeccably attired in an expensive navy-blue silk suit, blood-red power tie, glossy black dress shoes, black onyx and silver cufflinks, and a Rolex watch. His thick, dark, slightly graying hair was stylishly raked away from his smooth-shaven face. He looked to be the epitome of power and style.

His top three executives were gathered around the table and their attention was fixed intently on him. He considered them for a moment. They were his inner circle and the only people privy to his larger plans. They were corporate kings in their own right and wielded great power and influence on his behalf.

The other executives and board members were only allowed partial views of what the future held for the global giant. Jordan believed in doling out information to departments and individuals on a need to know basis and only enough to accomplish the task they were assigned to. Compartmentalization was a key component to maintaining secrecy. It worked well enough for the best intelligence agencies around the world, so it was good enough for him. None of them were allowed to see the big picture, except these three.

Jordan Dominion stood up at the head of the table and opened the meeting.

"I called this meeting to bring you up to date on Project Atlantech. To recap, we have made steady progress over the last five years. We have diligently followed up on rumors and myths that suggested the Atlantis technology had not only existed, but records of it may have survived. We believe some of these stories originated with sailors and citizens of Atlantis who were not on the continent when it met it's demise through whatever means. Therefore, I decided it to be a venture worth investing in.

We investigated every lead and followed the trail of every person who has been known to do serious research into the history of Atlantis."

"Our inquiries eventually lead us to where we are today. We know Professors Flannery and Bart of the University of Florida had quietly worked to identify the area where they believed Atlantis once existed. Furthermore, we know they made multiple expeditions to the Bahamas. We believe they spent a lot of time in the vicinity of the Bimini Islands, but they spent time in other island areas as well. We interviewed some of the residents on Bimini that were known to have assisted archeological missions or historical expeditions to that area and they remembered Professors Bart and Flannery. But it seems the professors never revealed anything of interest to these locals."

"We then questioned their peers at the university. They remembered Flannery and Bart being quite excited about some finds they had made, but Atlantis was never mentioned. Eventually, the situation went quiet."

"After running exhaustive background investigations on these two professors, who are now deceased, an important common link was discovered. Both men had cultivated a close relationship with a grandson. It seems likely to me that if any vital research or information had been uncovered by the professors, it may have been passed on to their grandsons. Of course, we began continuous surveillance on both of the grandsons which yielded no results, until now."

"Lucien Bart, the grandson of James Bart, lives the life of a drifter onboard a sailboat. He recently traveled from St. Petersburg, Florida to Anna Maria Island, Florida where Matthew Flannery lives. He is the grandson of Professor Bill Flannery. At this point, I felt we had sufficient reason to believe these two grandsons were holding relics or information given to them by their grandfathers. Information directly pertaining to the ancient continent and technology of Atlantis."

"I authorized one of our best field operatives to enter the home of Mr. Flannery to locate and secure the items. Mr. Bart was due to arrive in the area at about the same time, so it was our plan to subdue Mr. Flannery and do the same with Mr. Bart when he arrived at Flannery's house. Simple plan. Use whatever force needed to secure the relics and leave no trace of our incursion other than two inexplicable deaths."

"However, Mr. Bart's arrival was delayed due to a storm. We decided to move forward with handling Mr. Flannery and deal with Mr. Bart when he arrived. What we did not account for, were the survival skills of Mr. Flannery. He overcame our operative and terminated him. This was not anticipated."

"Mr. Bart's boat washed up on shore the next day at Anna Maria Island during a tropical storm. In a strange twist of fate, he landed on the beach in back of Mr. Flannery's house. He was assisted by Mr. Flannery and they have been together since that time. This further confirms what we had theorized. They both have information or relics and are working together now to further the work their grandfathers had begun."

"Mr. Flannery and Mr. Bart boarded Mr. Flannery's charter fishing boat and were joined by a friend of Flannery's, Jake Preston. Preston owns the local marina and Flannery keeps his boat at that marina. Mr. Flannery's lady friend, Kelli Renner, joined them on the boat as well. She operates a dive school in Siesta Key, Florida.

We continued our surveillance of them as they left the area and moved to the south. We felt reasonably certain they were going to travel around the southern tip of Florida and then to the islands, probably the Bahamas."

"We arranged a greeting party to be waiting for them at the Ten Thousand Island chain south of Marco Island. It was a perfect spot to stage the intercept. An obscure area with multiple places to deploy assets with minimal chance of discovery."

"Again, our people underestimated the capabilities of the targets. Our two chase boats were met with highly accurate sniper fire resulting in the deaths of five of our six operatives. The sixth one took his own life just prior to capture as he had been indoctrinated to do. Mr. Flannery and company proceeded to tow both chase boats, with the dead bodies aboard, to the Key West Coast Guard Station. None of our operatives carried anything that could link them to us and as far as we can ascertain, no association was made. They were all members of The Brotherhood, whose creation has served us well."

"I have just spoken to our lead operative and I expressed my displeasure at his failure to obtain the relics and information we seek. He assured me there will be no further failures. I have ordered him to upgrade his forces and tactical weapons. We must not continue to underestimate these targets. They have shown extreme resilience and unexpected capabilities."

"Mr. Flannery and his traveling party have now exited the Coast Guard Station at Key West and are proceeding north along the coast toward Miami. We have them under surveillance from the water and the air."

"I expect we will successfully interdict them soon, recover the relics, and complete this phase of Project Atlantech."

CHAPTER 78

MATT PLACED A CALL to Ken at the station and informed him they would be taking a detour up the east coast before heading east to the Bahamas. He thanked the Commander for his offer of protection but would not need the cutter escort any longer as they would be staying relatively close to the heavily populated coastline on this leg of their journey. The cutter soon dropped back and turned about.

Ghost had suggested they pick him up at a public dock near a restaurant at the south end of Key Biscayne. The pickup point was to be at a restaurant at No Name Harbor—aptly named for a clandestine meeting such as this. It was also an easy in and out for the *Catch* and would not attract any undue attention as the location was fairly isolated.

Matt set in a new course for Key Biscayne, brought the boat up to cruising speed and on optimum plane, and engaged the autopilot. He was alone on the bridge for the moment and he took a moment to enjoy the quiet morning and the soothing, cool breeze. He looked out at the turquoise waters of the Keys, the pelicans beginning their day of dive bombing, the occasional fish leaping joyfully into the air, and an osprey making a lazy circle high above them on the lookout for breakfast. That's when Matt noticed a small plane making similar circles in the sky over their position.

Perhaps, it's nothing. Or maybe we're under aerial surveillance. It would make sense that someone with deep resources would keep an eye in the sky on the Catch. It would be less conspicuous and the plane's crew could dispatch water or ground personnel to wherever the Catch goes. Let's see if it continues to fly overhead as the day goes on or if it's just a coincidence.

Matt already knew in his heart it was not a coincidence. He called below for Jake who joined him on the bridge. Matt pointed up at the plane.

"What do you think, Jake?"

"Too early to say, but it would be logical for them to track us from the air. I think we assume it to be hostile until we have reason to believe otherwise. In fact, we should assume almost anyone or anything to be hostile at this point. We don't know who our enemy is or how they will come at us."

"I believe you're right, friend. That plane isn't really the threat. It's the people they're talking to on the ground that are going to be a problem."

"Right on pardner. Right on."

CHAPTER 79

On Board the Nice Catch
The Florida Keys

THE *CATCH* CONTINUED TO make its way north along the southeast Florida coastline. Matt decided to run up the Atlantic side of the Keys to steer clear of most of the leisure boat traffic and to avoid the inlets and outlets that would lend themselves to an ambush.

The plane circling overhead had disappeared for a short while but another one had taken its place. Matt was now certain it was tracking their movements.

Jake alternated between manning the lookout tower high above the bridge and hanging out with Matt at the helm. So far, he had not spotted anything suspicious, but he knew it was just a matter of time before their unknown enemy would make another run at them.

Kelli had donned a two-piece swimsuit and sat out in the sun for a while on the back of the boat to freshen her tan, but was now checking over the diving gear in case it was needed.

Lucien continued to perch on the bow of the boat and enjoy the tropical scenery passing by like a slideshow. After a while, he went below to his cabin saying he wanted to check his e-mail.

The *Catch* cleared the Keys and was angling over toward Biscayne Bay when Jake approached Matt on the bridge.

"Doin' okay, Matt?"

"Fine as frog's hair."

"I think we should discuss our schedule so I can figure out the best way to secure the boat."

"Good idea. Here's what I'm thinking. It will be mid-afternoon when we make No Name Harbor and pick up Ghost. I don't really want to head back out on the open water that late in the day if I can help it. It starts getting dark around six now and it seems we would be better off traveling during daylight if we can. We can start our run to Bimini first thing tomorrow morning and make it easily by early afternoon. I'm not too worried about storms this time of year. We're well into the dry season and I don't see anything big enough to worry about on radar or the weather forecast."

"Well thought out plan, Matt. So, we'll pick up Ghost this afternoon and hunker down for the night in No Name Harbor. With the Boater's Grill located there, should be quite a bit of boat traffic and people around us most of the evening. We shouldn't have anything to worry about until the restaurant closes and the people clear out. I don't think these people who are chasing us want to draw attention if they can avoid it. They've went to great lengths to remain anonymous and not leave a trail. My biggest concern is the time from around midnight to daybreak. If I were them, that's when I'd make my move."

"Makes sense. What tactic do you think they'll try this time?"

"All I can do is take a wild-ass guess. Since they're ex-special forces, I try to think like they would. Special ops guys like to operate in the dark whenever they can. So, I think they'll try a raid under the cover of darkness."

"What's the best way to defend ourselves against that?"

"Well, we can do it one of two ways. We can use our night vision gear and stay up all night looking over the side of the boat in a strictly defensive posture, or we can stop them before they start. I'm partial to offense rather than defense myself."

"How can we do a preemptive strike if we don't know where they are?"

Jake chuckled a little and said, "You leave that up to me and Ghost. We enjoy nothing more than spoiling a bad guy's party, and we've spoiled quite a few of them. The fact is, they can't launch a mission out of thin air, no matter how good they are. It will most likely come from nearby land or water. Remember, they aren't trying to blow us up, at least not yet. They're trying to rob us. Then, they want to blow us up and leave no witnesses. At least that's what I would do."

"So, what you're saying is they need to keep the *Catch* intact and board it so they can get what they want?"

"Bingo. They might figure we would keep a lookout for them all night, but I doubt they'll be expecting an offensive strike on our part. That's the way I want to play it. Offense, not defense."

"Alright, let's take the fight to them. I'll call a meeting with everybody and let them know what the plan is?"

"Not so fast."

"Why?"

"First of all, the fewer people who know the plan, the less likely someone will screw it up, especially if they're not involved in it. Second, in a worst-case scenario, one of them is captured and forced to tell what they know. They can't confess what they don't know."

"Damn Jake, that's pretty hardcore. I feel a lot better knowing you're on my side…I think."

"You might start feeling sorry for the bad guys before the night is over."

"I hope it works out that way." Matt replied with an uneasy grin. "How're you going to head them off?"

"I'll figure that out once we get to No Name Harbor and pick up Ghost. We'll recon the area and make a plan. They aren't expecting this and I'm counting on them being a little sloppy with their mission prep. Don't worry, Matt. We'll still be alive come tomorrow morning, but I won't guarantee *they* will."

With that statement, Jake grabbed a cold beer out of the bridge fridge and climbed back up to the observation tower.

CHAPTER 80

No Name Harbor
Key Biscayne, Florida

MATT MANEUVERED THE *CATCH* into the mouth of the picturesque No Name Harbor located at the southern end of Key Biscayne. The harbor borders the western edge of Bill Baggs Cape Florida State Park which occupies the entire southern third of Key Biscayne. Only one bridge connects Key Biscayne to the mainland and the City of Miami, the Rickenbacker Causeway.

The harbor is well protected with only one passage in and out. Other than that, it is surrounded by land and mangroves which provide much needed shelter to the boaters and birds during storms.

Matt thought about the layout of the harbor. He was not sure there being one entrance and exit was a good thing or bad. He decided it was good. Only one way for boats to get in and only one entrance to have to keep an eye on. That is, if their enemies decided to use boats.

Everyone on the *Catch* was now topside, grabbing ropes to secure the boat to dock pilings. There was no way for Matt to determine at this point where to park the boat to gain a strategic advantage, so he chose the easiest spot to dock. He pulled alongside a long, unoccupied stretch of pilings with no other boat nearby and eased on in using his bow thrusters. Kelli and Lucien quickly tied off and secured the *Catch*. Jake was in the observation tower scanning the area with his high-powered binoculars.

As he was making a sweep, he suddenly stopped and let out a hoot. He scrambled down from his lofty perch and hopped off the boat and onto the dock. He hit the decking at a trot and made his way toward the restaurant area and parking lot.

The other three were surprised and amused at Jake's demeanor. It seemed a little out of character for him.

Jake continued jogging along the dock until he reached a spot where the sidewalk from the parking lot intersected with the dock walkway. There stood a smallish man dressed in green cargo pants and brown tee shirt. A military style camo cap was hanging off his belt and he was wearing a grin as big as the harbor. He had blue-black hair with a touch of gray scattered through it. The black hair, high cheekbones, and dark piercing eyes confirmed his Cherokee heritage.

The two men laughed heartily, embraced warmly, and started towards the *Catch*.

Upon reaching the boat and jumping over to the rear deck, Jake introduced the man known as Ghost.

"My friends, I would like you to meet the man I owe my life to several times over. The man you will know as Ghost."

"Glad to have you aboard, Ghost!" Matt said while offering a handshake and a smile.

"Thanks, Captain. Glad to be here. Glad to be anywhere, actually."

"Ghost, this is my girlfriend Kelli and our friend Lucien."

Ghost shook their hands and smiled warmly at each of them, holding his look at Lucien just a moment longer.

"Glad to meet both of you as well. Matt, this is quite a boat you have here."

Jake interrupted.

"Yeah, he uses it to fleece the snowbirds who have more money than sense. But as much as it pains me to say it, he runs the best charter boat on the other coast."

Matt ignored his remarks as usual.

"Ghost, where's your gear? Don't you have any bags to bring on board?"

Ghost looked at Jake, winked, and chuckled.

"Yeah, I have a few things back in my pickup. Jake, you want to give me a hand?"

The two of them headed toward the parking lot while everyone else went back to securing the boat for the night.

Before long, Jake and Ghost reappeared on the dock alongside the *Catch*. They were struggling with one large duffel and two slightly smaller ones that obviously held more than a couple changes of underwear and a toothbrush.

"Permission to come aboard, Captain." Ghost called out.

"Permission granted". Matt replied. "What the hell you guys got in those bags? On second thought, you can tell me later, maybe. I'm not sure I want to know".

That brought a large grin from both Jake and Ghost as they tossed their cargo over the side of the boat and climbed in after it.

CHAPTER 81

Executive Offices
Dominion Transglobal Headquarters
Dallas, Texas

"What do you have to report, Mr. Petrov?"

"Things are proceeding as planned, Mr. Dominion."

"What is the current situation?"

"We have tracked the targets from the air since they left the Coast Guard Station in Key West. They have now entered a small harbor in Key Biscayne near Miami."

"Have you kept assets staged and ready to go as I instructed?"

"Yes, sir. We have assets staged both on water and on land. We have kept all key assets on the move as we followed the targets."

"Do you think the targets are going to stay put for the night?"

"I am not sure, but they have secured their boat and do not seem to be preparing to leave the harbor anytime soon. Based on what we are seeing, I would guess they are going to spend the night there."

"Very good. Do you have a plan to secure the artifacts and dispose of the targets?"

"Yes, Mr. Dominion."

"Would you care to share that with me?"

"Of course, sir. The place where they docked is near a park and a restaurant, so there are quite a few people coming and going as well as some light boat traffic in and out of the harbor. It is our plan to wait until the restaurant closes and the public has vacated the area for the night, then launch our mission. We are trucking in a couple inflatables. We will hide them in some mangroves not far from the harbor. They will be launched sometime after midnight with a full complement of armed operators aboard and they will approach the target boat in total darkness. The moon will not be a major factor tonight and there should be intermittent cloud cover which we will use to our advantage. Even if they detect us as we approach, they will be no match for us numerically or in any other way. Once we have subdued the targets, we will extract from them the whereabouts of the relics, secure them, execute the targets, and set their boat on fire. There will be nothing left behind. It will appear to be a leaky fuel tank and accidental explosion."

"Very well, Mr. Petrov. You *do* understand that you must not destroy their boat or severely damage it before we can recover the artifacts? The last thing I want is for the relics we have worked so hard to obtain to end up at the bottom of the harbor. Or worse yet, destroyed in a fire or explosion."

"I understand, Mr. Dominion. I will make sure the recovery team is fully aware of your instructions."

"One more thing, Mr. Petrov. How confident are you that this latest plan will succeed?"

"I am completely confident. I would bet my life on it."

"Good. You might say…*you already have.*"

CHAPTER 82

No Name Harbor
Key Biscayne, Florida

IT WAS A PICTURE-PERFECT evening.

The surface of the water was black glass and the gentle breeze cool, but not cold. It was peaceful other than the sound of voices from the restaurant and parking area. The mangroves were still as were the resting birds who take shelter there.

An ideal evening to be alive and on a great ship with good friends. Matt and Kelli sat on the stern of the boat holding hands. He was nursing a cold beer and she a glass of chilled chardonnay.

Everyone had shared a sumptuous dinner. Lucien and Matt had caught snapper and grouper and grilled them for the main course.

Kelli had prepared the salad and a side dish of seasoned rice.

Right up until dinner was served, Jake and Ghost had cloistered themselves in their stateroom with the door closed. From the metallic noises that came through the door, it appeared they were rummaging through the goody bags they had brought on board. Once in a while, they could be heard giggling like a couple of schoolboys who had just discovered a secret stash of Playboy magazines.

Presently, Matt and Kelli were the only ones left on the *Catch*. Lucien had pleaded cabin fever and went off to the restaurant bar to get off the boat for a while. Jake and Ghost had taken a couple of small duffel bags and gone off into the night to do what they do.

Matt squeezed Kelli's hand.

"Please, don't get mad at me for saying this again, but it's not too late to get off this boat and go home where you're safe. I'll run you over to Miami where you can catch a direct flight to Sarasota or you can rent a car. Whichever you prefer."

Kelli thought about it for a moment.

"I know Matt, and I'm not upset that you worry about me, but there's one thing you're not thinking about. You know we're being watched and I believe the minute I am by myself on the mainland, they'll kidnap me and use me as leverage against you. How would that make me or you safer?"

Matt chewed on his lip and tried to think of a flaw in her logic. He hated to admit it, but she was right.

"You know, I hate it sometimes that you're so damn smart! You could stay with Ken and Cindy 'till this blows over?"

"And put them and the twins in danger? You know what kind of people we're dealing with. And if I were so damn smart, I would have married a billionaire and be living the big life somewhere."

"Oh hell, Kelli. You would hate that life and you know it. You'd be bored to death."

"So, I guess it's either be bored to death or shot to death."

Matt looked at her with sad, surprised eyes, looking guilty and hurt. Kelli burst out laughing and gave him a big kiss while grabbing both sides of his face in her hands.

"Don't worry Mr. Flannery, it'll be alright. I wouldn't have it any other way and I wouldn't be anywhere else right now. So, can I get you another beer?"

"Any other night, that would be a yes. But I better keep a clear head. I'm not sure what this night holds for us."

CHAPTER 83

No Name Harbor
Biscayne Bay, Florida

KELLI WENT INSIDE TO the galley to do some final clean up and Matt went to the restaurant to reclaim Lucien. When Matt slipped up behind Lucien at the bar, he was spinning quite the story to a lovely lady who was perched on an adjoining barstool, leaning forward, fascinated by Lucien's tale. It sounded as if Lucien was claiming the *Catch* was his boat in an attempt to impress his attentive conquest. He was also giving sketchy details of adventures that made him sound like a modern-day pirate. It appeared to be working from the way she was making goo-goo eyes at him and hanging on every word. Unfortunately, Matt had to burst both their bubbles and pull Lucien away, citing a pressing situation that needed Captain Lucien back on board without delay.

Once outside, Matt apologized for being a party pooper but reminded Lucien that it was not a good time to overdo the partying and everyone needed to remain vigilant.

He decided not to call him out for claiming to be the *Catch*'s captain.

Once back on board, Matt returned to the bridge to keep an eye out for any suspicious activity in the harbor. Jake and Ghost had been gone a couple of hours and Matt was starting to feel anxious.

Then, Jake suddenly appeared next to him.

"Damn it, Jake! You shouldn't sneak up on me like that, especially right now. You could give somebody a heart attack. I was starting to worry about you two. Everything alright?"

"Sorry, pardner. Just brushing up on my "sneaking up on people" skills. Yeah, everything's fine. It took a little while to find our friends' staging area, but we found it."

"Where's Ghost?"

"He stayed on point to keep an eye on them while I came back to let you know what's going on."

"So, what are our "friends" up to?"

"Pretty much what I expected. They brought in a couple of military-grade inflatables, night vision gear, wetsuits, and assault weapons. They are staging all of it on the other side of the harbor, back in a wooded area. They used an unmarked truck to bring in their equipment, carried their gear through the woods from a service road where nobody could see them, and then they sent the truck away."

"How many of them are there?"

"We counted twelve. Six-man assault teams for each boat."

"Twelve against our five…not the best odds."

"Yeah Matt, you're right. They're at a serious disadvantage." Jake retorted with a defiant snort.

"I like your style, Jake. Plus, we do have the element of surprise on our side."

"Offense is always more fun than defense, pardner."

"How're you going to take them down?"

"Me and Ghost have a plan but we're still working out the details. Don't worry, that bunch of operators won't be bothering anybody after tonight. They got sloppy like I predicted. They should never have set up their staging area in broad daylight without better perimeter lookouts or patrols, but they don't realize who they're messin' with. They assumed we'd be busy setting up a defense around our boat rather than looking for them."

"What can I do to help?"

"I need you to move the *Catch* out into the middle of the harbor and anchor there. That will cut off their ability to reach your boat from land. One less possibility to game plan for. Me and Ghost will take care of those inflatable crews. It'll be dark soon and I'll take the dinghy back to land. I'll use oars so they won't hear any motor noise. We'll use the dinghy later to return to the *Catch*. When we approach the boat, I'll signal three times with my flashlight to let you know it's us. Other than that, keep a low profile and leave the 2-way radio on in case I need to send you a message."

"Anything else?"

"Yeah, have a couple of cold beers ready when we get back."

CHAPTER 84

No Name Harbor
Key Biscayne, Florida

It was dark with little moonlight overhead. What natural light there was had been obscured by the puffy clouds floating around the sky. Jake silently paddled the dinghy over to the shore closest to the rendezvous site where he would reunite with Ghost.

Jake had applied night camo makeup to his face, was attired in black clothing from head to toe, and was carrying a black bag. He stealthily moved through a wooded area for about a half mile where he was to meet up with Ghost. When he arrived at the agreed upon spot, he did not see Ghost anywhere. He stood still for a moment to listen for any unusual sounds and to consider his next move. He felt something lightly land on his head and grabbed it off his stocking cap to see what it was. It was a twig and he looked up to see where it came from. There was Ghost sitting on a tree limb, smiling from ear to ear. The only thing Jake could see of him was white teeth.

Ghost shinnied down the tree trunk and joined Jake in the small clearing. He had already put on his dark clothing and face makeup.

"Good thing I'm a "friendly" Jake, or you'd be a goner."

"Yeah, I've always been glad you're a "friendly", Ghost. Maybe I'll start calling you Casper. You creep me out a little with the way you disappear any time you want. But I'm damn glad to have you along on this trip. Matt and Kelli are good people and I'm not sure I can protect them by myself."

"You said, Matt and Kelli. How about Lucien?"

"I don't know. Just a gut feeling, but I'm not sure about him yet. He's not done anything to make me suspicious but there's something about him that bugs me. I could be wrong, but I've learned not to ignore my gut when it's talkin' to me."

"Yeah, I'm with you on that, Jake. My gut has saved my ass more than a few times."

Jake and Ghost both had a quiet laugh at that one.

"Okay Ghost, time to show these amateurs how the pros do it. It's been dark for a while and we don't know when these operators are going to saddle up and launch. I brought the wetsuits and rebreathers. We need to finalize our plan and get into position near their staging area."

"Roger that. Let's move."

CHAPTER 85

The Brotherhood Staging Area
Key Biscayne, Florida

Jake and Ghost had finalized the details of their plan to neutralize the opposition and were now in position to put it into operation.

They watched the twelve members of the assault team casually prepare their equipment and inflate their small boats. They were dressed in blackout clothing and had applied night camo makeup to their faces. The operatives wore night vision goggles which they had pulled back on top of their heads. Their inflatables and weapons were also flat black. They were all armed with high-tech automatic assault weapons similar to the M4's the SEALs use but made by a different manufacturer. Potent and deadly, nevertheless.

It was now a little after midnight and the assault teams were stepping up the pace, preparing to launch their mission. Jake and Ghost shrugged into their wetsuits and rebreathers. The rebreathers allowed them to operate underwater without conventional oxygen tanks which emitted bubbles which could be seen on the surface. They checked and double-checked their equipment, including the weapons and night vision goggles. You could never have too many toys at a time like this. That was Jake's other motto.

The assault teams were lining up alongside their boats, three on each side of each boat, preparing to lift them above their heads and carry them the short distance from the woods to the water's edge. The inflatables did not have motors as the plan was to paddle quietly into the harbor and attempt to sneak up on the *Catch* and take it with overwhelming force and numbers, hoping to minimize the chance of a firefight.

It would have been a solid plan had the opposition been typical.

Jake and Ghost had chosen a little cove not far from the assault teams' staging area as the optimum spot to slip into the dark water. They made no sound as they glided under the surface to a position where the assault boats would soon be launched. Their night vision goggles were the only thing above the water line. They checked their rebreathers again and gave each other the thumbs up indicating everything was working. Their deadly M4's with silencers were slung across their backs, combat knives strapped to their legs. The two of them had practiced these maneuvers hundreds of times and executed them flawlessly in missions all over the planet under more demanding conditions than this. They were a seamless, lethal pair operating as one.

Twelve against these two was not fair...*for the twelve.*

CHAPTER 86

No Name Harbor
Biscayne Bay, Florida

JAKE AND GHOST WAITED silently just below the waterline, watching their prey leisurely walk their boats into the dark harbor waters, totally unaware of the danger lurking in the liquid blackness nearby.

The assault team waded out until they were about waist deep, lowered their inflatables into the water, then pulled themselves over and into their respective boats. Six in each boat, three on each side. The team members picked up short, black, folded paddles, unfolded them, and began rowing quietly toward the *Catch* as it lay anchored in the deserted harbor.

The assault team observed the target boat was blacked out and there was no discernable movement above decks. Perfect. The occupants had either gone to bed or were not expecting trouble. This was going to be quick and easy. Mr. Dominion would be pleased and The Brotherhood would fulfill its promise on this historic night. The assault boats were now moving along at a slow but steady pace. They barely disturbed the water and made almost no sound. Nothing looked or sounded out of place on this quiet night in paradise. The would-be assassins were relaxed and confident.

Jake and Ghost were completely submerged and by looking through their night vision goggles, they were able to track the inflatables and swim underneath them to escape detection. The assault boats were running side-by-side which made it easy for Jake and Ghost to coordinate their actions.

Jake waited until Ghost looked his way and emitted three quick signal bursts from a tiny black-out light attached to his dive suit. Ghost gave a single burst in acknowledgement and kept his eyes focused on Jake's signal light. Jake began a countdown. Now two bursts, now one.

It was go time…

CHAPTER 87

On Board the Catch
No Name Harbor

MATT WAS OUT OF sight behind the helm and console on the flying bridge. His sidearm was secured in a holster attached to his belt and thigh. He strained his eyes and ears for anything that would indicate what was going on out there in the darkness. The waiting was torture but he had confidence in Jake and Ghost and knew to stay out of the way and stick to the plan. All he could do for the moment was stay vigilant and chew on his lower left lip.

Kelli was staying low on the deck behind the stern bulwark and was outfitted in full scuba gear in the event she needed to go into the water. Kelli knew she was more valuable in the water than on land. Her pistol and spear gun lay beside her.

Lucien was pacing the floor of the main salon in total darkness per Matt's orders. He also had a weapon holstered to his side and was biting his fingernails and muttering to himself. He was scared to the point of wetting himself and his nerves were on edge.

It was now after midnight. Matt knew they were nearing the time when things would break loose. The breeze was slight. The harbor like black onyx. No sound other than water lightly lapping against the hull of the *Catch*. It was quiet alright…too quiet.

Then death emerged from the darkness.

CHAPTER 88

No Name Harbor
Key Biscayne, Florida

TWO BLINDING WHITE FLASHES accompanied by mind-numbing concussive booms exploded inside the assault boats simultaneously. The assault teams were sightless and stunned. The flash was made more vivid through the teams' night vision goggles which greatly intensified the light burning into their retinas. Jake and Ghost had thrown flash bang grenades into the inflatables at exactly the same moment while they shielded their own eyes and were kept safe from the concussion waves by protective ear plugs.

Jake and Ghost moved to address the threats before they had a chance to recover. The assault team members had thrown off their goggles and were rubbing their eyes in an attempt to regain their vision. It would take at least a minute for them to regain their eyesight in these lowlight conditions, probably longer. More than enough time for Jake and Ghost to finish their lethal mission.

Jake and Ghost quickly emerged between the two inflatables, back to back, so as to stay out of each other's line of fire. They pointed their silenced M4's away from each other and with practiced speed and efficiency, put a round to the head of each of their twelve adversaries. Six kills each. Took less than thirty seconds. The assault teams never knew what hit them.

Some of the dying bodies slid overboard into the water. Others slumped into the bottom of the boats. Jake and Ghost took hold of the ones still in the boats and pulled them into the water as well. They looked for cell phones and tracking devices on the bodies and found only one active cell phone. Ghost opened it, removed the battery, and smashed what was left with the shoulder stock of his weapon.

Jake and Ghost moved from body to body, checking for vital signs. They found none. The well-placed shots had done their deadly jobs. It would not be a good thing to have dead bodies floating around the harbor the next morning, so Jake and Ghost set about the grisly task of making sure the bodies would not be discovered.

They unsheathed their combat knives and inflicted strategic puncture wounds on each corpse. One in each lung to allow the oxygen to escape so it could be replaced with incoming sea water. Other deep cuts were made in places where gasses would eventually gather in body cavities such as the stomach and bowel areas. These openings would act as vents to allow the gasses to escape as they accumulated, preventing the gasses from creating buoyancy in the bodies through the days ahead. The corpses began to sink into the dark water as their lungs filled with water and their equipment pulled them downward into murky, watery graves.

Next, Jake and Ghost used their knives to gash the inflatables and send them to the bottom, joining their previous occupants.

The two looked around as they treaded water. It was as if nothing had ever happened. They gave each other a thumbs up and swam toward the staging area that the assault teams had used. They picked up the few items that had been left behind and put it all in an equipment bag they found. They weighted the bag down with rocks from the beach and made sure it went to the bottom as well.

Nothing they found contained any identifying logos or documents that might indicate who these guys were. This group never left trails. Jake did notice that a couple of them had the triangles tattooed on the back of their hands. He had not been able to look at their necks as they had been covered up to their chin in their black shirts and he did not want to take the time to strip them down. It was possible the local authorities might receive a report of an explosion in this area and come to check it out.

Jake looked at Ghost and they nodded at each other, agreeing they were done here.

"Ready for a cold beer, Ghost?"

"You bet your sweet ass I am!"

CHAPTER 89

On Board the Catch
No Name Harbor
Key Biscayne, Florida

AFTER SEEING THE BRIGHT flashes and hearing the loud booms, Matt had not seen or heard anything further. He had expected to hear gunfire but did not. He had no idea what the situation was and whether Jake had succeeded or if they would have to defend themselves here at the boat.

He scurried down from the bridge and called Lucien to come out of the salon and join him and Kelli on the aft deck.

"Kelli, I know you saw and heard the explosions. Did you Lucien?"

"Yeah, they sounded pretty intense."

"Listen, I don't know what the situation is at the moment so we have to be prepared for the worst and hope for the best. Have you got your weapons and plenty of ammo?"

Lucien and Kelli both nodded they did.

"Okay, good. I'm going below to get Jake's sniper rifle with the night scope. I noticed he didn't take it with him. I'll position myself in the observation tower. Lucien, I want you to grab all the flare guns out of the storage locker and be prepared to shoot them straight up in the air over the boat if I give you the signal. We'll need to see what we're shooting at if it comes to that. In the meantime, stay low to the deck and out of sight. Kelli, I want you to stay in your scuba gear and close to the dive platform. Be sure you keep your knife and spear gun ready. Jake said they would be using inflatables and if they get close to us, I want you to slip into the water and put a knife or spear into those boats. That would put the bad guys in the water and give us a fighting chance to pick them off as they try to board us. Any questions?"

"What if some of them do make it aboard?" Kelli asked.

"Then I want you to swim to shore as quickly as you can and break into that restaurant. Hopefully, they have a security system that will automatically call the police. In case they don't, use their phone to call 911. Hell, call 911 whether they have a security system or not. Me and Lucien will try to hold them off 'till help arrives."

Everyone took their positions and anxiously waited to learn the outcome of Jake's mission. There was nerve-wracking silence in the harbor once again.

Matt employed the night scope on the rifle to survey the area around the boat. A little moonlight would have come in handy about now, but there was none.

Thirty long minutes dragged by but it seemed like hours. Everyone was on edge, not knowing what to expect. Matt continued to sweep the area with the night scope. Was that movement in the water he was seeing? Friend or foe?

He focused on the area where he thought he saw movement and picked up three distinct flashes of light. Then three more.

It was Jake. Matt scrambled down from the observation tower and onto the bridge where he remotely engaged the powerful spotlight on the bow of the *Catch*. He pointed it toward the area where he saw the flashes of light and it lit up the dinghy like it was the middle of the day. Jake and Ghost were both aboard.

He turned off the spotlight and hustled down to the aft deck where he shared the good news with Kelli and Lucien. Both looked deeply relieved, as was Matt.

They turned on the aft deck and underwater lights, preparing to welcome the dinghy and its occupants aboard.

As the little boat came alongside the *Catch*, the first thing Matt heard was, "I hope you've got those cold beers handy, pardner?"

"Yeah, Jake, we got all the cold beers you can drink. I never thought I'd be this happy to see your ugly mug! You guys in one piece?"

"We are."

The two heroes climbed aboard the *Catch* and Jake noticed everyone looking at him with relieved but questioning faces.

"What?"

Kelli ran up and gave him a big hug, paused, and decided to give one to Ghost as well.

"It's just that you guys look like something out of a movie or something." Matt commented.

"Oh, these old things? Just some stuff we found at the Army Surplus Store."

Everyone shared a laugh that helped break the tension of the moment.

"I'm assuming you guys were successful and we're okay for now?"

"That would be the correct assumption, Captain Flannery," Jake replied with the grin still on his face.

"Then get out of those ninja suits and let's break out the cold beer. I want to know what the hell happened out there." Matt said.

"Aye aye, Captain." Jake replied.

CHAPTER 90

Executive Offices
Dominion Transglobal Headquarters
Dallas, Texas

"WHAT DO YOU MEAN they disappeared?"

"I know this does not seem possible Mr. Dominion, but they just vanished."

"You're telling me that twelve highly-trained, elite members of The Brotherhood just dissipated into thin air right after they launched their mission?"

"I don't know what happened to them."

"Have you sent someone in to look for them?"

"Yes, of course. My last contact with them was by phone and they were staged and ready. I spoke with their Team Leader just as they were getting ready to launch boats. Everything was a go and they had the target in sight. It was a sitting duck in the middle of the harbor with no obvious defenses. He was to check back with me every fifteen minutes for a status report. After he did not check in with me on schedule, I called him and his phone was dead. I tried to track his cell phone GPS signal, but it was no longer transmitting. None of the other operatives were carrying communication devices per your orders. I immediately ordered two standby operatives to recon the area. They searched the staging area but found no trace of the two teams whatsoever."

"Did you maintain surveillance on the target boat leading up to the time you were to initiate?"

"Yes, we did."

"Did you notice anything unusual?"

"No, sir. The targets docked their boat and did some fishing. Mr. Bart left the boat to have drinks at the restaurant bar but Mr. Flannery brought him back to the boat just before dark. The only other time someone left the boat was when Mr. Preston met someone at the parking lot and accompanied him to the target boat for a short visit. He then escorted him back to the parking lot where he disappeared from our view. It appeared he was just an acquaintance of Mr. Preston who visited and left. Mr. Preston returned to the boat and was still there until after dark. Mr. Flannery proceeded to move his boat into the middle of the harbor shortly after nightfall and dropped anchor. This would be an expected precaution as he was probably expecting we might approach from land at some point."

"Are you sure nobody saw you unloading the truck and setting up the staging area?"

"It does not seem likely, sir. We posted a guard throughout the lead up to the mission and detected no one in the area."

"Then how do you explain this, Mr. Petrov?"

"I cannot, Mr. Dominion. If our assault teams had reached the target boat, I would have been notified. If there had been a firefight, I would have been notified or there would be evidence of that event. Our two operatives currently on the ground in that area have found nothing unusual and reported that the target boat does not look as if it has been under attack. No debris has been found along the shoreline and no assault boats or wreckage on the surface. It is as if our operatives were intercepted and captured before they could report in."

"Let's hope for your sake, Mr. Petrov, that's not the case. I would rather they were killed than captured. Even your vaunted members of The Brotherhood could be made to talk with the right encouragement."

"They are sworn to secrecy, Mr. Dominion."

"I know that, Petrov! Who do you think dreamed up this whole Brotherhood of Atlantis thing to create a deeper commitment from our operatives?"

"You did, sir. I am sorry. I just believe they would die before they would betray us."

"They are still men, Petrov. Everyone has a price and a breaking point if discovered. I know. I built an empire utilizing that philosophy. However, I cannot accept this theory they were intercepted and captured by forces who did not exist in the area nor can I deny the fact of their disappearance. I promised to hold you personally responsible for the success or failure of this mission Mr. Petrov, but until I know what happened to our assault teams, I do not know where to place the blame for this fiasco. Therefore, you are off the hook for the moment, so to speak."

"Thank you, Mr. Dominion."

"How many men have we lost so far?"

"Nineteen, sir."

"Nineteen out of the original group of thirty special ops recruits?"

"That is correct, sir."

"Do we have enough manpower to continue Mr. Petrov, or do we need to recruit additional forces?"

"We have sufficient manpower to continue, sir. Some of our best operatives are among those remaining. If we had to recruit more men, it would require us to bring in less desirable mercenaries who have little loyalty and are harder to control."

"Very well. Make these eleven remaining men count, Mr. Petrov. What is your next move?"

"With your permission, I would like to attempt another assault from the water when they are out in the open. We will be better prepared this time and bring more sophisticated weaponry. It is much easier to carry out these attacks and dispose of the evidence when we are on open water and away from witnesses."

"I will agree to your plan as long as you do not blow up or sink their boat until we have the relics and maps in hand."

"Of course, Mr. Dominion. I am positive they will make for the Bahamas soon, probably tomorrow. That would be a good opportunity for us. We can stage our boats just off the coast of Miami by morning, put a surveillance plane overhead, and be ready to pursue them should they leave the harbor. It would be less risky than capturing them on land where there are more people."

"Make it happen, Petrov. And don't fail me this time. I want you personally up in that eye in the sky coordinating every move. Do you understand?"

"Yes, Mr. Dominion. You can count on me."

"I have been, Petrov. I have been. I am still waiting to be rewarded for my faith in you."

CHAPTER 91

On Board the Catch
Biscayne Bay, Florida

Matt was at the helm of the *Catch*, easing her out of the mouth of No Name Harbor just as the first rays of sunlight illuminated the eastern horizon. The weather reports were favorable and the day looked to be clear and mild with a moderate breeze and light seas. Ideal conditions for making the crossing to Bimini Island.

Kelli climbed up to the flying bridge and presented Matt with a fresh cup of coffee and a good morning smile. If they were not in constant danger, this would be a perfect morning to enjoy together. Sunrise on the Atlantic, awesome boat under his feet, fresh cup of coffee, and his lover at his side. He returned Kelli's smile and clicked coffee mugs with her to toast another day of life. Life that he no longer took for granted the way he once had.

"That was quite a story Jake and Ghost told last night." Kelli ventured.

"It was. Remind me not to piss those guys off anytime soon."

"But Matt, they talked about what they did like it was just another day at the office."

"With their backgrounds and training, I believe that is pretty much how it is."

"Don't get me wrong. I am grateful for all they're doing to keep us safe. But the Jake I know just doesn't seem capable of doing those things."

"Men like Jake are still good men, Kelli. I knew quite a few of them during my hitch in Naval Intelligence. We had to support them in the field from time to time and I started to understand what made them tick. They're able and willing to wall off a part of their minds so they can do the terrible things they have to do in order to protect the people and the country they love. Ironically, it's their deep level of caring and loyalty that allows them to walk on the dark side when necessary. I always sensed those traits in Jake and I guess that's why I was drawn to be friends with him. But I had no clue to his background. It wouldn't have made any difference had I known and it makes no difference now. If anything, I respect him even more because I know what he's had to do to preserve our freedom and security. And here he is doing it again out of friendship, expecting nothing in return but friendship. And how about Ghost? He doesn't know us at all. Yet, he's willing to put his life on the line for us out of friendship to Jake. You don't see that sort of loyalty and friendship every day."

Kelli nodded her head a little as she considered Matt's words.

"After all these dead guys, you think there's any more left to come after us?"

"I don't know, but we have to assume there are until we know different. We know this organization, whoever they are, has deep resources so we have to figure they'll stay on our trail until they get what they're after. I wish we knew what we're after and why it's so valuable. I guess we'll find out soon enough if we can keep these bastards off our backs."

Jake joined them on the bridge.

"Top of the mornin', ladies and gents! Damned if it doesn't look like the beauty and the beast up here. For the life of me I don't know what you see in him, Miss Kelli."

"Well Jake, the truth of the matter is, I knew he was friends with you and I got in tight with him so I could hang around with you."

"Ha! I knew it. Now it all makes sense to me and I won't have to go around scratching my head trying to figure it out."

Jake sipped his coffee with a twinkle in his eye and Matt just shook his head as always.

"Captain, how far to the Bahamas from here?"

"Well 007, we have to go north for a few miles to fuel up at a yacht club and then we head back down and around the southern tip of Key Biscayne to get out into the open water. The bridge to the north is too low for us to pass under. We should get out past Biscayne about eleven o'clock and then it's no more than two hours over to Bimini. Less than fifty nautical miles. Should be an easy run with good weather and calm seas."

"Hmmm." Jake mumbled.

"Hmmm what?" Matt queried.

"I don't expect them to be reset in time to make a run at us this early in the morning. They're still trying to figure out what happened to their boys last night. Of that, I'm sure. That should've kept them busy overnight but I bet they're already working on their next move. Our next window of vulnerability will come in the stretch of water between here and Bimini."

"You think they'll try another one of those open water attacks like the one back near Marco Island?" Kelli asked.

"Don't know for sure darlin', but they might. That was their Plan A after the guy failed to take out Matt back at his house. The only thing that was wrong with their plan was they weren't prepared for organized resistance. If they try it again, they'll come loaded for bear and take a few more risks in my opinion. If it were me, I would prefer to carry out a mission like that on open water, too. We can't hide out there, especially with their aerial surveillance, and there's less chance of witnesses. Easy to dispose of us and the boat too."

Matt and Kelli both spoke at the same time.

"What can we do?"

"I'm gonna have to give that some thought my friends before we get out in the open. I have a couple of hours yet to ponder on it. We'll figure something out."

Jake seemed a little less sure of himself than normal, even as he said it.

Kelli and Matt picked up on it and exchanged worried glances.

Matt knew that Jake did not like playing defense.

They all looked up at the sound of a small plane buzzing in a circle overhead.

The watchers had returned.

CHAPTER 92

The Brotherhood Assault Boats
Government Cut
Miami, Florida

"Yes, Mr. Petrov. The pursuit boats are ready and waiting at Government Cut near the Cruise Terminal in Miami. We can be on station on the other side of Key Biscayne in less than an hour."

"Make it so, Dmitri. We must be ready when the target boat gets outside U.S. territorial waters and away from the Coast Guard patrols. The target boat is refueling on the west side of Key Biscayne at present, but I expect them to move toward the Bahamas very soon."

"I will be ready to intercept on your command, sir."

"Make sure that you are. Do not underestimate the resourcefulness of our adversaries. We have already lost too many good men. I will continue to monitor their course from the air and keep you informed. Are your weapons checked and ready?"

"Yes, sir. We have everything on board as planned. We will not be outgunned this time."

"Excellent, Dmitri. Just be sure not to sink the target boat until after we recover the artifacts. Your brothers' blood will have been shed in vain should we lose the relics. Are your defensive shields in place as well?"

"Half-inch armor plate shields on the bow of both vessels."

"Excellent. Move your forces into position, Dmitri. Today we claim our heritage and honor our fallen comrades. The Brotherhood must be victorious on this day. We must not fail."

"Yes, Mr. Petrov. We will prevail."

CHAPTER 93

Coast Guard Station
Key West, Florida

"Joe Hillman in Operations, please."

"May I tell him who's calling?"

"Ken Spader. Coast Guard Station Key West."

"Yes, sir. Please hold."

After a short session of on-hold music, Joe Hillman came on the line.

"Ken, you old swabbie, is that you?"

"Been a long time, Joe. How are you?"

"Doing great, and you?"

"Couldn't be better."

"Outstanding! Now to what do I owe the pleasure of this call? Must be business or you would have called me at home or on my cell."

"You're right, Joe. I'll get right down to it. I need your help."

"Sure, Ken. What do you need?"

"I need surveillance on a boat heading from Key Biscayne to North Bimini Island. It's in serious danger and I can't track it from down here in Key West. I know you guys have satellites that can see that area."

"Why is that boat so important that you would try to hijack a satellite from me? Big drug deal?"

"No. The boat belongs to my brother-in-law, Matt Flannery, and there are some bad people after him."

"Why are they after him and who are these bad people?"

"We've been investigating but haven't turned up any information on them yet. I already have six of them in my freezer down here but we don't know where they came from or who's behind it. I think they're trying to steal something that Matt's grandfather left to him. Really weird situation."

"Six of them! He took 'em out by himself?"

"Not exactly. He has a buddy on board that's an ex-CIA operative and he did a number on them with a sniper rifle. Matt's girlfriend and another guy are on the boat with him as well."

"So, what exactly do you need me to do, Ken?"

"I need eyes on them while they make that run over to the Bahamas across open water and some way to intercede should things turn ugly. Do you still run the Predator drone program from up there?"

"Yes, I do. I'm head of Operations now, but there's a problem. All our satellite time is booked for today and I don't have the authority to pull them off the projects they are assigned to. They're designated as Level One priority missions from higher ups. I do have armed Predators at my command though and can authorize a training exercise to keep them airborne in that general area, but I will need to have a fix on your brother-in-law's position and an active satellite feed to pull it off."

"I understand. I appreciate your help with this. I can't move Coast Guard assets out into that area either without being able to substantiate a threat and I currently have no way to prove there will be another attack. But I really believe Matt could be in deep trouble today."

"I'm with you, Ken. I know you wouldn't ask if it wasn't critical. Is there any way you can get access to another space bird to allow me to monitor the area?"

"I'll call you right back."

CHAPTER 94

NASA Headquarters Building
Kennedy Space Center

"DEPUTY DIRECTOR FLANNERY'S OFFICE. How may I help you?"

"Ken Spader here. I need to speak with Director Flannery. It is urgent."

"Please hold and I will try to reach him for you."

"Mr. Flannery, you have a call from Ken Spader. Can you take it or should I tell him you will call him back?"

"Ask him if it's urgent or if it would be okay if I call him back this evening?"

"He said it's urgent."

"Very well, I'll pick up."

"Ken, are you and the family alright?"

"Yes Brad, we're all fine. It's not us that I'm calling about."

"What is it then? Official business or personal?"

"A little of both, I'm afraid. It's Matt. He's in imminent danger."

"What? What kind of danger?"

"Well, I suppose Cindy filled you in on what transpired at Matt's house a few days ago?

"Yes she did. Made no sense at all. I've been meaning to call him and talk about it. Has something else happened?"

"Yes. Evidently, your father left him some artifacts and a map and made Matt promise to follow up on what he had found over in Bimini. Whatever it is, it seems somebody else wants to get their hands on it real bad. After Matt headed out on his boat to try to get to the bottom of it, two boats carrying six more assailants tried to board him just south of Marco. Fortunately, he had his buddy Jake with him who we found out is ex-CIA black ops. As it turns out, Matt didn't know Jake's background either. Jake took them all out with a sniper rifle except one and he took a cyanide pill before they could capture him. I have the bodies here at my station but we have not been able to turn up any information on these bad guys yet. They carried no ID but we checked their fingerprints and were able to trace them back to the old USSR and Soviet Special Forces. But they have been off the grid for years before turning up here."

"Holy Christ! Why didn't Matt call me?"

"You know how he is, Brad. He's always had it in his head you are too busy and he doesn't want to bother you with his problems."

"Damn it. I should have called him a couple days ago like I was going to. You know I would drop whatever I'm doing and be there for him if he said he needed me?"

"Yeah, I know it but *he* doesn't seem to know it."

"I guess I'm going to have to talk this through with him before long. So, how can I help?"

"Matt is heading across open water today from Key Biscayne to North Bimini Island and I can't substantiate a threat large enough to allow me to divert Coast Guard assets to escort or monitor him. I need satellite surveillance on him while he makes the crossing so we can send help if he gets into trouble. I have an old friend who runs the Navy Predator program for that sector and he has agreed to help if I can get him a satellite link."

"How will I know what his exact location is so I can direct a satellite to his coordinates?"

"I put a GPS transponder on his boat while he was here without him knowing it. So, I have his exact coordinates at all times."

"So, you want me to get you some time on one of our birds?"

"I'm hoping."

"This will be tricky, Ken. But after what you just told me, I *will* find a way to get it done. Where do you want me to send the live feed when I have it available?"

"I want it sent to me and Joe Hillman at SOUTHCOM. He's going to stage a Predator or two in the area, just in case. But he couldn't get any satellite time today."

"Alright, consider it done. E-mail me the links to you and your contact at SOUTHCOM as well as the transponder number for Matt's boat then I will link the satellite to that transponder. One more question, who else is on that boat with Matt?"

"Kelli, Jake, Lucien Bart, who is the grandson of Professor Bart and who was also tasked with going on this mission by his grandfather, and a friend of Jake's who is also ex-CIA. They picked him up on Key Biscayne for extra support. Matt texted me an update yesterday afternoon."

"Damn. This is more serious than I thought. I'll get a satellite feed to you as soon as possible. Should be established within a half an hour. Keep me informed, please. I may not be able to monitor the feed as much as I would like but I will instruct my staff to interrupt me for your call no matter what I'm doing at the time."

"Yes, Brad. I sure will."

"And Ken, thanks for putting me in the loop and giving me a chance to help."

"I knew you'd want to be involved. Any father would. Talk to you later."

CHAPTER 95

On Board the Catch
Atlantic Ocean
West of Bimini Island

THE *NICE CATCH* HAD full fuel tanks and was rounding the southern tip of Key Biscayne, on a direct course to North Bimini Island. The water was morphing from aqua to indigo blue, indicating the deeper waters of the ocean. The Atlantic opens into a trench in this area that reaches depths exceeding six-thousand feet.

Matt called for a full crew meeting on the bridge. "I know you all realize the seriousness of our situation. But I'm going to spell it out to make sure we're all on the same page. We're going to make a run for North Bimini and hope for the best on the open water. I don't know for sure that anything will happen, but we have to assume it will and that trouble could start at any time. I have no doubt that if they hit us out there, it will be hard and fast because of what happened to them last time. They won't underestimate us again. I don't believe they want us to make it to Bimini because it will be harder to engage us on land with people around, and it's a lot more problematic to dispose of people, boats, and evidence on a populated island. As you can see, that plane is still circling over us which indicates to me that they are planning something. We just don't know what yet. I want to remind you that they could care less about us and if they're able to stop us and take the maps and artifacts, they will no doubt kill us and burn the boat. This group has no conscience. I don't expect them to try anything within the thirteen mile territorial limits off Key Biscayne, but we will be past that line very soon. It is less than two hours to Bimini and I will make the best time I can, but I believe they'll do everything in their power to prevent us from making it there. Jake has been working on our defensive plan and I'll let him explain it to you."

Jake stepped forward and looked each of them directly in the eyes. His eyes were intense, his jaw set.

"I agree with everything Matt told you. Unfortunately, we'll have a tough time playing offense this time. We don't know when or if they will come or what their game plan is. So, we are forced to play defense. We will prepare the best we can and respond to threats as they occur."

Jake paused for effect and continued.

"Matt will remain on the bridge and man the helm. But Matt, I want you off that bridge at the first sign of gunfire. You'll be a sitting duck up there and you almost took a bullet when we engaged these assholes over by Marco. They'll be looking to take out our driver first and slow us down. It would be best if you control the boat from the lower helm in the salon if shooting starts."

"Lucien, I need you to stay up front toward the bow for two reasons. You will be protected from gunfire if they approach from the rear, which they probably will, and you can be ready to lower the dinghy if it becomes necessary."

"Kelli, I want you to suit up in scuba gear like you did last time. We may need a diver in the water to counter something they're doing. You're as good as anyone in the water and I have complete faith in you."

"Ghost is going to take up a defensive fire position at the stern of the boat like I did at Marco. He will use his M4 assault weapon which also has a grenade launcher."

"I will man the observation tower with the sniper rifle and try to keep them at bay. The further we can keep them away, the better chance we have to make it to Bimini. However, if they get within weapons range, I will have to abandon that position because it will be too exposed, just like the bridge. In that scenario, I will join Ghost at the rear of the boat and reinforce his defensive fire position."

"Any questions?"

Nobody spoke.

"Very well. Check your weapons and ammo one more time and prepare for the worst and hope for the best. I won't blow smoke up your ass, this could be a tough fight. They have us at a disadvantage. We don't know anything about them and they pretty much know everything we're bringing to the party. So, we'll find out how much smarter they are this time. I promise you this, they will pay dearly for everything they get."

CHAPTER 96

EVERYONE MOVED INTO THEIR assigned defensive positions and re-checked their weapons and ammo. Kelli prepared her scuba gear and Lucien familiarized himself with the system that lowers the dinghy into the water off the side of the bow. Jake climbed the ladder to the observation tower and began sweeping the horizon for any signs of approaching vessels. Ghost settled into his defensive fire position on the stern of the boat and positioned ammo and grenades nearby for quick reloads.

Matt kicked up the engine throttles and soon the *Catch* was running fast and on plane. However, he had a full load of fuel and several people on board which slowed them down somewhat. He was actively scanning all instruments, monitoring the engines and checking the radar screens. He had just glanced at the radar displays when he noticed a couple of new things on different screens. The *Catch* had a "bird" radar which could scan the sky and a horizon radar that scanned all around the boat at water level. Both could "see" for miles in all directions.

The bird radar had consistently displayed a singular blip that represented the small plane circling them all morning. Now there was a similar size blip entering the radar field but at a higher altitude than the first plane.

The horizon radar was now revealing two blips moving quickly on an intercept course from the west and approaching the *Catch* from the rear.

Matt stepped out to the back of the bridge and yelled up at Jake.

"Jake, I think the fun is about to begin. We have an unidentified aircraft flying above the surveillance plane and we have two bogies closing fast from the west. They'll come up on our stern if they stay on their current heading."

Jake gazed up in the air but could not make out the second flying craft. But from his high position, he could now see the low outline of two boats appearing on the horizon to the rear of the *Catch*.

He looked down at Matt and shouted back.

"No real surprises other than that second aircraft. That's an outlier. Not sure what to make of it. Maybe they've brought in a second plane to relieve the first one and they're just going to trade places."

"That might explain it." Matt yelled back. "I know these bad guys have a lot of resources, but I don't think warplanes are one of them. It looks like they're doing exactly what we expected."

"Yeah." Jake growled. "But that doesn't make me feel any better. The big question now is what kind of firepower are they packing and how will they deploy and use it? Guess we'll know soon enough."

"Yeah, guess we will."

"How long do you think before they catch up to us?"

Matt looked back at his radar and replied.

"They're about five miles out and closing fast. Those boats must have big engines because I'm moving at just over thirty knots, so they have to be doing over forty knots. My guess is they will be within a mile of us in about fifteen minutes. I'll go to full throttle to squeeze out more speed, but I can't outrun them."

"Okay. Let me know when they're about a mile out. That's when I expect the games to begin."

Jake swiveled around in the small chair atop the observation tower and positioned his rifle to the rear where he could watch their pursuers through his high-powered scope. He would be within accurate firing range at roughly a mile out, but he had no way of knowing what their pursuers' capabilities would be.

Matt picked up the microphone for the ship's external PA system and keyed it on.

"Listen up. We have company coming up fast on our stern. Two craft about five miles out. I estimate they'll close to within a mile of us in approximately fifteen minutes. We also have a second small aircraft circling higher above us than the first one, but we don't know what kind of airplane it is or what it's doing. Stay alert and be ready for anything."

Matt counted off the distance as the pursuers closed on their position, keeping Jake informed.

He keyed the PA mic again.

"One mile out. We have them in visual range and they do not look friendly."

Jake was observing them and whistled out loud.

"Hey, Matt. Grab your binoculars and check out the front of those boats."

Matt quickly raised the binoculars to his eyes and dialed them in for a closer look.

"What the hell is that on the front decks of those boats?"

Jake studied them a few moments longer and cursed under his breath.

"Those are armored shields. They learned from our first dance together. The shields have gun ports cut out in them and our new friends can fire at us from behind those shields without exposing themselves to my sniper rifle again. That takes away our stand-off strategy."

"What about Ghost's grenade launcher?"

"Problem with grenade launchers is they don't have a long range and are not real accurate until you get a lot closer. I'm not sure we'll get close enough for it to be effective. I'm betting they have some long-distance firepower behind those shields."

"Holy shit, Jake. How're we going to get out of this one?"

"Not sure we will, old buddy."

CHAPTER 97

Operations Center
SOUTHCOM
Doral, Florida

"Joe, have you received the satellite feed from NASA and the GPS transponder link for the friendlies?"

"Yes Ken, I did. I have fed those links directly to the controller for the Predator. It is now on station with a back-up nearby if needed. But I have to ask you a question. How in the hell did you get access to a NASA bird?

"You know me, Joe, I've always had friends in low places."

"Seriously, Ken. That's almost impossible to do."

"Yeah, you're right. But my father-in-law is a Deputy Administrator at NASA. I implied we could use some help on this one. Matt's his son."

"Are you serious? What's going on here? I think there's more to this story than you're telling me."

"Yes and no. I've told you most of what I know. But this situation is definitely growing arms and legs and we still don't know who and what is behind this mess. All I know for sure is a good man and his friends are at risk and until we know the rest of the story, I'm going to do all I can to keep them alive. Matt's my wife's only sibling and she wouldn't and I couldn't ever forgive myself if I let something happen to him knowing I could have prevented it."

"Roger that, Ken. I get it. Rest assured, we will have your back on this one. I can tell you with certainty that the Predator we have on station is one of our newest versions and it is a nasty little weapons platform. The Predator has now established visual contact with our friendlies and I will be monitoring the situation live through both the satellite feed as well as the Predator's nose camera. We'll be ready to get involved if things get sticky. In fact, I'll share the Predator live feed with you so you can see what's going on in real time."

"That would be great, Joe. We go way back and have been through a lot of tough situations together. I appreciate this more than you know. If you authorize offensive action by the Predator, how will you spin it to your supervisors?"

"I've been thinking about that. Here's how I think we should play it. I'm going to write it up as a sea piracy incident. I will document the Coast Guard had alerted me to a possible piracy threat in the area and the suspects were armed and dangerous and currently under investigation for other similar crimes. All that is true and I will have you to corroborate my story. If I have to intervene with the Predator, I'll be able to show the video feed playback from its camera confirming that the friendly was being attacked by pirates whose intention was to commit piracy, robbery, and possibly murder. I think we can build our case well enough to make it fully justifiable."

"You're smarter than you look, Joe. The scary thing is…*that's exactly what's taking place out there.*"

CHAPTER 98

On Board the Catch
Atlantic Ocean
Thirty Miles West of Bimini Island

THE SECOND PURSUIT BOAT had ducked in behind the first one for additional cover and to present a smaller target profile to the defenders of the *Catch*.

A thunderous shot rang out from the lead boat, blew a hole through the lounge on the bridge, then lodged itself in the forward bulkhead.

"Sonofabitch!" Jake yelled. "Matt, get the hell off that bridge! I think that was a .50 caliber rifle round."

Jake quickly moved to abandon his exposed position as well. He half jumped and half climbed down from the observation tower to the deck below.

Matt took a quick look at the damage that single bullet had caused and scrambled down from the flying bridge, taking up a new position at the lower helm in the salon. He left the rear sliding door open so he could hear what was going on at the aft deck.

He ducked out and looked at Jake who was kneeling behind the stern bulwark.

"Did you say a .50 cal?"

"Looked and sounded like it. That damn thing can penetrate tank armor."

"I guess you were right. They came loaded for bear this time."

A second muzzle flash and a puff of smoke appeared through one of the armored shields on the lead pursuit boat. Another high-powered round smashed into the flying bridge helm console, rendering it useless. Radar screens and gauges shattered and sparks erupted. If Matt had still been there, he would likely be dead. It was obvious they were trying to take out the control systems of the boat so it would be forced to slow down or stop.

Jake fired off a couple of quick rounds from his sniper rifle, but as he feared, they glanced harmlessly off the pursuit boat's forward shielding. Jake's rifle was the most powerful weapon aboard the *Catch*, yet it had no effect.

The chase boats maintained a cautious distance behind the *Catch* while they probed its defenses. Now a loud bullhorn blasted from the lead pursuit boat.

"Prepare to be boarded. Surrender without resistance and you will not be harmed. Come to a full stop, throw your weapons overboard, and raise your hands where we can see them. You have one minute to comply."

Silence.

Ghost launched a rifle grenade towards them as an answer. It fell short of its target and disappeared into the sea.

The bullhorn blared again.

"This is your final warning. Stop, disarm, and show your hands. We will release you unharmed if you comply. If you do not surrender, we will be forced to take more aggressive action."

Silence.

The crew of the *Catch* already knew they were dead if they surrendered. They had no choice but to fight it out.

Jake, Ghost, and Kelli opened up with their weapons delivering a fearsome volley of bullets aimed toward their attackers. Ghost's M4 rattled off hundreds of rounds in short order while Jake pumped numerous high impact bullets into the pursuing boat's forward armor. A few of their bullets hit the pursuing boat nearer the waterline, but the bilge pumps would be able to handle the inflow of water long enough for the battle to be decided.

The response from the assailants was swift and deadly.

A man's head popped up over the armor of the lead pursuit boat and he quickly hoisted something up on his shoulder.

Jake was observing through his scope and suddenly screamed at his friends.

"Hit the deck…NOW! Incoming!"

There was a loud whistle and whoosh as a projectile passed over their heads and slammed with tremendous force into the observation tower. The shell exploded on contact taking the radar and communications array with it.

Matt ran out onto the rear deck and looked at where his observation tower used to be. He was stunned. It was reduced to mangled wreckage hanging over the side of the boat. Debris was raining down on their heads and floating on the water all around the *Catch*.

Jake jumped up and grabbed Matt by the shoulders, snapping him back to the situation at hand.

"Matt, listen to me. Do we still have the ability to navigate?"

Matt looked back at him and blinked back to reality.

"Yeah, I think so. I have the handheld GPS unit inside and it still works. I also have the sat phone and it should still work. It has its own power supply and satellite connection. But we're blind on radar and the rest of our comm units are dead."

"Okay. Good."

"What do you mean "good"? Jake, we're about to get blown out of the water?"

"Things aren't looking so hot right now Matt, but I don't think they'll sink us until they have what they came for. That's the only reason we're still afloat."

"Great. They won't sink us until *after* we're dead. What do we do next? They will board us shortly if we don't do something. They'll start picking us off one by one."

"I know."

Ghost cried out from the rear of the boat.

"Incoming!"

Another screaming whoosh as they all hit the aft deck again. The flying bridge took a direct hit and the explosion penetrated all the way through the roof of the salon and lower helm. Fiberglass, wood, and glass shards flew everywhere. The main drive controls were damaged and the *Catch* began to slow as the engines came down to idle.

Matt ran inside, dodging the debris and trying to wave away the smoke. He frantically opened his locked safe and grabbed the relics and maps. He stuffed them into a waterproof bag along with some heavy cans of vegetables from the galley.

By God, if he did not survive this, those bastards would not get their hands on the artifacts either.

He ran out on the stern deck and stood along the side railing with the bag in his hands, waiting to see what the attackers would do next. Everyone was staring at him, wondering what he was doing.

"If we go down, the relics go with us."

He knew the end was coming and he held the bag out over the water, daring the low-life scum to come after them.

CHAPTER 99

Operations Center
SOUTHCOM
Doral, Florida

Joe Hillman intently watched the live feed from the Predator circling above the *Catch*. He instructed the drone operator to zoom in for a closer view.

Clearly, things were heating up. He could see weapons fire being exchanged between the friendlies and the bogies and he could tell the friendly fire was having no effect on the pursuit boat. It was then that he saw a shoulder-fired missile launcher appear on the lead pursuit boat and a projectile was launched towards the friendly. It took out the upper superstructure of the entire bridge area. The friendlies were laying down more fire, but with no effect. Then another projectile was launched from the pursuit boat and it took out the rest of the upper bridge and part of the main cabin.

Joe Hillman had seen enough.

"Control One?"

"Yes, sir?

"Prepare for weapons launch."

"Weapons armed and ready, sir."

"Lock Hellfire One onto Bogey One and lock Hellfire Two onto Bogey Two."

"Hellfire One and Two locked on targets, sir."

"On my command."

Joe looked at the live feed again and could see the crew of the friendly standing around on the stern of the boat. They were out of options and were preparing to go down with the ship. Sitting ducks at this point.

Not on my watch, Joe Hillman thought to himself.

"Control One." Hillman said with authority.

"Yes, sir."

"Release Hellfire One and Two…NOW!"

"Missiles away, sir."

CHAPTER 100

Coast Guard Station Key West
Key West, Florida

COMMANDER SPADER WAS HUNCHED over the screen watching the Predator live feed and holding his breath.

"Why aren't you intervening, Joe?" he said through clenched teeth. "For God's sake, do something!"

He watched in growing horror as the pursuit boat took out the tower and the bridge. He was reaching for the phone to call Hillman when he saw two white streaks pass in front of the Predator's camera. He pumped his fist and waited…

CHAPTER 101

On Board the Catch
Atlantic Ocean
West of Bimini Island

THE TRAILING PURSUIT BOAT had now moved up beside the lead boat and they were starting to separate in order to position themselves on either side of the *Catch*.

They were moving in for the kill and there was little the five people aboard The *Catch* could do about it. If Jake raised his rifle or Ghost his grenade launcher or assault weapon, the shooters on the pursuit boats would kill them instantly. They were facing certain death either way they played it.

Jake, Ghost, Kelli, and Lucien were now standing, their body language and faces reflecting their growing apprehension and sense of hopelessness. They were fixated on Matt, who was dangling the bag of relics over the side of the boat. It was one hell of a predicament.

Matt looked at all of them with sorrow and regret in his eyes. Deeply saddened that he had involved them in this ill-fated venture. He locked eyes with Kelli and he felt his heart breaking in half and melting down into his shoes at the thought of harm coming to her, all because of his own selfishness and foolishness. But Kelli being Kelli, looked back at him with a nervous smile and mouthed the words, "*It's okay…I love you.*"

Matt noticed the others were now turning their attention to the sky. He could hear a faint whistle like that of a distant jet engine. It seemed to be growing louder and closer.

The activity on the pursuing boats had paused as well while they searched for the source of the new sound in the air over their heads.

Jake and Ghost raised their binoculars to try to see what they were hearing.

Jake screamed, "Incoming!", and they all flattened themselves on the deck again except Matt who remained at the rail, poised to take the relics with him as his last act of defiance.

As everyone onboard the *Catch* waited for the end to come, knowing another missile would probably do them in, two ear-splitting explosions and billowing fireballs erupted into the air around them. They were all curled up in defensive positions on the aft deck, waiting to be blown into oblivion. But a couple of seconds after the massive explosions, they opened their eyes and realized they were not only still alive, but everything around them was still intact. That is when they noticed that Matt was no longer there.

As they looked around to see what happened to Matt, they surveyed the scene around them. The two pursuit boats had been annihilated. Only burning wreckage and debris floated where the attackers had been a few seconds ago.

Jake and Ghost were shaking their heads and trying to make sense of what had just happened while Kelli ran to the rail where Matt had been standing. Lucien was a statue with his mouth open; motionless, in an obvious state of shock.

Kelli leaned out and looked over the side of the boat, then cried out with relief and joy. Matt was floating not far from the boat and was conscious. But she could tell he was in distress over something.

"I'll throw you a life ring, Matt. Hang on!"

Matt screamed at the top of his lungs.

"No, Kelli. I'll be fine. The blast knocked me overboard and I lost the bag. We need to find it before it sinks to the bottom!"

Kelli nodded and sprang into action.

"One of you guys throw Matt a life ring. I'm going after the bag."

Kelli was still outfitted in scuba gear since that had been her defensive assignment prior to the attack. She quickly grabbed her facemask and mouthpiece and turned on her oxygen supply. She moved to the spot Matt had gone overboard and jumped feet first into the water. With a quick wave toward Matt, she submerged.

Kelli turned on the powerful headlight built into her scuba mask, flipped over, and went straight down. She swam as fast as she could, hoping the bag would sink slower than she could swim. The water was too deep here for her to safely dive to the bottom without getting the bends or lose consciousness, so she had to retrieve it before it fell beyond her safe range. Hopefully, the waterproof bag had air trapped in it which would provide a small amount of buoyancy and slow it's descent.

The water became darker and murkier as she moved further away from the surface. Down and down she went, depending on her solitary light to show the way.

I have to find that bag or all of this will have been in vain. I can't let Matt down. She redoubled her efforts and swam even harder, deeper into the darkness, hoping for a miracle. It would truly be a miracle if she were able to locate the bag in this growing gloominess.

She was becoming winded and muscle cramps were threatening to stop her advance. But perhaps this was a day for miracles.

Her light momentarily hit something that glimmered enough to catch her eye.

Was that just a shiny fish?

She moved her head around to cast the light back in the direction of the reflection.

Could that be it?

She kept her head and light pointed toward the shadowy object and swam desperately to catch up to it while it descended deeper and deeper into the inky depths.

Kelli knew she was gaining on it but after glancing at her depth gauge, she was not sure if she could get to it before losing consciousness. The depth and exertion were taking a serious toll on her.

She could now make out the object's shape and it was definitely the bag.

She kicked her fins desperately and fought off exhaustion and lightheadedness as she moved toward the bag. She was seeing spots in front of her eyes and blackness was threatening to move in from the corners of her vision, but she would not be denied.

"Got it!" she exclaimed to herself and quickly attached it to a clip on her utility belt. She was fading closer and closer to unconsciousness and knew she had to get to a lower depth or else. She unfastened the weight belt that was around her waist and let it fall to facilitate her ascent. Even if she blacked out, she might still rise to the surface and be recovered.

Kelli felt her limbs growing numb and cold as her body began to direct blood to her core to maintain the primary functions needed to stay alive. Exhaustion had taken over, but she was moving upward and had enough mental clarity left to control her ascent speed to prevent the bends from disabling and possibly killing her.

After what seemed like an eternity, Matt spotted Kelli's head popping through the surface. She was about twenty-five yards away from the boat and not showing any signs of consciousness.

Matt grabbed a life ring and he and Jake immediately dove into the water. They swam like madmen and soon reached her unmoving body, now floating horizontally on the surface. Jake checked her pulse and indicated that she had one. Matt removed her mask and mouthpiece, then slipped the life ring over her head and shoulders. They towed her back to the *Catch* where Lucien and Ghost swiftly pulled her aboard. Matt pulled himself over the side after her and sat her in an upright position to help her breath more efficiently.

"Kelli, wake up! This is Matt. You're safe now and back on the boat. Please wake up! You have to wake up! Kelli, you saved the relics! You're my hero. Please, come back!"

Matt did not care who was listening or how mushy he sounded. Kelli was all that mattered to him in that moment.

Matt pinched her nose so she would be forced to take in deep breaths through her mouth. After several swallows of fresh sea air, her eyelids began to flutter and blinked open.

She looked up at Matt and gave him a weak smile. She widened her view to see the other three beaming down at her, relieved expressions on their faces.

"Did the bag make it to the surface with me?" Kelli asked in a raspy, whispering voice.

"Damn right it did! You are absolutely incredible. I don't know how you did it, Kelli." Matt replied.

Kelli attempted a weak laugh and reply.

"Just tryin' to earn my keep, Captain."

Matt wrapped her into a long hug. Jake retrieved a blanket from the wreckage of the rear salon and draped it around her shoulders.

"Welcome back to the world, darlin'." Jake said. "How're you feeling?"

"I have a headache and I'm exhausted, but other than that, I think I'm good to go."

"You just rest for now. Matt, we need to see if we have any helm control left and try to get this old girl underway again. Any idea where those missiles came from that saved our asses?"

"Not a clue."

CHAPTER 102

Operations Center
SOUTHCOM
Doral, Florida

"Bogies One and Two destroyed, sir. Direct hits."

"I see that. Fine work young man!"

"Thank you, sir."

Joe Hillman let out a sigh of **relief** and took the call that came in from Ken Spader.

"You had me scared there for a minute, Joe."

"Yeah, I figured as much. Hell, I scared myself. But I had to let the situation play out until it would confirm on video that I had no choice but to intercede."

"I understand. Bottom line is you saved their bacon out there today and I will always be in your debt."

"Glad to help. Reducing the world's population of bad guys is my job, old friend. I'll let you repay that debt with some top shelf whiskey next time I see you."

"You got it, Joe. Let me know what you need from me to corroborate your incident report and I will shoot it to you right away. I better go. I have an anxious father-in-law at NASA waiting for an update."

CHAPTER 103

Dominion Transglobal Corporate Jet
Destination: Miami, Florida

"I TRUST YOU HAVE positive news to report, Mr. Petrov?"

"Unfortunately, I do not, Mr. Dominion."

"Are you saying that you do not have possession of my artifacts? That you have failed again?"

"That is correct, sir."

"And exactly why is that? Did I not give you all the resources you requested?"

"Yes sir, you did. That was not the problem."

"What exactly *is* the problem, Mr. Petrov? I am starting to believe that *you* are the problem."

"It seems the U.S. Navy has become our problem."

"What do you mean?"

"A Navy drone blew our two boats out of the water just as they were ready to board the target boat."

"What? How can that be?"

"I am just guessing sir, but we have determined that Matt Flannery does have connections in strategic places. His brother-in-law commands the Coast Guard Station at Key West and his father is a top manager at NASA. It is my belief that our boats were being monitored and when they moved in for the attack, the drone strike was called in by someone."

"Were you not on station in an airplane yourself, Petrov?"

"Yes, sir. Just as you had instructed. But the drone was flying at a much higher altitude and we never saw it. Our plan had worked to perfection until the drone interfered."

"I see. How many members of The Brotherhood did we lose this time?"

"Six, sir."

"By my calculations, that leaves five remaining, not counting yourself?"

"That is correct, Mr. Dominion."

"What is your next step, Petrov?"

"We do not have water-based assets available at this time and it is obvious we are being monitored over the Atlantic. Therefore, we will have to make another interception attempt after they make landfall."

"Make it happen, Petrov. Move the remaining members of The Brotherhood into position when the targets arrive in the Bahamas. Is their boat disabled?"

"I am not sure, sir. We hit it hard, but it is a sturdy boat and it is possible the drive systems survived. As you ordered, we were careful not to damage it enough to sink it."

"Very well. Give me an update once they reach land and I will want to know your plan to intercept them at that time. I am on my way to Miami so I can personally receive the relics once you have secured them."

"I understand, Mr. Dominion."

"And Mr. Petrov, try not to involve the U.S. Government any further."

"Yes, Mr. Dominion. I will be cautious."

CHAPTER 104

On Board the Catch
Atlantic Ocean
West of Bimini Island

THE SAT PHONE RANG.

"Hello?" Matt answered.

"Matt, it's Ken. Everyone alright?"

"For the moment. But things were pretty hairy out here a few minutes ago."

"Yeah, I know. I watched it all go down, live and in color."

"What do you mean you watched it?"

"Your little helper in the air had a live camera feed coming back."

"What and who was that?"

"It was a Navy Predator drone. It had new Hellfire missiles onboard that Uncle Sam needed to test on somebody and we graciously volunteered your friends."

"A Predator? How did you know we were in trouble and who was running that drone?"

"Believe it or not, I told your old man that you might be in some deep shit and he pulled some satellite time off a NASA bird. Then, my old buddy Joe Hillman, who runs drone operations at SOUTHCOM, linked to the satellite feed and we tracked you. That, and I stuck a GPS locator on your boat while you were here.

By the strangest coincidence, Joe just happened to have a Predator in your general vicinity and neither of us care much for pirates."

"Dad pulled a satellite for me?"

"Didn't hesitate. Put his reputation on the line with NASA. The way I see it, the average citizen ought to get something in return for all those taxes they pay."

"I thought we were goners, Ken."

"You would've been without a little help from your friends. Don't try to be such a lone ranger. You've got some good people around you and they want to help. So, let 'em."

"I hear you."

"Is your boat seaworthy?"

"Jake's working on it. I have my handheld GPS unit to navigate by. The engines don't appear damaged but the control systems were nicked up. With any luck, we can patch them together well enough to get over to the Bahamas."

"I hope your boat insurance is paid up."

Matt laughed, "That's affirmative. First bill I pay every month."

"Alright then, let me know if you need anything and stay in touch from now on."

"Will do, and from all of us, thanks Ken. We owe you and Joe big time."

"You're quite welcome. And you owe your old man, too. Talk to you soon."

Jake had raised up from his work on the controls and was listening to Matt's phone conversation.

"Did you say that a NASA satellite has been tracking us?

"Yes, and that's not all. That was a Navy Predator drone that saved our ass with a couple Hellfire missiles. Ken's friend at SOUTHCOM was monitoring the satellite feed and had the drone on standby."

"So, Ken set all that up?"

"Yep. Seems he went to my old man for the satellite. Unbelievable. Guess he didn't want to explain to my sister why he let something happen to her brother. She can be a tough one to deal with when the situation calls for it."

"Well, I owe Ken a night out when I see him again. Hell, I owe him my life."

"We all do, Jake. We all do."

"I found a throttle control cable that snapped. That's why the engines idled back down to neutral when we were attacked. I've about got it patched back together so we can get off this open water."

"That would be outstanding. I'll help you finish up and we'll get underway. We can still make port before dark."

CHAPTER 105

THE CROSSING TO THE Bahamas was without further incident or surprises. Kelli had agreed to retire to her cabin, grabbing some much-needed rest after her exhausting dive.

Matt approached the docks at Brown's Marina at a snail's pace. The *Catch*'s helm was sluggish and the rigged throttle controls were slow to respond. Jake suspected some hydraulic damage had occurred in the steering system and it was likely other systems had been affected as well. The good news was the *Catch* had not been compromised below the water line and was not taking on water. The engines appeared to be operating normally though the dashboard gauges were offline and it was only an educated guess.

All radar and communications systems on the boat were destroyed when the observation tower and flying bridge were blown up. The wreckage of the observation tower was still draped over the port side of the ship and the flying bridge was reduced to fragments and debris. A haunting reminder of the fate they all barely escaped.

There was a jagged, gaping hole in the back end of the main cabin and many of the salon furnishings had been damaged. Lucien and Ghost were busy spreading a tarpaulin over the area exposed to the outside elements. The galley was located forward of the salon and remained intact and usable. The sleeping cabins were unaffected since they were below decks.

Matt could not dwell on the destruction that had been inflicted on his beloved boat. At least everyone had survived and now he had to focus on the final leg of their journey. He had come this far and would not turn back now. Too many had risked too much not to see it through.

With great difficulty, he turned the *Catch* until it aligned with the dock, then let it inch closer until they could throw ropes out to the man who was working the marina. They secured the boat from the front and the rear. The *Catch* was safe, at least for the moment. The marina hand was staring at the damaged boat in front of him with a look of bewilderment all over his perspiring face.

Normally, Matt would have called the harbormaster prior to arrival to check in and secure a berth, but since his ship to shore radio no longer existed, he had not been able to do so. He explained to the dock worker how they had suffered a terrible accident at sea and he would see the harbormaster as soon as he registered with customs. The man looked at the condition of the *Catch* and was visibly sympathetic. He offered to let the harbormaster know the situation.

Matt gathered his passport and ship's registration and left the boat to register with customs. Only the Captain of a boat is allowed to come ashore until he has cleared customs.

In Alice Town, customs is located in a small pink building near the Government Center. It was close by and Matt walked there in less than five minutes. The whole town could be navigated entirely on foot. The island of North Bimini only had a couple thousand permanent residents. Matt filled out the required paperwork, paid the entry fee, and moved on to the harbormaster's office at Brown's Marina.

He had chosen this marina because it not only had a good reputation but was right inside the harbor entrance. Easy entrance and easy exit—that is if the *Catch* would ever be able to exit.

An uneasy thought had been festering in the back of Matt's brain. The insurance company could declare the *Catch* a total loss, and if they did, he would have to leave it here and sign it over to a salvage company. He shook his head and refocused away from the unhappy thought.

He gave the harbormaster, Johnny, his credit card information and explained that due to the accident, he was not sure how long they would be there or what would happen with the boat. Johnny listened and nodded and assured Matt of his help and cooperation. Johnny informed Matt he could leave the *Catch* right where it was for the time being as it was out of the way of the other boats coming and going. It was winter which is the slower season on Bimini, so there were plenty of slips available. He also showed Matt the elaborate system of security cameras and gate codes employed by the marina.

Matt thought about the security systems for a moment but decided it might be of little help against these guys. Best to get off the boat as soon as possible and move on to the map coordinates. Time to find out what was so damned important to Grandpa Flannery and Mr. Bart, and the growing number of dead assailants.

CHAPTER 106

On Board the Catch
North Bimini Island, Bahamas

THE FIVE SURVIVORS ONBOARD the *Catch* were gathered on the aft deck. It was late afternoon on the day of their arrival at North Bimini but not yet dark. It was time to work up a plan for the rest of the day and tomorrow.

Matt began the conversation. "First, it's impossible for me to express how much respect I have for each of you. We've been to hell and back the last few days and somehow, we're still standing. I appreciate your friendship more than I can tell you. We owe a debt of gratitude to some of our other friends who provided some unexpected help when we needed it most."

"Next, after looking at the coordinates on the map, the location of the rest of these artifacts should be near the northern tip of this island. I talked to the harbormaster about that particular area and he described it as isolated and mostly wooded with thick undergrowth. The good news is that it's not far inland from the water, so we can get there by boat and only have a short hike to the site."

"What are we going to use for a boat?" Lucien asked. "The *Catch* is pretty beat up and the dinghy is kind of small for all of us."

"You're right on both counts, Lucien." Matt replied. "There are several boat rental businesses nearby so I'll check them out and find a boat that's right for the job. Jake, what's your gut telling you about future threats?"

"Well, other than picking up a stomach virus from local food, my gut is finding it hard to assess the threat at this point. They could hit us here, but there are security cameras and people all around us. They could follow us on the rental boat and attack, but it will be a short ride to the north end of the island and their opportunities will be limited. Or they might wait until we get back here with the relics and try to take them after we've done all the heavy lifting. Bottom line is we have to be prepared at all times and assume we're being watched twenty-four seven. I do like our chances better here than I did on the open water. It will be hard for them to mount a large-scale offensive against us here without a lot of witnesses, and there is an active harbor patrol as well. So, I expect them to try something quiet and fast somewhere along the way. I need all of you to check your weapons. Let's clean 'em up and let me know if you need more ammo. There's probably a gun store in town, but if not, we'll have to share and conserve what we have."

"Anybody else have something to add?" Matt asked.

"Yeah." Lucien replied. "How 'bout we get off the boat and take a break? Lots of places to eat and drink nearby."

"Lucien." Matt replied. "One thing I can say about you is you're consistent. Always lookin' for your next meal and a party. But I'm inclined to agree with you this time. I think we can all use a little R&R after what we went through today. So, let's pick a spot to hang out, stay together, and try not to get too wasted. We still have to be careful, even in town. We will leave the boat together, have fun together, and return to the boat together. We can set up a night watch rotation and we should all try to get some shuteye. I'll find us a rental boat in the morning and we'll head to the north end of the island. Sound good?"

Everyone smiled and said as one, "Sounds good!"

CHAPTER 107

Big John's Restaurant and Bar
Alice Town
North Bimini Island, Bahamas

BIMINI BIG JOHN'S BAR and Grill is a two-story, bright-blue building located waterside overlooking the clear, aqua waters of the Lower Lagoon. The open dining and drinking area occupies the lower level and spills out onto a wooden deck offering additional seating. The upper level houses a few nondescript hotel rooms.

The island is rich in history and the locals are more than happy to tell you about it.

Ernest Hemingway came here often and during his visits to North Bimini, was inspired to write "The Old Man and The Sea" as well as "Islands in the Stream". During the Prohibition Era in the United States, Bimini served as a warehouse for staging and shipping illegal liquor into Florida. There is a natural spring called the Healing Hole on the east side of the island which is reputed to have healing powers to those who soak in it. There is also the Bimini Road which is a mysterious stone formation located on the ocean bottom just off the northwest side of the island. It is also called the Atlantis Road by some who believe it to be an ancient roadway that led to the lost continent of Atlantis. Bimini is a fishing and boating paradise drawing a steady stream of visitors from the east coast of the States as well as from all over the world. The summer months are the busiest.

The crew of the *Catch* had chosen seats at a large table waterside and decided to order Big John's specialty drink, the Big John's Swingers. Nobody was sure what it had in it, but "when in Rome…"

Whatever the ingredients, they all agreed it was potent. There was lots of laughter and retelling of the day's events from each person's viewpoint as the alcohol took effect and they let their shoulders down. They felt more secure in this busy public place and the tired crew took full advantage of this opportunity to relax.

Jake and Ghost would occasionally point out people who looked a little out of place at the bar but saw nothing indicating they were spies. Kelli had fully recovered from her dangerous dive earlier in the day and had slipped on a low-cut sundress and placed a matching flower in her sun lightened hair, so it was not surprising to see men stealing glances at her from time to time.

Everyone had a good buzz going after the Big John's Swingers took effect and they agreed it was time to order food.

The waiter was an affable local fellow named Pender who looked to be in his late twenties, thin as a rail, and quick to point out the freshest seafood on the menu. In the end, they could not decide what they wanted most, so they had the waiter bring orders of all their favorites and they shared the meal family style.

After they had stuffed themselves on the freshest seafood imaginable, after dinner drinks were ordered to complete the banquet.

The conversation continued to be lively but had settled into a lower key and transitioned into side conversations.

As everyone was nursing their drinks and talking, Lucien excused himself to visit the restroom. They all nodded and went back to their conversations. After about five minutes, the ever-vigilant Jake noticed Lucien had not returned. He leaned back in his chair to get a better look at the hallway that led around to the men's room but saw no lines of people or anything that would explain Lucien's prolonged absence. Jake stood up with a worried look clouding his face.

"I'm going to check on Lucien. He should've been back by now." Jake stated.

Everyone else at the table looked up and realized that it had been awhile since Lucien had left. Jake headed to the restroom with Ghost right behind him. A couple more minutes passed and Matt was glancing anxiously toward the back hallway to the men's room while he chewed on his lip. Jake and Ghost were now headed back to the table with a grim look on their faces.

"He's not there. If he's run off somewhere to party without telling us, I'm goin' to kick his ass into the middle of next week." Jake growled.

Matt and Kelli stood up and Matt signaled the waiter to bring the check.

"I was going to stick Lucien with the check but it appears he figured as much and ducked out on me," Matt offered as a weak attempt at humor. "Okay, guys. Let's look around the area nearby first and not assume anything bad has happened, other than his poor judgment, until we know different."

They fanned out in pairs and checked all the restaurants and bars in the vicinity. Nothing. They widened their search area to all the drinking establishments in Alice Town. No sign of Lucien anywhere and nobody remembered seeing him.

They returned to Big John's and questioned everyone there, including guests, to see if they could offer any clues to Lucien's whereabouts. Nobody had seen him leave the premises or noticed anything out of the ordinary. This was not a surprise because the staff was far too busy to be paying attention to patrons' restroom visits. The patrons themselves were mostly drunk and not watching anything other than the amount of alcohol left in their glasses and the sun sinking into the water.

The four of them made another wide sweep around Alice Town but found no trace of Lucien.

Not good.

They headed back to the *Nice Catch* to regroup.

CHAPTER 108

On Board the Catch
Brown's Marina
North Bimini Island, Bahamas

DARKNESS HAD BLANKETED THE island and the remaining four crew members of the *Nice Catch* gathered in the galley to discuss what to do about Lucien's disappearance.

"So, what's everybody thinking? Did he take off on his own or did somebody grab him?" Matt asked.

Ghost was a man of few words, but he spoke next.

"I believe they have him. It's what I would do in their situation. They can either hold him hostage and offer to exchange him for the relics, or they can try to sweat information out of him and go after the relics before we do."

"Yeah, you're probably right. I don't think even Lucien is dumb enough to take off partying on his own after what he's seen the last few days." Jake added. "Matt, do you think he would try to beat us to the artifacts and keep them for himself?"

"No, I don't think so. I have the maps and the relics locked up in the safe and I'm the only one with the combination. And it's in my head, not written down. He might have a general idea of what part of the island we are headed to, but not the exact location."

Kelli joined in.

"Well, I'm worried sick about Lucien. If they do have him, I hate to think about what he might be going through. We can't just do nothing. What do we do next? Go to the police?"

Matt let her question hang in the air for a moment, then addressed it.

"I want to find Lucien too, but I don't think going to the police would be our best move at this point. No telling how the police would react. They would probably start an investigation and make us stay put until it's completed. On island time, that could take weeks or months. And, if the bad guys do have Lucien, the police are not likely to find him. These guys are too smart for that. I think the best option is to stick with our plan. We rent a boat in the morning and go. If they have Lucien, we'll hear from them soon enough. If they don't, he'll resurface on his own. I will let the harbormaster know to keep an eye out for him in case he turns up. Johnny has my cell number and can call me if that happens. Agreed?"

The other three nodded their heads in agreement.

"It's settled then. Let's work out the rotation for night watch and get some sleep. No telling what tomorrow will bring and we need to be rested and ready."

CHAPTER 109

Brown's Marina
Alice Town
North Bimini Island, Bahamas

THE NIGHT PASSED WITHOUT incident and Matt was up at daybreak. Kelli stirred as Matt pulled himself out of bed. She rubbed her eyes and stretched like a cat, forcing herself to become fully awake. Her muscles were still sore after the punishing dive she endured the day before. She followed Matt out of bed and after they dressed in comfortable clothes and walking shoes, the two of them headed up to the galley to make coffee. As they climbed the stairs and emerged into the galley, they discovered Jake and Ghost had already made a pot of coffee, feeling the same sense of urgency as Matt and Kelli.

"I guess I don't need to ask if everyone's ready to move out early this morning?" Matt asked.

"I don't know about the rest of you," Jake replied, "but I'm gettin' a real itch to see what the hell this is all about. The sooner we get to the bottom of it, the better, as far as I'm concerned."

"Won't argue with that, Jake." Matt answered.

"I can't help being worried about Lucien." Kelli added. "I kept waking up thinking about what might have happened to him. He's one of us."

"Just another reason to force this thing to a head. They'll play their hand before long and then we'll know. Remember, we need to play offense, not defense." Jake stated.

"Let's down this coffee and a quick breakfast and get a move on." Matt said. "You guys button up the *Catch* best you can while I go down the street and find a decent boat to rent. Pack up some drinks and snacks and throw in a set of basic tools. I don't know what we'll need when we get there."

Jake nodded and added...

"And our guns and ammo. Always better to be a hammer than a nail."

CHAPTER 110

Cayce Point
Northern Tip of North Bimini Island

MATT FOUND A TWENTY-FIVE foot fishing boat for rent. It was a walk around with open cabin and twin 250 HP outboards hanging off the stern. It was fast and sturdy. Perfect for this mission. It was ironically named, *Island Treasure*.

When he returned with the rental boat, Matt noticed the dinghy was missing from the foredeck of the *Catch*. He also noticed that Ghost was no longer with Jake and Kelli. When Matt asked Jake where Ghost and the dinghy were, Jake looked at him with a twinkle in his eye and a sly smile. He told Matt not to worry, Ghost was doing his thing. Matt decided it best to let it ride. Jake and Ghost knew what they were doing.

Jake slipped the sniper rifle and his bag of tricks on board the rental boat without anyone at the marina taking notice. Jake, Matt, and Kelli buckled their holstered sidearms to their hips once they cleared the port and were out of the harbor patrol's line of sight. All three had strapped sheathed knives to their legs as well. Matt had retrieved the relics and maps from his ship's safe and put them back into the waterproof bag they had been in when they had fallen overboard. He stashed the relics and maps under the helm controls of the *Island Treasure* along with some extra storage bags in anticipation of finding more artifacts.

They proceeded to make the short trip north following the west side of the island. They anchored the boat in a couple feet of water just off a white sandy beach. The water was clear and warm, the day sunny with only a few cottony clouds meandering across the sky. They were at the northernmost point of the island at a spot called Cayce Point.

The Atlantis Road, or Stones as they were sometimes called, was located just west and south of Cayce Point and lay barely off the coastline of North Bimini. Edgar Cayce was well known for predicting the reemergence of Atlantis at some point in the future. It was impossible to be in this part of the Bahamas and not be aware of the Atlantis connection. Jake had struck up another conversation about the Atlantis myths and legends as their boat passed over the Atlantis Road on the way to Cayce Point. Jake's Atlantis stories made an appropriate backdrop as they considered the mysteries that awaited them.

The *Island Treasure* was now rocking gently at anchor and Matt pulled the maps out of the waterproof bag. Kelli and Jake carefully aligned the two pieces of the map to reveal the exact coordinates they would hike to. Matt produced his hand-held GPS unit and punched the coordinates into the keypad. It linked to a satellite and brought up the direction for them to follow from their current position.

Jake slung the rifle over his shoulder and they strapped carry bags across their shoulders and backs. Matt made sure the bag with the relics in it was doubly secured to his body. They crawled over the side of the boat and splashed feet first into the shallow water. Matt pointed in the direction the GPS indicated they should go, and they sloshed onto the narrow beach.

The openness and bright light of the beach soon gave way to deep shade and shadows as they made their way into the trees and scrubby brush. Jake took the lead, pulled out his knife, and cut away undergrowth to allow them easier passage. They did not see any clear paths or trails in the area, so they fought their way through it the best they could. The good news was they would not have to go far. Less than a mile inland was where they would find the target site according to the GPS.

As they drew closer to the coordinates, their anticipation began to build. Matt pondered whether this was all a wild goose chase his grandfather had sent him on or a day that would change his life forever? He was about to find out…

CHAPTER 111

Matt, Kelli, and Jake now arrived at a point matching the coordinates on the GPS. If there was something here, it should be nearby.

Matt and Kelli unsheathed their knives and joined Jake in cutting through the thick undergrowth, looking for a sign of anything out of the ordinary. After several minutes of whacking and clearing underbrush, nothing noteworthy revealed itself in the mangle of vines, trees, and bushes.

On a whim, Matt pulled a compass out of one of his bags and stood still, observing it. It was behaving strangely as if something was having an unusual effect on it. The compass needle was swinging wildly and unable to settle on any points on the dial.

"Kelli, Jake…look at this." he said.

They moved to his side and watched the curiously unsettled compass needle.

"What do you make of this?" Matt asked.

"I've never seen a compass act like that out in the open with nothing to interfere with it." Jake said.

"What if there *is* something interfering with it?" Kelli offered. "We don't know the nature of what we're looking for and there could be some unusual magnetic properties involved. That could cause the compass to act up."

Matt thought about what Kelli said for a moment.

"Kelli, you could be on to something. If that's true, the compass might lead us to the objects."

Matt began walking around in a circle, watching the compass dial for any clues to where they should search. As he continued to circle around, a definite pattern began to show itself. The compass behaved more wildly when he pointed it toward one particular area.

Matt lead the way and they all began to move slowly toward the area that was causing the magnetic fluctuation. The dense undergrowth still hid whatever the source was but the more they zeroed in, the crazier the compass behaved. They emerged into an open area with few trees but a lot of bothersome bushes and groundcover. It was there that the compass exploded with crazy directional swings.

Matt looked at the others and nodded to indicate this would be the spot to focus their search. He unslung the backpack containing a general assortment of tools and laid it on the ground. He opened it up and pulled out a folding shovel he always kept on the *Catch* for clam digging or to make holes for beach umbrellas.

Matt used the shovel to open small pilot holes to see if he might uncover anything of interest. Kelli and Jake were using their knives to cut into the undergrowth and make jabs into the sandy dirt for the same purpose.

They had dug and jabbed around a perimeter roughly ten yards in diameter when Kelli heard a muffled metallic clunk from one of her knife probes.

The other two ran to her position and watched as she stabbed the ground again, producing a more pronounced clank. She had clearly hit something metallic.

Matt jumped in with his camp shovel and began digging cautiously while Kelli and Jake continued to cut the undergrowth away from the spot. It was now midday and a fair amount of light was penetrating the forest canopy. Little by little, the light revealed a metallic object being uncovered.

Matt dug carefully but with urgency as the mystery began to reveal itself. He trenched along its sides to determine the length of the item. It seemed to be about twelve feet long and two feet across. As Matt continued to uncover the object, it showed itself to be in the shape of a rocket or missile of some kind. He began to wonder if it was an old military weapon that had been tested in this area years ago and never recovered. He knew a lot of U.S. weapons testing had occurred near Bimini in years past. But the more the digging revealed, the less it looked like anything that Matt had seen in the U.S. military's inventory of weapons.

They could now see a propulsion system of some sort on the back end of the object and it took up about two feet of its overall length. Matt used his shovel to tap on the body of the object in front of the motor area, and it seemed hollow from the sound emanating from it.

The three of them worked together to finish clearing away all the sandy soil and undergrowth from the entire length of the thing before them.

It was now in clear view and they stood and stared at it, trying to decide what it was they had uncovered. They visually inspected the object for a while and then looked at each other.

"I know it looks like a missile, but I don't remember seeing anything exactly like this when I was in Naval Intelligence." Matt offered.

"Yeah, I don't recognize it either." Jake replied. "I was trained to identify high-end weaponry from all countries during my time in ops. But I don't remember a propulsion system like this one and I don't see any of the identifying marks I would expect to see if it was military, except it has stabilizer fins on the back like a typical rocket."

"But missiles and rockets typically would have no effect on a compass." Matt replied.

"It sounded hollow when you tapped on it, Matt." Kelli said. "Is there an access door or something that would allow us to look inside for more clues as to where it came from or what it is?"

Matt extracted a flashlight from his tool bag and began to examine the surface of the cylinder, looking for any sign of a break or seam in the smooth metal casing.

Jake cautioned, "Matt, be careful in case this thing has unexploded ordinance inside that is still viable."

Matt nodded and continued to move slowly over the surface of the cylinder. He stopped, using his hand to scrape away dust from the spot where his flashlight was pointed.

"I might have found something." Matt said.

They all huddled over the object as Matt continued to brush away dust and debris. They could now see the clear outline of a long hatch that ran half the length of the object and about a third of its circumference. As Matt traced the outline of the access door with his flashlight, he made out four spots that seemed to be the lockdown points for sealing the hatch. As he examined them more closely, it appeared they had once been welded shut, but no more.

Matt thought about that for a moment and shared his thoughts about it.

"If this is the object that Grandpa Flannery wanted me to find, that means he and Bart were here at some point and examined it. They were probably the ones who broke these welds, then covered it back up with dirt and brush and left it for us to find later."

"Could be." Jake said. "But not until they took some souvenirs from it. I would guess that's where those little triangles came from."

"Only one way to find out." Matt said.

He reached back into his tool bag and pulled out a long flathead screwdriver and began to pry the hatch open.

CHAPTER 112

Dig Site near Cayce Point
North Bimini Island, Bahamas

MATT SELECTED A SPOT along the hatch seam and carefully slipped the end of the screwdriver into the thin gap between the hatch and the body of the missile. He tapped the back of the screwdriver with the open palm of his other hand and forced it deeper into the crack, then levered it up. The hatch lifted slightly with the upward push of the screwdriver and Jake inserted the edge of his knife blade into the opening to hold it. Kelli pushed her knife blade into the gap and they all began to lift up. It was a long, heavy hatch door but it soon began to give way to the three levers acting on it. Matt removed his screwdriver and was able to slip his fingers into the opening, lifting the cover up and over and out of the way. He grabbed his flashlight and pointed it towards the darkness inside the cylinder.

It looked to be a large, hollow compartment designed to carry a warhead but had been adapted for another purpose.

Matt handed Kelli the flashlight and began extracting the contents of the storage compartment. He removed multiple containers that all seemed to be designed to protect what was inside of them. They were made of a shiny metal and simple clasp locks held them shut. They looked like small toolboxes. Matt worked until he had removed all the containers that were visible. He laid them side by side on the ground. There were ten of them of various sizes.

Anticipation and uncertainty coursed through the minds of the three explorers as they took in the articles before them and prepared to unlock the secrets drawing them to this time and place.

Matt looked at Kelli and Jake, searching their faces as he considered the next move. They looked as unsure as he felt.

"Your move, Matt. I believe this is the stuff we came here for and your grandpa started all this. So, you should be the one to open the containers and see what the big deal is." Jake said.

"He's right, Jake." Kelli added. "Time to see what was so important to your grandfather."

Matt stood silent for about thirty seconds as he considered their words and remembered the look in his grandpa's eyes the day in the barn when he first showed the relics to him. A mixture of fear and trust. He would never forget it. It was forever burned into his mind and heart.

Matt knelt beside one of the larger containers and cautiously manipulated the clasps holding it shut. The lid gave way with a click and he lifted it up and to the side, revealing the contents. It was a crystalline device of some sort attached to a base with three openings in its face. They were triangular. The realization hit the three of them simultaneously. The openings looked like perfect fits for the little pyramids Matt had in his bag.

Matt anxiously took three of the six triangles out of his bag and noticed they were glowing with more intensity than they had when he held them previously. They were growing warmer and seemed to be coming alive.

He placed them into the corresponding slots in the base of the device and waited. Nothing happened.

He pulled the little triangles out again and examined them more closely. They had symbols inscribed on them which might be instructions he mused. He made sure the symbols were all pointed outward towards him and reinserted them in a different combination.

A brilliant flash shot out the top of the device, causing a surprised Matt to fall over backward. They watched in wide-eyed astonishment as 3-D holographic images hung in the air over the device. The images were in a slideshow format as they changed every few seconds. The depictions were detailed and realistic, as though you could reach out and touch what you saw.

The images being shown were sweeping views of several different cities, majestic in their beauty and scope. Tall, colorful city towers and lush landscapes shared the same spaces. People moved about in an orderly and purposeful fashion. Some were being transported in glass enclosed public trams, while others leisurely walked down tree-lined boulevards. Equally beautiful neighborhoods ringed the downtown area, efficient and elegant. Waterways permeated the landscape and tropical coastlines lay near each urban center. There seemed to be four cities that were rotating in sequence in the hologram.

Matt's mind was excitedly searching for answers.

Is this some architect's dream that has been created on computer and turned into a slideshow? This couldn't be a real place, could it? Nothing like this has ever existed on Earth to my knowledge. Nothing in my travels around the world looked like this. What the hell are we seeing? Where is this place? What's the meaning behind it? Why would Grandpa place such value on me discovering it?

Matt paused to consider the location of this discovery and the history of the area, looking for a connection.

No, it couldn't be, could it? Atlantis? That's just a myth that people love to believe in. They say that myths have their basis in fact. But Atlantis? Oh my God, could that be what we are seeing? If it is, I know why Grandpa acted the way he did. This would be…

Matt looked at Kelli and Jake for a reaction. They were mesmerized by the realistic images rotating before them.

"Uh, hello you two. Earth calling Jake and Kelli."

They pulled their eyes away from the breathtaking spectacle and looked at Matt with unspoken questions written on their faces.

"What do you think we're looking at here?" Matt asked.

"I don't know, but our government doesn't have the ability to create holographs this realistic yet. And, if we can't make them, I don't think anyone else can either." Jake offered.

"Those cities are unbelievable. They couldn't be real places, could they?" Kelli wondered aloud.

"I don't know for sure. I have an idea to throw out there, but you might think I'm losin' it." Matt stated.

"Well, we don't have a clue what's going on here Matt, so after all that's happened, I doubt that we will think anything is crazy at this point. So out with it." Jake said.

"Alright. Here it is. Think of where we are right now and the history of this area. The stories and myths and legends. What are most of them about? Jake, you should be able to answer this one. You've been the one educating me on the background of this place."

"You talking about Atlantis?" Jake asked.

"Why not?" Matt replied. I can't think of anything else that makes sense or I can connect this to."

"Whoa, Pardner. That's a pretty big leap you're taking. Those are just myths I told you about."

"Yeah, but you said yourself that myths usually have their origin in fact. What else could we be dealing with here?"

"Jesus, Matt. I can't even begin to imagine the ramifications of this if these are real artifacts from Atlantis." Jake stated. "This would turn history upside down. I wonder what else is stored inside the projector, or whatever it is?"

Matt examined the base of the device more closely and found there to be small buttons around the base. He pushed the last one on the row. What they saw next caused them to recoil. It was a horror show beyond their comprehension.

A new set of images began to rotate in front of them. Images of the four beautiful cities being shaken, tossed, thrown down, and annihilated right in front of their eyes. They watched in silent disbelief, unable to look away. The devastation was total and complete. The people in the projection were screaming and running everywhere in blind panic. Many held small children in their arms and others were trying to help the elderly move out of harm's way. But it was to no avail. In the end, they were all being claimed by the yawing mouth of the earth opening to claim them.

Kelli cried out, "Turn that thing off, I can't watch it anymore. All those poor people…" Tears were trickling down her cheeks.

Matt and Jake were stunned at the visions in front of them and shaken to their core. Matt reached back to the base and touched the first button in the row, restoring the images they first beheld.

Matt now touched the second button and images of a large assembly appeared before them. It looked like a government body or something similar. He touched the third button and they saw people constructing new buildings and scientists working on projects in laboratories. He touched the fourth button and they saw the inside of a large control center with people gathered around consoles and what appeared to be computer stations. There were view screens all around the front of the room monitoring events happening in different locations. Matt touched the fifth button and images appeared depicting large ships and aircraft under construction. They were unlike anything currently on Earth. Matt depressed the sixth button and images came up showing a large cannon of some type that was being moved into place near a large opening that looked like a mineshaft.

Matt already knew what the seventh button held. He did not push it again.

CHAPTER 113

MATT SELECTED THE FIRST button once more. As the images of the beautiful cities rotated in front of them, Matt spoke in a subdued voice.

"That is either the best 3D movie ever made or we just watched the destruction of a world. Again, based on the myths, much of what we just saw would be consistent with the story of Atlantis."

Jake responded.

"The prevailing theory is that Atlantis was destroyed by a natural disaster, like an earthquake or volcano. We just saw what looked like a massive earthquake in those pictures. Maybe the projection wasn't just a movie. Maybe it was real."

"I think we should see what else is in these containers." Kelli said. "Maybe that will answer some of our questions." Her voice was still laden with the emotion of what she had witnessed.

Matt opened another container like the first one. It also held a crystalline device. He took out the remaining three triangles from his bag and inserted them into the slots the way he had learned to do with the first one.

It immediately sprang to life and opened a hologram in front of them. This time, the images were of drawings, mathematical formulas, and schematics for devices unfamiliar to them and the language was not one they recognized. Matt chose each of the seven buttons and each revealed more of the same. It was an endless array of detailed plans of advanced technological devices.

Matt narrowed his eyes and realized the import of what they were looking at. An electrical feeling coursed through him and he felt his blood run cold.

"Now, I understand what Grandpa was afraid of and why people are willing to kill us to get their hands on this. It's the technology they're after. From what we saw on the first device, these people were very advanced technologically. Whoever controls this technology, could conceivably control the world."

Jake's face now took on a look that reflected the same feelings that Matt was experiencing. He understood the import of their discovery.

"This is some serious shit we're dealing with, Matt. This is a matter of national security. Even if we get this stuff off the island and safely back home, what are you going to do with it? Are you going to give it to your father and NASA? Or do you want me to call the big boys at the CIA to get down here and help us? They could be here within an hour. What do you think?"

Matt only took a second to offer his answer. The one he knew to be right.

"None of those options feel right to me. We have to think about the bigger picture. If any government or organization gets their hands on this knowledge, it could end very badly. I have no reason to believe any of them can be trusted to do the right thing with this kind of power and technology. I'm not convinced any of them would do the right thing."

Kelli was watching Matt as he spoke with unwavering conviction and passion. She said with a loving smile, "Now I understand why your grandfather trusted you to be the one to make this discovery."

CHAPTER 114

Dig Site near Cayce Point
North Bimini Island, Bahamas

"Okay, pardner. It's your call. I hope you know what you're doing." Jake said.

"I don't have a clue what I'm doing. But I know what I'm *not* doing. I say we open some of these other containers and see what else is here." Matt said.

Matt opened the third one and it contained personal items from the people who had lived in those beautiful cities. There were pictures of families, notes and cards written in their unfamiliar language, jewelry, and smaller crystalline information devices with single triangular keys still inserted in their slots. Matt pushed a button on one of the devices and scenes of families, holidays, vacations, sports events, and festivals unfolded before them. A record of who they were as people and how they lived their personal lives.

He put it back into its container and opened a fourth one. It also held an information storage device. When activated, it showed newscasts and historical records dating back to the early origins of the nation and the people who lived at that time. The earliest records showed something else very interesting. There were several drawings and pictures of a group of people who were similar to, but not exactly like the ones they had been seeing. They were depicted as people who had arrived in flying craft of some sort and were helping the other people build things.

Matt quickly skimmed from container to container. He opened them all and found each of them contained storage crystals with a different set of information to impart. There was a record of legislative sessions over many years. There were images of their educational system and what was taught there. There were images referring to their spiritual beliefs and how they practiced them.

As Matt put the last one back in its container, Kelli asked a question.

"Do you think this rocket might have been their last-ditch effort to leave a record of who they were before they died?"

"It would seem that way." Matt replied. "They must have gathered all the records they could before the end and fired them off in this rocket hoping that someday, someone would find it and discover who they were and what they accomplished."

"It'll take years of translation and studying these records to fully understand what all they knew and what happened at the end," Jake said. "And what about those different looking people who seemed to be helping them in the beginning? What was that all about?"

"Hell, if I know. We're creating more questions than answers at this point, but we can't worry about all that right now. We have to get these relics out of here and go somewhere we can think it through without anyone else getting involved or trying to kill us. You may have to help me find a safe house, Jake," Matt stated.

Jake nodded his head up and down but he was conflicted, not sure where his loyalties should lie at this moment. With his friend Matt, or the CIA.

The three of them hurriedly packed up all the artifacts in the extra bags they had brought and covered up the empty rocket again with dirt and brush. They threw a couple of good size rocks on top as a marker to help identify the spot should they return.

Matt, Kelli, and Jake retraced their steps in the direction of the waiting rental boat waiting to take them back to the *Nice Catch* where they could formulate a plan to get home in one piece. They were hoping Lucien would be waiting there when they returned.

Matt was already thinking he may have to call on Ken or some of Jake's connections to help get them home safely.

But how can I ask for help without divulging too much information about this discovery.

He did not want government interference to become a problem right now. He was not sure how he would pull it off, but he had to focus on getting back to the relative safety of the *Nice Catch* for the moment.

The trio worked their way through the thick brush, made easier by their having cleared some of it on the way in. They could see the light growing brighter as they approached the beach area where their boat was anchored. They were in a subdued and serious frame of mind because of what they had witnessed and the weight of the knowledge they were carrying.

They broke through the lush growth and spilled out onto the beach only to discover that a second boat was anchored near theirs.

Not good.

Jake quickly barked out orders.

"Let's get off this beach! We're exposed out here. Quick, back into the woods until we figure out what we're dealing with."

The three of them quickly retreated toward the shelter of the undergrowth only to be greeted with another unexpected surprise.

They stopped dead in their tracks. Disbelief and confusion spread across their faces.

There stood Lucien at the edge of the woods flanked by two other men holding assault rifles aimed in their direction. It happened so quickly that neither Matt, Jake, nor Kelli had been able to draw their weapons in defense.

"Lucien, what the hell are you doing? Where did you disappear to?" Matt questioned with a tinge of anger in his voice.

"Well, it's a long story, old friend. I didn't mean for it to end like this, but they made me an offer I couldn't refuse."

"You were planning this all along?" Matt asked.

"No dude, not at all. They snatched me at that restaurant the other night and I thought they were going to torture and kill me."

"Obviously they didn't." Matt retorted.

"Well, not in the end. They threatened to, slapped me around a little bit, and then offered me a choice. They would either torture me to find out where the relics were or I could help them and they would make me rich and spare all our lives. Seemed like an easy decision to me."

"Lucien, you didn't have the maps. How did you know where we would be?" Matt asked.

Lucien chuckled, shook his head, and replied.

"I wasn't born yesterday, Matt. I gave you the original but I made a copy of the coordinates just in case something happened to you or the maps."

Matt gritted his teeth.

"Lucien, you don't honestly believe they will pay you a bunch of money and let us all walk out of here alive after they get what they want?"

"I'm willing to take my chances. They seem like an honorable bunch of guys to me, in their own way. The whole "honor among thieves" thing you know. Hell, you ought to be thanking me! I've done you a favor. They would have eventually chased us down and taken the relics anyway and you would have probably died trying to hang onto them. This way, all of us get to live and do it in style!"

"Don't do this, Lucien," Matt pleaded in a lowered voice. "You have no idea what you're doing. You can't even comprehend the consequences if they get their hands on this stuff. This discovery is bigger than anything we could have imagined. We absolutely cannot let them, or anyone, have these artifacts. Our grandfathers already knew what was at stake and that's why they trusted us with this."

"Yeah, I do feel kinda bad about not sticking to my promise to Grandpa Bart, but he wasn't the one with a gun pointed in his face."

Lucien took a step towards them and spoke in a calm voice, trying to reason with them.

"Alright guys, listen. Let's do this all peaceful like, okay? No need to make this difficult. They're gonna take them, one way or another. So, let's just do it the easy way. Okay? Come on, just hand 'em over and let's get the hell out of here."

Matt, Jake, and Kelli glared at Lucien and stood their ground without moving.

"Damn it, guys!" Lucien yelled. "They're gonna kill you if you don't give them the relics. Please, JUST DO IT!"

As if to accent Lucien's words, the two gunmen stepped closer to the three captives and trained both deadly gun barrels straight at their heads, moving the weapons side to side to cover all three of them.

"I'm telling you all, stop messin' around! These guys mean business. Hand that shit over here before it's too late. Please!"

"It's already too late, Lucien." Matt replied.

The gunmen moved forward and a shot rang out, then another, clear and deadly, in that perfect afternoon in paradise.

…to be continued in *Critical Mass* Book
Two of the Atlantis Legacy Series

ACKNOWLEDGMENTS

Writing a novel, as in any major endeavor, usually involves a support group of people that work to make the writer a success. I want to thank the following individuals who have pushed and prodded me along *"the long and winding road"* (tip of the hat to the Beatles) that led me to publishing this, my first full length novel. I am pretty sure that without the unselfish support of the person or persons who have to live with a writer, facing a blank page might be the least of an author's problems. A writer often has to be selfish with their time in order to appease the author beast within and the readers without. In my life, the person who has chosen to not only deal with it but actually support my occasional disappearing act, is my wife Karole. She is also the first to hear of my great and not-so-great ideas and ride the roller coaster with me. So Karole … my heartfelt thanks and appreciation for all you do. Your encouragement is only known to me, but it's monumental. I look forward to seeing your children's books introduced in the not too distant future. They will be stellar.

Cindy is my sister. For some reason, she has chosen to be my constant cheerleader from the time we were young. I don't fully understand it and sometimes think I must have convinced her of my greatness as a person before she was old enough to think for herself. But yet even now that we are older … she persists. Thank You for always being the loudest voice in my cheering section.

Matthew Hamilton is my son. He is a fine young man who has found his way to a good life.

I take no credit for that but I am proud of him and happy for him. Yes, the main character in this novel was named after him as a tribute. May the wind always be at your back son …

Stephen King … you are a force. Not because of what you write, but how you write. I have re-read your book "On Writing" numerous times and it has given me inspiration, guidance, and permission to write the way that is best for me. You are a fearless author and authentic person and I Thank You for that.

John Locke … you are a groundbreaker and way shower. You flipped the publishing paradigm on it's head and never looked back. You even answered my e-mails! Thank You for doing things your way and giving us all courage to pursue our publishing dreams in whatever way we choose.

Thank You to the team at Mindstir Media, my publisher. JJ, Jen, Monica, and others who I do not know the names of, have worked with me for months to produce books I can be proud of and then make sure they are not the best kept secret in the publishing world. Last, I want to thank the readers of my books even before you have purchased one or discovered who I am. I have always been a voracious reader and I know who you are … I think. I share your appreciation of the written word and hope you will be entertained if nothing else…and maybe even given pause to think more deeply about some of the things I write about.

I look forward to meeting you. You are why I write.

Larry Hamilton

Postscript

The Atlantis Codes

Who survives to walk away from the beach at North Bimini? Who does not? What fate befalls Matt and his friends? What happens to the relics that could determine the future of mankind on Earth?

The sweeping saga continues in *Critical Mass,* the second book in the Atlantis Legacy Series.

This astounding adventure continues with more twists and turns and dilemmas presenting themselves in every chapter.

Larger truths will reveal themselves as the series continues,truths of universal scope and importance. The very origins of mankind come into focus as the story unfolds. Continue the journey … seek the truth.

Author's Note: I invite you to leave reviews on *The Atlantis Codes* at your bookseller's website.

You may e-mail me at larry@hamiltonhousebooks.com, or visit my new website www.hamiltonhousebooks.com.

I look forward to hearing from you and making some new friends!